Grimgar of Fantasy and Ash

level. 1 — Whisper, Chant, Prayer, Awaken

Presented by Ao Jyumonji   Illustrated by Eiri Shirai

Merry
Class Priest

Yume
Class Hunter

Renji
Class Warrior

Chibi
Class Priest

Soma
Class Samurai

Moguzo
Class Warrior

Grimgar of Fantasy and Ash

level. 1 — Whisper, Chant, Prayer, Awaken

Presented by
AO JYUMONJI

Illustrated by
EIRI SHIRAI

GRIMGAR OF FANTASY AND ASH, LEVEL. 1

© 2013 Ao Jyumonji
© 2013 Eiri Shirai

First published in Japan in 2013 by Overlap Co., Ltd., Tokyo.
English translation rights arranged with Overlap Co., Ltd., Tokyo.

Seven Seas books may be purchased in bulk for promotional, educational, or business use. Please contact your local bookseller or the Macmillan Corporate and Premium Sales Department at 1-800-221-7945, extension 5442, or by e-mail at MacmillanSpecialMarkets@macmillan.com.

Follow Seven Seas Entertainment online at gomanga.com.
Experience J-Novel Club books online at j-novel.club.

Translation: Sean McCann
J-Novel Editor: Emily Sorensen
Book Layout: Karis Page
Cover Design: Nicky Lim
Copy Editor: Tom Speelman
Light Novel Editor: Jenn Grunigen
Production Assistant: CK Russell
Production Manager: Lissa Pattillo
Editor-in-Chief: Adam Arnold
Publisher: Jason DeAngelis

ISBN: 978-1-626926-58-5
Printed in Canada
First Printing: June 2017
10 9 8 7 6 5 4 3 2 1

[TABLE OF CONTENTS]

[GEOGRAPHY]

GRIMGAR

The word that refers to this "world." Nobody knows whether it refers to an entire continent, an entire island, part of one of those, or if it encompasses everything. Basically, when those who live in this "world" refer to the "world," they use this name. Generally, it refers to the area south of the Tenryu Mountains (the homeland) and north of them (the frontier) in a single word.

ARABAKIA KINGDOM

(Almost) The only human kingdom (city states and micronations do exist). Though they once held territory in what is now called the frontier and were highly prosperous, they were defeated by the Undying Empire and retreated south of the Tenryu Mountains, maintaining their power. Since that time, they have come to call the areas south of the Tenryus the "homeland" and the area north of them the "frontier."

THE FORTRESS CITY ALTERNA

The Arabakia Kingdom's sole fortified stronghold north of the Tenryu Mountains. The town of the beginning. The fortress of humanity. With lodgings, taverns, weapon shops, guilds, and more, it has all of the necessary facilities in place. The margrave of Alterna, Garlan Vedoy, rules the city. It shelters the Alterna

Frontier Army led by General Rasentra. By forming alliances with the elves of the Shadow Forest, the dwarves of the Black Gold Mountain Range, and the centaurs of Quickwind Plains, they have somehow managed to sustain their power. They have hostile relations with all other races.

[MONSTERS]

GOBLIN

Ugly diminutive humanoids. Height tends to be 140cm at most. Many individuals are around 120cm. They have greenish skin and pointed ears. Though they can vary, they tend to be clever and won't engage in battles when they are at a disadvantage. Prefer to act in groups. Have formed a kingdom ruled by a royal bloodline. They give birth in litters, have a short gestation period of around three months, and mature quickly, so their species has an extraordinarily large number of individuals. One trait they have is that they carry a small bag called a goblin pouch slung over one shoulder in which they keep items of value. High-ranked goblins decorate their pouches; these can sell for a high amount. They seem to have a liking for fashion as they often wear expensive items on themselves. Something to target.

HOBGOBLIN

A subrace of goblins which are less common compared to the standard goblin. They resemble goblins but are built larger, being roughly human size. They are more fierce than goblins but less intelligent, sometimes being tamed by goblins and turned into slave warriors.

They are generally bullied for being taller than the other goblins. Some intelligent hobgoblins have formed a tribal society and regard goblins as enemies. Occasionally there is a submissive hobgoblin that has been tamed by goblins, armed as a bodyguard, and will fight fiercely on their behalf. Most important goblins have such a hobgoblin protecting them.

PIT RAT

Rats that are roughly the size of cats. They are speedy and have exceptionally hard hair. Similar to porcupines. They have the trait of curling into a ball and rolling away at high speed. Many subspecies exist. They are omnivorous but like meat and there are pit rats that will target larger animals (including humans) as prey. Their meat is not very tasty. Their pelts are of little use. They are vermin.

UNDEAD

One faction of the undead. A new race created by No-Life King. Skeletons, zombies, and ghosts are not technically undead (though humans often view them as undead). Undead are creatures that have died but are not dead and do not rot. They have powerful regenerative abilities and even when their brains are destroyed or they are burned, it does not destroy them. It is said that dead bodies given No-Life King's black blood became the undead, but even now with No-Life King gone, the priests and bishops of the undead perform the "ritual of undeath" to undeathen corpses. Those who are undeathened lose most of the memories that they had in life, pledging allegiance to No-Life King. This remains unchanged even now that No-Life King is no more.

ZOMBIE ···

Due to "No-Life King's curse," those who die in Grimgar, unless proper measures are taken, become "servants of No-Life King." Zombies are the servants "with meat" while those that have fully rotted become skeletons. Severing the head or destroying the brain will stop them from moving, but left alone, they will become either partial skeleton parts or ghosts.

[CLASS LISTING]

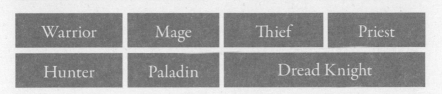

Warrior	Mage	Thief	Priest
Hunter	Paladin	Dread Knight	

※ There are also other specialized classes such as Samurai.

[ACQUISITION OF SKILLS AND MAGIC]

When a skill or magic is first learned through training, what is learned is only the basics: enough to execute it, but not enough to use it with sufficient power and effect. Through practice or use in battle (which is said to be ten times as effective) your degree of skill builds and gradually you become able to execute it with the power and effect it was meant to have. It takes considerable time and effort to master it fully.

[CLANS]

A team or group formed by volunteer soldiers, primarily those working toward the same goal. Members are all comrades. When assaulting a fortress or labyrinth that is too large for a single party, a number of parties must band together. It is thought that these sorts of circumstances are what lead to the formation of clans. In the Volunteer Soldier Corps, there are no fixed regulations for them, but it is recommended to report it to the office when forming a clan.

[GUILDS]

There are a number of guilds in this world. Most are organizations for a designated trade and a pact between all of the guilds ensures that an individual may only hold membership in one guild. In almost all guilds, there is a code that all members must follow. This is not written down, but passed verbally to the members. Those who break the code are expelled. Expelled members may never return to the guild. Furthermore, whether expulsion is the worst that happens to the offender depends on the guild. In some guilds, pursuers will chase down the expelled, seeking their lives.

Grimgar of Fantasy and Ash

"Awaken."

He opened his eyes, feeling like he'd heard someone's voice.

It was dark. Nighttime, maybe? But not pitch black. There were lights. Fire. Above him. Some kind of lighting. Candles, it looked like. Small ones affixed to the wall. Not just one, but many, spaced evenly, continuing as far as he could see.

Where was this place?

It was kind of hard to breathe.

When he tried touching the wall, it was hard and rocky. This was no wall. It was just bare rock. Little wonder his back was sore after lying against it. His butt hurt, too.

Maybe he was in a cave... A cave? Why would he be in a cave...?

Those candles were pretty high up. He might be able to reach one if he stood; that was how high they were. Moreover, they didn't even give off enough light for him to see his hands and feet.

But he sensed the presence of others nearby. When he listened closely, there was a faint noise that sounded like breathing.

Humans? What if they weren't? He might be in trouble. But they sounded human, somehow.

"Is anyone there?" he asked hesitantly.

"Uh, yeah," a man's voice shot back.

"I'm here..." came another response, likely that of a woman.

Another man's voice gave a short, "Yeah."

"I figured as much," another person added.

"How many of us are there?"

"Should we count?"

"And...where are we, anyway?"

"Dunno..."

"What? Doesn't anyone know where we are?"

"What's going on?"

"What is this?"

Seriously. What the hell was this? What was he doing in a place like this? And why? How long had he been here?

He clutched at his chest tightly as if trying to claw something off of it.

He had no clue what was going on. How long had he been here? Why was he here?

When he began to consider his situation, something began to tug at the back of his mind. But it suddenly vanished before he could latch on to it.

He didn't know. He didn't know anything. He was at a complete loss.

"Sitting here won't solve anything," said one man in a low, husky voice.

There was a sound, like someone stepping on pebbles. It sounded like the man had stood up.

"Going somewhere...?" a woman's voice asked.

"Following the wall," the man answered. "Going to try heading towards the light." The man's tone was surprisingly calm.

Wasn't he scared? Why wasn't he shaken up by this?

The man was now beneath the second candle from him and he seemed very tall.

He could make out a bit of the man's head in the candlelight. The man's hair wasn't black. Was it...silver?

"I'm going, too," the woman said.

"Me too, I guess," a man's voice said.

"H-hold on, guys! I'm coming, too, then!" called another man.

"There's the other direction too," said yet another person. The voice sounded slightly high-pitched, but it was probably another male. "We can probably go that way. There's no candles, though."

The silver-haired man said, "If you want to go that way, be my guest," and started walking.

It looked like everyone would be following the silver-haired man. *I had better go too, then,* he thought. He stood up hurriedly, not wanting to be left alone.

He nervously stepped forward, keeping a hand on the rock wall. The ground wasn't smooth. It was uneven but easy enough to walk on.

There was someone in front of him and someone behind. He didn't know who, though.

Judging by their voices, nobody here was all that old. *I don't know any of these people...at least, I don't think so,* he thought.

Who were the people he knew? Acquaintances. Friends. But just exactly who were they?

Strange. He couldn't think of anyone. No, it was more like whenever he tried to work backwards from the faces that did come to mind, they would suddenly vanish.

He didn't know.

It didn't just happen with friends. Family, too. It wasn't that he didn't know them at all. It was more that he ought to have known them, but he was forgetting.

"Maybe it's best not to think about it," he said out loud.

"Did you..." asked a voice from behind. Definitely a young girl's voice. "Did you say something?"

"No, it was nothing—"

He stopped.

Nothing important? Really? Nothing important? How was it not important?

He shook his head to clear it.

At some point, he seemed to have stopped walking. *I should continue on,* he thought.

He needed to keep walking. It was better not to think about it. The more he tried to remember, the less he felt like he knew.

The row of candles continued. There was no end in sight.

How long had he been walking? Had he walked a long way or not? He couldn't say which. His sense of time and space had become dulled.

"There's something here," said someone up ahead. "It's bright. There are...lamps?"

The silver-haired man said, "It's an iron grate."

"D-do you think it's the exit?!" exclaimed a different man, his voice shrill and excited.

The sound of the heavy footfalls lightened. Even in the dark, he could tell that everyone was hurrying ahead.

He could see the light sources now. They were much brighter than the candles had been. Those were definitely lamps. Were they hanging on the wall? The lamps were illuminating what looked like an iron grate.

The silver-haired man grabbed the iron grate. Not only was his hair silver, the man was dressed like a gangster. He shook the iron grate violently—like a gangster would—and it began to move.

"I'm opening it," the gangster called, pulling the grate inwards. With a creaking noise, the iron grate door opened.

"Oh...!" several people cried out at the same time.

"Can we get out?!" exclaimed a woman dressed in flashy clothes who was standing behind the gangster.

The gangster headed through the door. "There are stairs. We can go up."

Through the door was a cramped, moldy corridor. Beyond that, there were stone steps. There was no light but some was shining down from above.

The group ascended the stairs in single file, one step at a time.

There was another iron grate at the top of the stairs. This one looked like it wouldn't open.

The gangster bashed the grate with his fist over and over again. "Is anybody there?! Open the door!" the gangster roared like a beast.

The flashy woman joined in, shouting, "Hey, someone, anyone, open up!"

From behind them, a guy with curly hair shouted, "Hey! Open the door! Hey!"

They didn't have to wait long. The gangster took his hand off the grate and stepped back. Apparently someone had come.

The flashy woman and guy with curly hair went quiet and there was the sound of a lock turning. The iron grate opened and a man's voice said, "Get out." He assumed the voice belonged to the man who had unlocked and opened the door.

They ascended the stairs and there was a stone room. It was windowless but brightly lit thanks to the lamps. In addition to the stairs they had come up, there was another set of stairs going up to a higher level.

The whole place feels too old, like it doesn't belong in the modern world, he thought. *The man who opened the gate is dressed weirdly, too.*

I mean, those aren't clothes he's wearing. That metal stuff he's wearing is...armor? I'd call that headgear he has on an armored helmet, too. And that object hanging from his waist, it doesn't look like a nightstick. Is it a sword...or something similar? Armor, a helmet, and a sword? What era did this guy come from? Then again, I guess that's not the problem here.

The man in armor pulled a blackish switch on the wall.

The wall and floor shook slightly and a heavy sound echoed through the room. The wall moved.

It opened. Part of the wall slowly opened.

It sunk down, leaving a hole. An oblong, rectangular hole.

The man in armor simply said, "Get out" again, gesturing towards the hole with his chin.

The gangster went outside first and the flashy woman followed. Everyone followed after them, going through the hole one after another as if being pulled along.

Outside.

This time, they were really outside.

It was either predawn or twilight. The dimly lit sky spread out as far as the eye could see.

This was the top of a small hill.

When they turned around, a large tower rose in front of them. They had been inside that tower...or perhaps, it would be more accurate to say, *beneath* it.

Counting everyone in the group, there were eight males including Gangster, Curly, and himself, and four females including Flashy. Twelve in total.

It was dark, so he couldn't see that much detail. Still, he could make out their figures, roughly what they were wearing, hairstyles, and general facial features. As he had thought, he didn't recognize anyone.

"You think that's a city?" asked a slender man with silky hair. He was pointing to the other side of the hill.

Looking in that direction, he could see buildings crowded together.

A town. It certainly looked like one. It had to be a town. Except that the town was surrounded by a high fence—no, not a fence. It was surrounded by high, solid walls.

"Rather than a town," said a thin man wearing black-rimmed glasses, "it's almost like a castle."

"A castle..." he whispered, but for some reason, his own voice sounded like someone else's.

"Um..." a petite girl behind him timidly asked, "where is this, do you think?"

"Look, asking me isn't going to help," he said.

"...Right, of course. Um, d-does anyone...know? Where is this place?"

No one said anything. Unless they were deliberately trying to trouble the girl or were concealing the information for some other reason, that meant none of them had any idea.

Curly scratched at his hair and said, "Seriously?"

"I've got it!" said a man who looked like a playboy, clapping his hands together. He wore a bordered cut-and-sew outfit. "Why don't we just ask that dude?! Y'know, the one who was in, like, armor or whatever!"

Everyone turned to look at the tower.

And then it happened.

The entrance began to shrink. The wall rose up again, filling in the hole.

"Whoa, whoa, wai—"

Playboy made a panicked run for it. He was too late.

The entrance vanished, leaving the spot where it had once been indistinguishable from the surrounding wall. Playboy tried touching and hitting the wall in all sorts of places while crying out things like, "Oh, come on, you can't be doing this! Wait, wait, stop it! Please, man..." But nothing happened.

After a while, Playboy sat down, dejected.

"Well, this is a problem," said a girl with her long hair in two braids. She said the word "problem" with a funny accent.

"You said it," replied Curly Hair, crouching down and hanging his head.

"Seriously...? Seriously?"

"And now, with that perfect tiiiiiiiming!" a high-pitched woman's voice rang out—

Wait, who...? he thought.

There were four girls in their group: Flashy, the one with braids, the petite and timid one, and an even tinier girl who had to be shorter than 150 centimeters. That high-pitched voice didn't sound like it belonged to Flashy, Braids, or Timid. It probably wasn't Tiny's voice, either.

"I appear, you know. I take the stage, you know. Where am I? I'm right heeeere!"

"Right where?!" cried Playboy, standing up and shouting.

"Don't paaaanic! Don't be alaaaarmed! But, still, don't relaaaax. Don't pull out your hair, eiiiither!"

Singing something like "Chararararararahn, chararararararahnrarahn." a woman poked her head out from the side of the tower where she had apparently been hiding.

Is her hairstyle what they call "twintails"? he wondered.

"Heeeey. Is everyone feeling fiiiine? Welcome to Grimgar. I'm your guide, Hiyomuuuu. Nice to meet youuuu. Let's get along! Kyapii!"

A man with a buzz-cut ground his teeth loudly. "What an annoying speech style," he muttered.

"Eek!" Hiyomu ducked her head back behind the tower but soon stuck it out again. "You're so scary. So dangerous. Don't get so maaaad. Okay? Okay? Okay? Okay?"

Buzz-Cut clicked his tongue in distaste. "Then don't piss me off."

"Yes sirreeee!" Hiyomu hopped out next to the tower, raising her hand in a salute. "I'll be careful from now on, sir! I'll be reeeeal careful, sir? Is this okay? It's okay, right? Teehee."

"You're doing that on purpose, aren't you?"

"Aw, you could teeeell? Ah! Ah! Don't get mad! Don't punch me, don't kick me! I don't like being hurt! Generally, I want you to be niiiice to me! Anyway, is it okay if I move things along now? Can I do my job now?"

"Hurry it up," said Gangster in a low voice. Unlike Buzz-Cut, he didn't look openly agitated. Still, his tone was intimidating.

"All righty, then," Hiyomu began with a grin. "I'm gonna do my job now, okay?"

The sky was getting brighter by the moment. It was much brighter now than it had been earlier, which meant it must be morning, not dusk. The dawn was breaking.

"For now, just follow after meeee. Don't get left behiiiind!"

Hiyomu started to walk, her twintails swaying behind her.

Looking around, they saw a path from the tower leading down the hill. Grass fields spread out on both sides of a dark path of exposed earth that had been hardened with use and there were large white stones scattered around the grass that covered the hill. A whole lot of them. Too many. It looked almost like they were in orderly rows.

It was as if someone had lined them up.

"Hey, are those..." Curly asked, pointing at the white stones. "Could they be...graves?"

He shuddered.

Speaking of which, he noticed some sort of writing carved into them. Flowers had been placed in front of some, as well. A graveyard. *Could* this hill be a graveyard?

At the head of the group, Hiyomu giggled without turning around. "I wondeeeer. Well, don't you worry about that now. Don't woooorry. It's too soon for any of you. I hope it's too soon for any of youuuu. Hee hee hee..."

Buzz-Cut clicked his tongue in distaste again, kicking the dirt. He seemed pretty ticked off, but it looked like he still planned to follow Hiyomu for now.

Gangster had already started walking. Glasses, Flashy, and Tiny followed him.

Playboy shouted, "Whoa! Me too, me too! Me too!" and began chasing after them, then tripped.

It looked like there was no choice but to go along. But where was Hiyomu planning to take them? Where was this place?

He sighed, looking up to the sky. "Ah..."

What's that? It's pretty low in the sky. It can't be the sun—and it's too big to be a distant star. It's not even a full circle, anyway, and it's shape is somewhere between a half and a crescent moon. Did that mean it's the moon, then? That'd be a weird moon, though...

"It's red," he said out loud. He blinked, taking another look at it. No matter how many times he looked, it was still ruby red.

Behind him, Timid gulped audibly. He turned around to see she was gazing at the moon, as well.

"Ahh," said Braids as she seemed to notice it, too. She blinked repeatedly, then chuckled. "Mr. Moon is red. That's super pretty."

The man with silky hair looked up to the red moon hanging in the dawn sky, standing still with an absent look on his face.

Curly said, "Whoa..." with a wide-eyed stare.

An excessively large, but seemingly quiet, man let out a low groan.

He didn't know where this was. Where had he come from? How had he gotten here? He didn't know those things, either. He couldn't recall. But... there was just one thing he was certain of.

The moon in that other place wasn't red.

A red moon was just weird.

Grimgar of Fantasy and Ash

1. All These Things We Don't Know

In some parts of the town, the streets were lined with stone buildings, while in others, there were nothing but wooden ones. The cobblestone street twisted and turned, making it hard to see far ahead. Next to the wide road, there was an aqueduct, with water flowing through it that was mostly pure. At times there was a foul odor, likely of excrement, but as they walked onwards, it stopped bothering them.

Hiyomu led the group of twelve men and women into the town beyond the hill. From what she had said, this town was called Alterna. There were people living here, as might be expected from something called a town, and though it was early morning, they passed no small number of people who seemed to be residents. The residents all stared at the twelve as if they were an unusual sight. But the twelve found themselves staring right back. After all, the people were all dressed weirdly.

Wait... weird how? Compared to the twelve, their clothes were simple and shabby, not showy at all.

"So, like, this place..." started Playboy, "is it, like, you know...

a foreign country or something...?"

"Uh..." Curly turned his head, trying to come up with an answer. "...A foreign country? A country? Come to think of it, what nationality am I, anyway? Huh? Weird, I can't remember... Actually, I can't remember my address and such either. Huh?"

"What, you hadn't noticed?" Gangster said in a low voice. "My name is about all I still know."

The phrase *still know* caught his attention. It probably meant something different than just not having known at all. Maybe Gangster had been hit with that feeling of trying to trace his memories back only to feel them vanishing, too.

"My name..." Curly thumped his chest. "My name is... Ranta. Other than that... Yeah. No clue. Whoa. Seriously? I've got memory disappearance..."

"I think you mean..." He broke in without meaning to, and then immediately regretted it. Still, he couldn't very well stop now. "... memory loss, right?"

"Listen, buddy..." Curly said with a sigh. "If you're going to be the smart guy, can't you do it better? It requires a certain spirit, you know. When you half-ass it like that, it's awkward for me as the guy playing the fool for you. It kills the mood. Well, whatever. I'll overlook it this once. So, who're you?"

"You'll... overlook it..."

In what way had Ranta been playing the fool? What a horrible attempt at humor. He wasn't fully convinced but...

A name.

What was his own name?

"...I'm Haruhiro. I think?"

Curly, a.k.a. Ranta, made an exaggerated tripping gesture, like a pratfall. "You think? Hold on, buddy, you don't even know your own name? Okay, I know we're talking about how my name's all I know, but..."

This guy's pretty annoying, Haruhiro thought, glancing over at Gangster, who was walking behind Hiyomu. He wondered what Gangster's name was. He kind of wanted to ask but he was too scared of the man. Though he didn't intend it as a replacement for asking Gangster, he turned to the slender man with silky hair and asked, "How about you?"

"Oh," replied Silky with a smile. He was a rather eloquent man. "I'm Manato. Do you mind if I call you Haruhiro? No honorifics or anything?"

"Oh, sure, that's fine. Then can I call you just Manato, too?"

"I'm fine with that, of course."

When Manato smiled at him, he couldn't help but smile, too. *He looks like a good guy. I can probably trust him,* he thought.

Ranta was annoying. Gangster scared him and Buzz-Cut had a scary face. Flashy felt like she came from a world far removed from his and it was hard to approach an intelligent-looking guy like Glasses. Braids, Timid, and Tiny: what about those three girls?

Timid he had talked to a little already and she was close by. He figured he'd at least try to get her name. But when it came to actually asking, he was a bundle of nerves.

Haruhiro cleared his throat. "Uh, hey."

"Y-Yes...?"

"N-Now, it's not anything important, but, uh..."

"I'm Kikkawa, yeah!" Playboy suddenly exclaimed, striking a

weird pose. "Hey, hey! Forget the guys, let's hear from the ladies! You want to shoot off some introductions or not?!"

Braids shook her head. "Not."

"No way!" Playboy, a.k.a. Kikkawa, looked pathetically shot down.

Haruhiro couldn't help but feel a little gleeful. Still, Kikkawa's attempt had given him the momentum he needed.

"Um," Haruhiro tried to ask as straight as he could. "What's your name? It'd be easier to address you if we knew. Well, compared to us not knowing, at least."

"Ah…" Timid looked down, pulling at her bangs. Was she trying to hide her face? Her eyes, nose and lips were modest but she was pretty cute. There was nothing she needed to hide at least. "…I'm…Shihoru. That's my name, I mean. More or less. Sorry…"

"No, you don't need to apologize."

"Sorry, it's a habit. I'm sorry, I'll try not to…" Shihoru was trembling like a newborn fawn.

Was this girl going to be okay? He was worried just looking at her. It stimulated a protective instinct in him.

"You're a big guy," said Manato, who was talking to the gentle giant. "How tall are you?"

"Huh?" said the big man, blinking absently. "My height? I'm 160 cm…"

"160?!" Ranta interjected. "That's smaller than me, the guy who's a self-proclaimed 170 cm, you know?!"

"I got it wrong. It was 180… 86? Around there. I think. Ah. My name is Moguzo. Probably."

"Give me 10 of your centimeters right now, Moguzo!" Ranta demanded, jabbing Moguzo in the side. As if that were possible.

"If I get 10 centimeters from you, I'll be 178! You'll be 176! What a turnaround! That'd be wonderful! Wouldn't it?!"

"If I could give them to you..." replied Moguzo.

"Hold on..." Haruhiro could only curse himself as he started to correct Ranta again. "In that case, your height isn't over 170; you're really 168."

"Oh, shut up. *Sorrrrr-ry!* You look like you're about the same height as me, anyway!" Ranta huffed.

"I'm just barely 170."

"You're a piece of work, you know that?! You're a fiend who discriminates against people over a measly two centimeters!"

"This guy is such a pain," Haruhiro muttered.

"Huh?! I didn't hear you quite right. Did you say something?! You did, didn't you?! You said something!"

"Nothing, nothing. I didn't say a thing, honest."

"You liar! You lying, perverted, deviant bastard! Don't underestimate my devilishly good hearing! This is what you said: 'You and your natural curls can go to hell, you bastard!'"

"No, I seriously did not say that."

"You called me 'Curly'! That's the one thing you can't call me! That word is banned, damn it!"

"Yeah, and I didn't say it. Listen when people are talking..."

"I *was* listening! I was listening so *well,* I've got callouses on my ears! Anyway, I don't forgive anyone who calls me 'Curly'! That's an executable offense! Don't you forget it!"

"Curly," Gangster turned around and said, "you're annoying. Shut up."

"...Yes, sir," said Curly, a.k.a. Ranta, in a tiny voice. "...Sorry. I'll shut up now."

Haruhiro shrugged. "Weren't you never going to forgive that?"

"You moron." Ranta said quietly. "I'm a guy who chooses the right time and place. They call me Master Choice. I'm gonna be the Decision King!"

"Yeah, you go ahead and do that..."

"I'll become a king of discernment! Not detergent, discernment! The Decision King! That's what I'll be!"

"Curly," Gangster stopped and turned around again. "Shut up."

"Eeek!" Ranta quickly did a jumping kowtow. "I-I'm sorry...!"

"Rather than the King of Decision," Haruhiro said, looking down at Ranta, "why not become the King of Kowtows, instead?"

"That's it!" Ranta raised his head and snapped his fingers. "Wait, no, that is *not* it! Being the King of Kowtows would be way too lame! No matter how high my kowtow skill is!"

"Curly." Gangster sounded ready to kill him. "This is the third time."

"Eeeeek!" Ranta did another kowtow, rubbing his forehead on the cobblestones. "I-I'm sorry! Won't happen again! Forgive me, pleeeeeease...!"

This guy's already the King of Kowtows, thought Haruhiro, but he decided not to say so. If he said anything, they'd probably just start arguing again, and that would be a pain. After that, they continued on in silence until Hiyomu stopped in front of a two-story stone building.

The building was flying a flag with a red crescent moon on a white field. There was a sign out front, as well. On the sign, it said, "Altern Fronter Arm Voluter Solder Cops Red Mon," which seemed weird.

On closer inspection, many of the letters had lost their color or peeled off.

"Ta-da!" said Hiyomu, pointing at the sign. "We've finally arrived, yes we have. Here. It. Is! The office of the famous Volunteer Soldier Corps of the Alterna Frontier Army, Red Moon!"

Haruhiro whispered, "Red Moon," and looked to the sign again. It made sense now. If you read it with the missing bits, it did say "Alterna Frontier Army Volunteer Soldier Corps Red Moon."

"Come in, come in!" Hiyomu gestured them into a large room that was like a beer hall, with tables and chairs scattered around and, at the back, a counter. Behind the counter was a man with his arms crossed. Haruhiro, the others and Hiyomu were the only other people there.

"Well, that's it for me!" Hiyomu said with a bow to the man behind the counter. "I know I do this every time, but give them the rundown, 'kay, Bri-chan?"

The man she called Bri-chan gave a light "Righty-o" in response, and waved good-bye to her with his arms still crossed. For some reason, he shook his hips as well as waving his hand.

"I'm leaving noooow! Bye-byeeee!" Hiyomu said as she left. Once she closed the door behind her, a strange tension spread through the room. Likely because Bri-chan was closely examining Haruhiro and the others. That must have been it. After all, Bri-chan looked pretty suspicious. Way too suspicious.

Bri-chan bent over, resting both elbows on the counter, and rested his chin on top of his clasped hands. It was a cleft chin. But, well, that detail didn't matter so much, because it was his hair color that set off warning flags. It was green. On top of that, he must have had lipstick or something on, because his lips were black. He had pale blue eyes surrounded by long, thick lashes, and though their color was beautiful, that only made him more terrifying. It seemed like he'd used rouge on his cheeks, too. He had thick makeup overall, even though, no matter how you looked at him, Bri-chan was a guy.

"Hm..." He nodded to himself a number of times, then stood up. "Very nice. Come here, my little kittens. Welcome. I'm Britney. I'm the chief and host here at the office of Red Moon, the Volunteer Soldier Corps of the Alterna Frontier Army. You can call me Chief, but Bri-chan is fine, too. Though, if you do call me that, make sure you say it with lots of love, okay?"

"Chief," Gangster walked straight up to the counter, cocking his head to one side. "Answer my questions. I know that this town is called Alterna. But what is this Frontier Army and Volunteer Soldier Corps stuff about? Why am I here? Do you know?"

"You've got spunk," Bri-chan said with a chuckle. "I've got a thing for boys like you. What's your name?"

"It's Renji. And I hate fags like you."

"Oh, *do* you now..."

For a moment, Haruhiro wasn't sure what Bri-chan had done. His movements had been not only fast, but smooth and all too natural.

"Renji, let me give you a tip." Bri-chan pressed a knife against Renji's throat, his eyes narrowing threateningly. "Nobody who calls me a fag lives for long. You look like a clever boy; I think you catch my meaning. Or do you want to try it again?"

"Well," Renji said.

Haruhiro gulped.

Renji seized the knife's blade with his bare hand. Though he had the blade fixed in place with his palm and fingers, there was blood dripping from the base of his thumb.

"I never wanted a long life, and I don't care to give in to threats," he said. "If you think you can take me, do it, Chief Fag."

"In due time," Bri-chan replied, licking his lips and stroking Renji's cheek. "I'll take you hard. As many times as I like. And when I'm done, you'll never be able to forget me."

"...Hey," Ranta whispered to Haruhiro. "When he says he'll take him, I'm pretty sure he means it a different way."

"What way?" Braids asked Ranta with a blank look.

"Huh? Uh, well, like putting something in a place where things are supposed to come out of... Basically, uh, how do I say this? Hey, Haruhiro?"

"Don't look to me to get you out of this. You dug this hole, get out of it by yourself."

"You're cold, man... You've got a kindness deficiency... You're at the absolute zero of human kindness..."

"Well, anyway!" Kikkawa the playboy got between Renji and Bri-chan. "It's our first meeting! There are bound to be misunderstandings! Let's settle this peacefully! Let's try to get along and be cheery? Okay? Okay? In deference to my good looks!"

"Your good looks?" Renji glared at Kikkawa and snorted derisively as he let go of the knife.

Bri-chan pulled back his knife, wiping the blood from it with a rag. "Looks like we have a few reckless ones here. Eight men, four women. There aren't quite enough women, but I prefer it that way, and men are more likely to be useful in battle anyway, so it's no problem."

Manato cocked an eyebrow. "In battle?"

"Right," Bri-chan said with a smile. It was pretty creepy, frankly.

"Useful in battle."

"This is a Volunteer Soldier office," Manato said, looking down. "So, does that mean we're becoming volunteer soldiers or something?"

"Oh, my!" Bri-chan clapped. "You've got some promise, too. That's exactly it. You're all going to be volunteer soldiers. You do have some freedom to decide, though, y'know?"

"Master Choice," Haruhiro said, slapping Ranta on the back. "You're up."

"O-Oh?! I... I am, aren't I?! Aren't... I...?"

"All of you can choose," Bri-chan said, lifting up his index finger and wiggling it around. "You can accept my offer or reject it. The offer is to join our Red Moon Volunteer Soldier Corps as part of the Alterna Frontier Army. Well, you'll be starting as trainees aiming to become fully fledged volunteer soldiers."

"Volunteer soldiers..." said Flashy, with a frightening look on her face. "What do they even do?"

"They fight," Bri-chan said with a wave of his hand, looking like he wanted to add a "you silly goose" afterward. "Here in the borderlands, there are races that are hostile to us humans, as well as lots and lots of monsters. The Frontier Army's duty is to exterminate them and secure the frontier. But, to be honest, it's not an easy job. As a matter of fact, the Frontier Army has its hands full just maintaining its front line base in Alterna. So, that's where our Volunteer Soldier Corps comes in."

"So, basically..." Glasses adjusted the position of his glasses with the middle finger of his right hand. "...while the regular forces protect the town, the Volunteer Soldier Corps strikes out to slay hostile races and monsters. Is that it?"

"To put it simply, yes," Bri-chan said, spreading his hands like a flower. He may have thought it looked cute, but it was pretty creepy.

"Though, that said, it isn't like the Frontier Army is purely defensive, you know? There are times when they launch expeditionary forces to assault the strongholds of hostile races. It's just that large-scale military operations have their limitations. With supply logistics and whatnot, lots of things need to be thought out in advance, after all. Volunteer soldiers aren't like that."

Kikkawa was following along with exaggerated nods. "Like, how are they different?"

"We volunteer soldiers..." Bri-chan began, bringing his hands together and wiggling the tips of his fingers. "...appear suddenly and unexpectedly, infiltrating enemy territory left and right, surveying, causing confusion and finding ways to weaken opposing forces. Though we cooperate with the main force, we very rarely engage in organized operations. Most volunteer soldiers act alone or in small parties of 3-6 people, I would think. Anyway, we use our own individual skills and judgment to gather intel and strike the enemy. That is the way the Volunteer Soldier Corps, Red Moon, works."

"And?" Renji asked, flexing the fingers of his right hand. There was no blood dripping from it. The bleeding had already stopped. "What happens if I turn down your offer?"

"Nothing, really, y'know?" Bri-chan tilted his head and shook his waist a little. Was he fooling around? Perhaps he was fooling around and threatening them at the same time. It was pretty scary, after all. "I already told you, you have room to decide. You can choose. If you don't want to be a volunteer soldier, you're welcome to leave right now and never come back."

"Heh..." Ranta said, scratching at his curly hair. "Maybe I'll pass, then. I don't really get it, but, you know, I'm fundamentally a pacifist and all."

"Fine. Bye, then. Take care."

"Yeah! You take care too, Bri-chan!" Ranta turned around, walked towards the exit, then stopped. "...Hold on, but once I leave here, what am I supposed to do?"

"I can't take responsibility for you after that," Bri-chan laughed. "If you aren't joining the Corps, you're free to do as you please. Those of you who become volunteer soldier trainees will each receive ten silver coins, 10 Silver. That will be enough for you to live on for the time being, I think."

"Silver coins..." Manato's eyes widened and he began fishing through his pockets. "Oh, yeah... money."

Haruhiro touched his hip and back pockets, too. They were empty. He had nothing on him. Which, of course, meant he was penniless.

"A part-time job, maybe..." Ranta's face twitched, and he hung his head. "I could look for one... That's about all I can do, for now..."

"Hopefully something conveniently falls into your lap," Bri-chan said with an exaggerated shrug. "But any other job you find will come with its own troubles, you know? Even if you luck into someone willing to hire you, they'll pay you barely anything, and you'll generally start out doing grueling menial tasks or looking after the owner or master's personal needs."

"Ack!" Kikkawa said, slapping his forehead. "It's a tough world, man. I dunno what to say. Do we have to, like, just go with the flow here?"

"I do believe I told you? Flow or no flow, the ones to decide whether you join or not are..." Bri-chan pointed at each of them. "You. Your. Selves."

Renji took a deep breath. "Be specific. What do we need to do first?"

"Oh, Renji. Don't disappoint me. Weren't you listening? Use your own individual skills and judgment to gather intel and strike the enemy. That's the volunteer soldier way."

"So, as trainees, we need to search and think for ourselves, too, then?"

"That's right," Bri-chan nodded and began lining something up on the counter. Reddish, coin-like objects and little leather pouches. Twelve sets in total.

Bri-chan held one of the coin-like objects, which had a crescent moon on it, between his fingers. "This badge identifies the holder as a trainee. It's known as a Trainee Badge. As such, it will be proof of your status as a volunteer soldier trainee. If you take one, don't lose it. Well, not that carrying it will do much for you, either. Though, once you buy your Corps Badge from me with 20 Silver and become a full member of the Volunteer Soldier Corps, that one will have some perks."

"Hold on," Buzz-Cut said in an agitated tone. "You want us to pay you for status?"

"Yes. Is that a problem?"

"I don't like it."

"Say what you like, but without money, you can't eat, you can't clothe yourself, you can't do anything. What choice do you have? You can go die in a ditch if you prefer."

Renji laughed a little at that one. "Even in Hell, money matters, huh?"

"Hell?" Bri-chan tilted his head to the side, quizzically. "Well, that's about right. Anyway, I know this is odd to say after telling you to figure things out yourselves, but I would think your first goal should be to buy a Corps Badge and become a volunteer soldier."

"Fair enough." Renji took a Trainee Badge and leather pouch. "I don't know about this volunteer soldier business or whatever but I'll do it. We'll talk after that."

After Renji, Buzz-Cut took a Trainee Badge and leather pouch. A little bit after him were Flashy, Manato, and Glasses.

Kikkawa said, "Okay then, I'm getting in on this, too!" then went to take two pouches, only to have his hand slapped by Bri-chan.

There wasn't much of a choice. But... why do this? To get money... or, in other words, to stay alive, maybe? If that was why, then he supposed he had to. It was unavoidable, but he still had a bad feeling about it.

Shihoru, Braids, and Tiny all seemed hesitant. Ranta and the big guy, Moguzo, hadn't decided yet either.

Bri-chan turned his pale blue eyes towards them. "What about you?"

"I dunno..." Ranta walked towards the counter, mumbling to himself. "I feel like I'm about to get screwed here. I've got a vaguely bad feeling about all this..."

"Hmm." Braids followed behind Ranta. "Where there's a will-will, there's a way-way, they say..."

"No," Haruhiro shook his head. "I don't think anybody says will-will or way-way..."

"Oh?" Braids turned back, her hand outstretched towards the badge and pouch. "They don't? Yume's always said it with will-will and way-way."

"You learned it wrong then. "It's just 'where there's a will, there's a way.'"

"Oh. But it sounds cuter with will-will and way-way. Yume thinks cute is important, too."

"...It definitely did sound cuter that way."

Braids, whose name was apparently Yume, giggled with genuine glee. "Isn't it, though?" While they'd been bantering, Tiny had taken a badge and pouch. Moguzo, Shihoru, and Haruhiro were the only ones left. Not wanting to be last, Haruhiro grabbed a badge and pouch. While he was opening his pouch to confirm there were ten tiny silver coins inside, Moguzo unhurriedly came and took a Trainee Badge and pouch. Shihoru was the last to do so.

"Congratulations," Bri-chan said, smiling and clapping. "Now, all of you are volunteer soldier trainees. Work hard and learn to stand on your own quickly. Once you're proper volunteer soldiers, I wouldn't be adverse to giving you some advice."

Then, suddenly—

"Hey!"

Thud!

"Urgh!"

They saw Buzz-Cut was now flat on the floor. It had happened in an instant, so they couldn't be sure, but maybe Renji had punched Buzz-Cut. Punched him? Why would he have done that?

"Get up," Renji said with a blank expression.

"You jerk!" Buzz-Cut shouted and tried to get up, only for Renji to immediately kick him, sending him sprawling across the floor.

"What's wrong? Get up."

"What's your problem, you ass?"

"From the first time I saw you, I wondered which of us was stronger. It's time for me to show you the answer. Get up."

"Dammit...!"

Renji was going to strike as soon as Buzz-Cut tried to spring up. Since it was obvious even to a bystander like Haruhiro, Buzz-Cut just needed to avoid it. Well, Buzz-Cut did try to dodge it but Renji moved ahead of where he was going and punched him, kicked him then grabbed him by the ear and pulled. As Buzz-Cut let out a scream of pain, he kneed him hard in the solar plexus. Not just once. Again and again. After that, Renji took Buzz-Cut's head in both hands. He swung his own head back and gave him a headbutt. There was a loud thud and Buzz-Cut slumped down and fell to one knee.

"You've got a hard head," Renji said, rubbing his forehead with one finger. It had gone red, and was bleeding a little. "Tell me your name."

Buzz-Cut kept his hands off the floor, putting them on his knee for support instead. He may have been bearing the pain out of a stubborn unwillingness to crawl. "...It's Ron. Damn, you're strong."

"You're pretty tough yourself. Come with me, Ron."

"Yeah. I'll stick with you for now."

"Good. Now, who else..." Renji looked around the office, stopping on Manato.

Manato reacted to Renji's glance with a narrowing of his eyes.

Renji moved right on, looking away from Manato to Glasses. "You look like you could be useful. Come with me."

Glasses crossed his arms and blinked a couple times in surprise. Then, adjusting the position of his glasses with the middle finger of his right hand, he gave a curt nod. "Sure. I'm Adachi. It's a pleasure, Renji."

Renji responded by raising one side of his mouth into a smirk, then turned his eyes on Haruhiro.

Huh? Maybe he wants me, too? thought Haruhiro, surprised and somewhat delighted. After all, Renji looked muscular, and he had demonstrated he was strong enough to easily take down Ron. He was a man of action. He could think on his feet, too. He was scary and seemed hard to get along with, but if Haruhiro could get past that, Renji was definitely reliable. If Renji was willing to take him along, it would probably make life easy from here out.

He couldn't deny that he felt that way. But those feelings soon shriveled up and died, because Renji looked elsewhere. He'd been ignored.

"You there, Chibi."

"Aye...?" The girl who was tiniest among the twelve of them had a tiny voice, too.

Renji said "Come," and gestured for her to follow.

Chibi-chan may have been staring off into space. She tottered over in his direction, and looked up at Renji.

Renji patted Chibi-chan on the head. "You look like you'll be useful. Come along."

Chibi-chan said "Aye..." and nodded. Her face flushed red. There was something about her that resembled a boiled egg. More than her looks, it was her little gestures and overall essence that lent her a mascot-like adorableness. But...useful? Haruhiro didn't know about that. And, wait, had Renji decided Chibi-chan would be more useful than him? He didn't know whether to feel humiliated or just sad.

"We're going," Renji gestured to the office door with his chin. As Ron, Adachi, Chibi-chan, and Renji began to walk away, Flashy shouted, "Wait! Take me, too!"

Renji let out a short sigh. "I don't need any useless baggage."

"I'll do anything!" Flashy said, clinging to Renji. "I'm Sassa. Please. Absolutely anything, I'll do it."

"Absolutely anything, huh?" Renji said, shoving Sassa away. "Don't forget those words."

"Yeah. I won't."

"And don't touch me."

"Gotcha..."

"Good. You come, too."

"Thanks, Renji!" Sassa opened the door, and Renji and his followers walked out. Sassa was the last to leave. When the door closed, the seven people remaining looked defeated, like they'd lost the lottery.

"Ack!" Kikkawa said, grimacing and scratching his head. "Wish I coulda gotten on Team Renji, too... Between Renji and Ron, they're probably unbeatable in a fight. Adachi looked smart, Chibi-chan's cute as a button and Sassa was smoking hot. Man, I'm so jealous. But, well, them's the breaks. I'm off to gather info. Toodles." Before he could say anything, Kikkawa had left the office.

Haruhiro exchanged glances with Shihoru. Shihoru hung her head in shame.

"Well, I'm off, too," said Manato, heading for the exit. "I won't learn anything staying here so I'm going outside to look around. See you all later."

"Yeah, see you." As Haruhiro was waving good-bye to Manato, it occurred to him maybe he should tag along. Manato was approachable unlike Renji. He seemed good-natured, and was probably reliable. But, even though he couldn't care less about Ranta, what would Shihoru and Yume do? Moguzo was here, too. Right.

If they all went together, that would solve the problem. Except, by the time Haruhiro figured that out, Manato was no longer in the office. But he was sure it was still not too late.

"Listen, us staying here really won't help, so let's all go after Manato, and..."

Haruhiro only got that far before the door opened. *Perhaps it's Manato coming back!*

But it wasn't. It was another man who had entered the office. He wore an outfit made out of hide, a cap with a feather in it and had a bow and arrows slung over his back. He looked a few years older than Haruhiro and the others. The man had eyes like a fox and a crooked mouth.

"Heya, Chief."

"Oh, my," Bri-chan looked at the man. "If it isn't Kuzuoka. What's going on? Did you need me for something?"

"No, that's not why I came," Kuzuoka said with a glance to Haruhiro and the others. "I heard we had some newbies so I came for a peek."

"News sure makes it to you fast. But we had twelve this time, and only five of them are still here."

"Oh. These are the leftovers, then, huh."

Ranta's face stiffened. "Well, *sorrrr-ry* for being left over."

"You ought to be sorry, you know?" Kuzuoka said with a glare at Ranta, then gave Haruhiro and the others the once-over to evaluate them. "Hmm... Well, it's the front-liners we're short on, anyway. Hey, big guy, you'll do."

Moguzo pointed at himself. "Me?"

"That's right. I mean you. When I say 'big guy,' you're the only one here I could mean. I'll let you join our party. I'll show you the ropes. I can even lend you a little money. It's a pretty sweet deal, don't you think? Now if you understand me, come along."

"Uh, okay..."

"Moguzo, you're going?!" Ranta grabbed Moguzo by the left arm. "Don't do it! This guy is clearly dodgy!"

"Ah, okay..."

"Just come already!" Kuzuoka pulled his right arm. "As a trainee, you should be grateful just to be let into a party! Also, I am *not* dodgy!"

"Uh, uh, okay..."

"Moguzo, don't let him trick you! A guy who's dodgy is never going to tell you he's dodgy!"

"Ah, ah, uh... Ow, ouch, that... hurts, you know..."

"Oh!" Ranta let go of his arm.

"Sorry, sorry, ah..." Moguzo apologized meekly.

"Okay, let's go now!" Kuzuoka said, savagely dragging Moguzo away.

Shihoru's shoulders slumped. "They left..."

"Now there're..." Yume counted one, two, three on her fingers as she pointed to Haruhiro, Ranta, Shihoru and finally herself. "...four of us, huh?"

"Darlings," Bri-chan said, stifling a yawn. "Just how long do you plan on standing there? I'm busy with work of my own. If you're just going to loiter around, I'll toss you out, you know?"

Ranta looked to Haruhiro and the others like a beaten dog. "... Should we get out of here?"

Haruhiro figured the look on his own face must have been at least as pathetic as Ranta's. "...Yeah."

2. Lost and Confused

They had left the office of the Red Moon Volunteer Soldier Corps. But where would they go now? There had been talk of gathering information, but Haruhiro and company knew absolutely nothing about this town called Alterna. None of them knew anyone here, so they had no connections to rely on and Renji, Kikkawa, Manato, and even Kuzuoka and Moguzo didn't seem to be around anymore, either. It looked like they had already taken off elsewhere.

No one knew what to do.

Haruhiro, Ranta, Yume, and Shihoru stood in front of the office a while in a daze.

"...What should we do?" Shihoru was first to speak.

Why are you asking me? I ought to be asking you, Haruhiro wanted to say, but then he thought, *She's a girl. I can't say it like that.*

"What...should we do?" he tried asking her.

"What...should we do, indeed?" Shihoru answered three seconds later.

"You people..." Ranta said with an exaggerated sigh. "Can't you come up with something a little better? Show a little more, I dunno, independence? Something like that. It's really not the time to be saying, 'What do we do?' now is it?"

"Well, since you're saying that," replied Haruhiro. "What do you suggest...?"

"I'm thinking about it, okay? About what to do next."

Yume chuckled to herself. "That sounds 'bout the same to Yume."

"Yeah, kinda," Ranta said, rubbing the underside of his nose like a mischievous child. "You could say that."

Honestly, this is pretty bad, Haruhiro couldn't help but think. *Kuzuoka called us the leftovers and he may have been absolutely right. The indecisive four of us were left behind and we aren't trying to come together to do something, we're just sort of here. Could this be the worst possible result...?*

"Moguzo's got it good..." said Ranta, giving voice to a thought Haruhiro couldn't say he didn't share. "Even if that Kuzuoka did seem scummy. He's got experience, you know? If you get into a party with a guy who seems like he knows stuff, you can relax a bit. It could be pretty breezy from there. And why Moguzo, anyway? He shoulda chosen me. I'm clearly way more useful. Seriously... Seriously..."

"You sure?" Yume asked in a soft voice.

"I have a hard time seeing it," Haruhiro concurred.

"You people..." Ranta said, pointing at Haruhiro and Yume. "You can only say that because you haven't seen what I can do! Let me tell you, I'm real capable! From the time I was a baby suckling at my mother's teat, I've been secretly famous as a man who would do great things!"

"If you were famous, it would hardly be a secret," rebutted Haruhiro.

"Don't sweat the details that much. You'll just tire yourself out, y'know?"

"Having to deal with you has already left me a little tired..."

"You've got no stamina. Haruhiro, you're so useless. You're no good. No good at all."

"I don't want to hear this from the guy whose only redeeming quality is his curly hair."

"Don't call it curly!"

"Hey, I said it was a redeeming quality. Your curly hair is the only thing you've got going for you. Curly hair is all you've got."

"R-Really? You think curly hair's good? I'm not so convinced, you know...?"

"Yume's hair is all straight, y'know," Yume piped in. "When Yume sees another girl with her hair up in curls, she gets jealous. Yume thinks you've got it good, Ranta."

"R-Really? My curly hair's that great? For real?"

"Yeah. When your hair's all curly like that, it makes it look like the inside of your head's all fluffy, too. It's kind of cute, y'know."

"What? Cute? Nah, are you sure? As a guy, having a girl call me cute, well, it doesn't feel bad, but—hey, wait! The inside of my head's all fluffy? Are you saying I look like an idiot?!"

They heard someone inhale sharply. When they looked, Shihoru's shoulders were trembling and she had her face in her hands.

Ranta's eyes popped out. "Whaa...?!"

Yume looked at Shihoru and blinked a few times.

Haruhiro was, of course, surprised as well.

Sh-She's crying...?

"Wh-What's... wrong?" Haruhiro went to put a supporting hand on her back but stopped himself. *Touching her's probably a bad idea. She is a girl, after all.*

"It... It's nothing..." Shihoru was obviously sobbing heavily. "Nothing...at all. I'm just...feeling a little worried..."

"Oh..." That made sense to Haruhiro, once he thought about it. In their situation, perhaps Haruhiro and the others who were bantering about trivial nonsense were the crazy ones. Shihoru might be the only normal one.

"There, there," Yume said, rubbing Shihoru's back to soothe her. "There, there. It'll be fine. Even if Yume isn't sure what exactly'll be fine, y'know."

Ranta grimaced. "You're not sounding reassuring there..."

"Well, still..." Haruhiro said, scratching his neck. "We've got to do something or we're in trouble, don't you think? Just standing here in silence is awkward. I dunno. Like, there've got to be other volunteer soldiers like that Kuzuoka guy. We could find one of them and ask questions...or something?"

"Okay, counting on you for that!" Ranta said, slapping Haruhiro on the shoulder. "Find one quick and ask them questions or whatever! Yep, Haruhiro! You're our man for this!"

"...It's almost refreshing how eager you are to make someone else do all the work."

"It's like a breath of fresh air, isn't it?"

"It really pisses me off."

"I'll come right out and say it: you getting pissed off won't bother me in the least!"

"You're the worst!"

"Oh, shove it. You suggested it, so you get to do it. That's how these things work, pretty much. But okay, fine, let's split up the workload. Haruhiro, you're in charge of finding a volunteer soldier and getting some answers. Shihoru's in charge of being depressed. Yume's in charge of consoling her. As for me, we'll say I'm in charge of waiting here for you to get back!"

"Ranta, man, are you really that eager to do nothing...?"

"If you're gonna insist, I can do something, but if it's not fun, I don't wanna."

"Don't we have...bigger things to worry about than whether you have fun or not?"

"Nah, that's the most important thing. I'm the kind of guy who wants to enjoy life. If I can't enjoy it, it ain't part of my life. What about you, Haruhiro? Are you the type that can't enjoy life? I'll bet you are, with those sleepy eyes of yours."

"I was born with these eyes!" Haruhiro shot back at Ranta, then sighed deeply. "Fine, I've had enough. I'll be right back. I'll go find us a volunteer soldier."

"Finally ready to do it, huh? Well, next time just do it to begin with. You're such a pain," said Ranta.

Maybe I should punch him, thought Haruhiro, but he decided against it. *If I punch a guy like this, I'd just get my fist, and my soul, dirty. He's not even worth hitting.*

With an "I'll be right back, so stay here," to Shihoru and Yume, he walked away from the front of the office. Though he still honestly had no clue where to go.

The sun should be to the East, so that way's North, that way's South, and that way's West.

To the north rose a tall building that looked like a tower or castle.

I can probably use that as a landmark, so I guess I'll look around a bit. He decided to go north based on that idea, but Haruhiro wasn't here as a tourist. *Is this going to be okay? I'm sure Renji's group is doing fine. Manato's probably getting by somehow, too. As for the overly exuberant Kikkawa, he's probably chatting up every person he comes across. I hope Moguzo isn't being tricked by Kuzuoka. If he's not being lied to, he may well have had the best start here of all of us.*

"...I'll have to ask someone, I guess," Haruhiro said to himself.

Anyone will do. I'll start with the couple over there—but what do I ask about? Volunteer soldiers? Right. I'll have them tell me about volunteer soldiers. About where the volunteer soldiers are.

Having found his resolve, he started people-watching. He wasn't concerned about age or gender. He just wanted someone who seemed friendly and approachable.

Most of the people who went by made eye contact with Haruhiro. They were all looking at him. Was he an unusual sight for them? He must be. The way he dressed was blatantly out of place.

None of them seem well-disposed towards me. They look at me like I don't belong here, you could say. Am I just imagining it? Maybe I'm reading too much into it.

"...Still, maybe I'm setting my expectations too high. Or is it that I'm being too much of a chicken...?"

Courage, come to me, please, Haruhiro prayed silently as he walked through the unfamiliar town. *After all, I figure once I get going, I can stop people with "Excuse me?" I just hope I can get into that mindset quickly since it looks like I didn't arrive with it.*

On the other side of a plaza completely free of any litter, that tall building rose into the sky. It looked like it was stonework. The buildings around it all had either one or two floors—three at most—so that made it stand out. But really, it would have stood out anyway because it really was tall. It looked solid, with windows and gates that were decorated in fine detail. It made a very impressive sight.

Positioned around the plaza and in front of the gates, there were men who looked like guards, dressed in armor and helmets, armed with spears and shields. The place seemed to be under tight guard, so maybe someone important lived there. Like the mayor, maybe.

As he stood in the middle of the plaza staring up at the building, one of the guards came over, his metal armor and equipment clanking.

"What are you doing there? Have you some business at Tenboro Tower?" the guard demanded.

"Huh? Tenboro? Uh, no, not really..."

"Then begone. Do you wish to be arrested for disturbing His Excellency, the Margrave?"

"G-Get arrested...? I'd rather not. That's for sure. Yeah. Sorry." Haruhiro left the plaza as quickly as he could.

I don't really get it, but His Excellency, the Margrave must be the name...no, the title...of whoever lives in that tower, Tenboro or whatever it was called.

It was the first piece of information he'd gotten. Though, considering how the place stood out, it was probably something every person in town knew.

"Alterna. Margrave. His Excellency. Tenboro Tower. Frontier... The Frontier Army. Volunteer Soldier Corps. Volunteer soldiers, huh..."

Mumbling the words he had learned to himself, he proceeded north and found a strangely lively area up ahead of him.

What could this be? Shops?

Both sides of the street were packed tightly with food carts and street stalls. It looked as if some were still setting up, but more than half seemed to be open for business. The stores had a wide variety of foods, clothing, sundries, and even more on display out front. Energetic voices from all directions called out to the people passing by, shouting at them to try each shop.

"Something like a market, maybe...?" As if being lured, Haruhiro walked in.

The hustle and bustle was incredible. The goods had tags saying things like 1C or 3C or 12C and though he could read them, he wasn't sure what any of it meant.

"C'mere and buy something, Mister!" and "Come on in, Mister!" people called out to him, and he hated the cowardice which caused him to ignore or run away from them every time. Still, it didn't take long for the wonderful scents to drift his way and get him excited.

"Meat..." He started to salivate.

There was meat. In one cart, they were cooking meat on skewers. The cart over there was cooking soup or something in a pot and yet another cart had mountains of bread piled up. There was a shop selling some kind of sandwiches, as well. In the shop across the way, they had something like steamed buns on display.

The steam. The smoke. The scents. It was all irresistible.

Haruhiro clutched his belly. His stomach was crying out for attention. Why had he not noticed it before? He was really hungry.

"But...Shihoru and Yume are waiting. I don't care about Ranta, but it feels wrong somehow to eat by myself... Still, they say you can't fight on an empty stomach... In fact, I don't think I can take another step without eating, or at least I don't want to... Sorry, girls!" Unable to resist, Haruhiro dashed for the stall selling meat skewers.

With hurried fingers, he clumsily withdrew a single silver coin from his leather pouch. Could he buy one with this? Would it be enough? Well, if it wasn't enough, he'd worry about it then.

"C-Can I buy one with this?!"

"Wh-what?!" The paunchy man cooking the skewers stared at him with wide eyes. "A silver coin? You don't need that much! My skewers are four copper apiece. Look, it's written right here. I don't give discounts, but we never take more than the price here at Dory's Skewers!"

"Four copper..." Haruhiro looked at the silver coin. "...Wait, um... does that mean I can't buy one using this?"

"Listen, a silver coin is one silver, yeah? One silver is a hundred copper, so that'd be twenty-five skewers. You can't eat that much, I'm sure, and since it's before noon, I only have about fifty copper on hand. I can't make change."

"Ah, so the copper you're talking about..."

"I mean the copper coins, obviously," the paunchy man said, showing him a copper coin that looked like his Trainee Badge but one half to one quarter the size. "One of these. You can't possibly not know this, can you? Although...you are dressed kinda funny. Ah! Could it be you're a volunteer soldier?"

"Huh? Yeah, I'm a volunteer soldier... No, a trainee, actually..."

"Oh, I see. So that's it. All you volunteer soldier types are a little weird, after all. So, what? You don't have any copper coins? Even though you've got a silver one?"

"Yeah...I don't. One silver is a hundred copper..."

Which meant the ten silver coins Haruhiro had were worth a

thousand copper. Enough for 250 meat skewers. The skewers were big enough that they could probably serve as a full meal. Which meant he could afford 250 meals. At three meals a day, he had enough for more than 80 days, so he could keep himself fed for quite a while.

"...I'm glad I became one. A volunteer soldier trainee."

"If you don't know about copper coins," the paunchy man said, twisting his mouth and exhaling through his nose, "of course you won't know about the Yorozu Deposit Company, either. Why not try going there? They'll convert your money there, and though they do charge a service fee, they'll hold your money for you."

"Yorozu Deposit Company..."

"To find it, go south from the market here, past Tenboro Tower, then take the first, second, and third left and you'll be right there. There's a sign for it out front. I'm sure you'll find it well enough."

3. Yorozu-chan

Yorozu Deposit Company. That was definitely what the sign out front of the warehouse-like building said. The way it was in gold relief was extravagant to the point that it seemed slightly tasteless.

Haruhiro had made it there without getting lost, so that put him in a bit of a better mood. The problem was, he was still famished. If he didn't get his money changed here, rush back to the skewer seller, and chow down on some nice meat skewers, he was going to die.

Entering through the front door, he reached an open hall with a counter at the end of some stone steps. A short line had formed at the counter. He got in line, waited, and soon enough someone called, "Next!" and it was Haruhiro's turn.

Across the counter from him was a massive leather chair and in complete contrast to its size, there was a girl of about ten plopped down on it, sitting there boldly. Wearing a gaudy red and white outfit accented with gold, she had gold-rimmed glasses, a golden pipe on top of that, and an attitude to match.

"Hmm," the girl held the pipe in her mouth, taking a puff as she scrutinized Haruhiro. "You're a new face. Is this your first time here?"

"Yes..." he replied, feeling somewhat pitiful. To think he'd have to be so polite to a little girl! Haruhiro cleared his throat. "It's my first time here, so..."

"From the look of you, I'd say you're a volunteer soldier trainee. I see. A newbie, huh." The girl slapped her raised thigh. "I am the Yorozu. The fourth Yorozu. As has been customary for the Yorozu, I know my clients' names, faces, balances, and transaction histories by heart. There is nothing the Yorozu cannot remember. Still, I do keep a ledger, because others are not blessed with the Yorozu's good memory. Allow me to enter you into the ledger at once. You, what is your name?"

"Ah...I'm Haruhiro."

"I see." The Yorozu leaned forward, opened the ledger book on the counter, and wrote something in it with a feather pen. "—There. Now you may make deals with the Yorozu Deposit Company." When he took a peek at the ledger, Haruhiro saw his own name written in a beautiful flowing script across a nearly blank page. Raising his eyes, he saw the Yorozu's face up close. She was short, but she couldn't actually be ten years old. Maybe she was a little older than that. When he looked closer, disregarding her bizarre apparel, she had a well-defined nose, blue eyes that reminded him of fine glasswork, and plump red lips. She was quite the young beauty.

"What?" She made a sour face and turned to the side. "The Yorozu's face is not something to be gawked at, insolent one."

"Ah, sorry."

"I will say this for your benefit," the Yorozu said, pointing her pipe at Haruhiro's face. "The fourth Yorozu is young, but flawless as a

Yorozu. Should you show me disrespect, you will pay for it dearly. You would do well to remember that. Also, Haruhiro, I shall remember you henceforth as the insolent one."

"...I'd really rather you forgot that."

"Impossible. The Yorozu is a Yorozu and so I cannot forget. If I were to forget, the Yorozu would have to cede the Yorozu position to the next Yorozu. Such is the code of the Yorozu."

"It sounds...kinda tough, being a Yorozu," Haruhiro said, looking around the hall. Perhaps by coincidence, Haruhiro was the only customer at the moment. He didn't see anyone who looked like an employee, either. "...Could it be that you run the deposit company by yourself?"

"Of course not. The Yorozu is the symbol of this company, as well as its chairperson and president. For the transportation of items and money, appraisals, warehouse management, and other duties, we employ a large number of clerks and apprentices. Do you know what sort of business this company does?"

"Well, I hear you take deposits of money and you can act as a money changer."

"We handle more than just money. This company can take deposits of items, as well. If your deposit is money, the deposit fee is 1/100th of the total. If it is an item, the deposit fee is 1/50th of the appraised value of the item."

"1/100th..." *So if I leave 100 copper coins with her, she'll charge me one for the privilege, huh.* "...Kinda expensive, isn't it?"

"If you feel that way," Yorozu said, drawing a long puff from her pipe, "you simply need not make a deposit. It matters not in the least to our company. Though as Yorozu, I will say that you, as a volunteer soldier trainee, will gradually come to understand how useful our company is. So, what business have you come for today, insolent one?"

"'Insolent one'..." He wondered if she was going to keep calling him that forever. Haruhiro withdrew one...no, two silver coins from his pouch. "I came because I wanted to convert these to copper coins."

"Hmm. Incidentally, our money changing is provided as a wonderfully free service, so your two silver coins will get you 200 copper coins. Do you understand how bulky all those coins will be, insolent one?"

"Ah." Haruhiro recalled the copper coin that the paunchy man at Dory's Skewers had shown him. It had been a pretty small coin, but 200 of them would add up to a good weight. "I see... Carrying around a large amount of money is a hassle. That's why people pay the deposit fee to deposit it here, huh?"

"Well, there you have it. Furthermore, the Yorozu can calculate down to 1/100th of a copper instantly, so if you leave just one copper coin with us, your deposit fee will be 1/100th of a copper. The Yorozu will remember this, and also note it down in the ledger. When it accumulates to a full copper, the amount will be taken from your funds on deposit. So you needn't try to get clever by depositing your copper 99 at a time."

"Basically, you're telling me there's no cheating the system. I get it." Haruhiro laid one silver coin down on the counter. "Okay, I'll have one silver coin converted, then."

"Very well." The Yorozu struck a bell sitting out on the counter with her pipe and a young boy in sparkling silver clothes came out from a door in the back. Yorozu didn't spare a glance in the boy's direction before gesturing with her fingers for him to do something.

When she did, the boy silently bowed, headed back through the door, then returned shortly with a black tray. Atop the tray were copper coins. The boy left the tray on the counter and then took his leave.

"100 copper coins. You may take them, insolent one."

"Can you drop the 'insolent one' thing already...?" Haruhiro muttered as he took the coins and slid them into his pouch. The coins were about the size of the tip of his little finger, but with 100 of them, the pouch was stuffed full. "It's pretty bulky. It might not fit in my pocket like this."

Yorozu snorted smugly. "I could take a deposit for you right now, if you like. Insolent you may be, but our company makes a policy of treasuring all its customers."

"Nah, I'm good for now. I can carry it in my hand. It's just a bit of a hassle."

"If you say so." The Yorozu took another puff on her pipe. "Then come again when you need us, insolent one. Our company is open year-round, never taking a holiday. We are open from 7:00 in the morning to 7:00 at night. At any time, for any purpose, I, the fourth Yorozu, will be waiting at this window to take your business."

"At any time, you say? What, you don't take lunch breaks?"

"I do no such thing. The Yorozu is here from 7:00 to 7:00. This, too, is the code of the Yorozu."

"Well, aren't you a hard worker..."

Thinking, *She seems to have it together, but it must be hard on a young girl,* Haruhiro went to leave the Yorozu Deposit Company and his stomach rumbled.

Meat. There were meat skewers waiting.

Haruhiro rushed back to Dory's Skewers in the market and, after taking a deep whiff of their delectable scent, he bought himself a freshly cooked skewer. Unable to resist, he chowed down right there, and the savory taste and juiciness of the meat scored a direct strike on his brain.

"De-*licious!*"

After polishing off that first skewer in no time, he agonized over whether or not he should buy another, but after a grueling battle, his self-control won out. *I don't care about Ranta, but I'll tell Shihoru and Yume, and I can come here again with them later.* Haruhiro danced through the market in high spirits, then came to a sudden stop.

"Oh, crap. This isn't the time to be munching on meat skewers. I need to be gathering information..."

He looked around the area, his eyes falling on an arch-shaped sign reading "Flower Garden Road." A man in whitish clothes was walking from that direction. While the man wore a cape over metal armor, with a shield over his back and what looked to be a sword at his hip, he had a different vibe from the guards at Tenboro Tower. Haruhiro had a vague sense that maybe, just maybe, he might be a volunteer soldier.

He exhaled deeply, trying to compose himself. Then, psyching himself up a bit, he hailed him with a "Hey!" and the man stopped and turned in Haruhiro's direction.

"Need something?" he asked.

"Um, well, excuse me, and sorry if I'm mistaken, but are you...a volunteer soldier, perhaps...?"

"Yes, I am, why?" the man said, blinking a few times before breaking into a smile. "Ohhh. Could it be you're a volunteer soldier trainee?"

"Ah, yes, yes I am! I just became one! I dunno what to say, I barely know left from right at this point, so I was hoping..."

"It's like that for all of us at first. I know you feel lost, but step by step, if you keep on moving forward, you'll gradually find your way."

"Is that...just how it is, you think? But, still, I'm feeling really uncertain about where I head from here..."

"I understand," the man said, nodding with a gentle smile. "However, this experience you're going through now is something you'll be able to put to use later. If you can't grope around blindly in the darkness, you'll never be able to reach anywhere."

"Is...that how it is? No, I mean, if you don't mind, could you..."

"I'm Shinohara of Orion."

"Oh, I'm Haruhiro."

"Haruhiro-kun, the members of Orion are often at a place called Sherry's Tavern. If something comes up, please come find us there."

"Huh? Uh... Yeah, Sh-Sherry's Tavern, was it? O-Orion...?"

"Yes. I wish you luck, Haruhiro-kun. Until we meet again."

Shinohara left, leaving behind only the bright, refreshing air he had brought with him.

"...Did I just fail at gathering information?" Haruhiro hung his head. He should have stopped him and been more insistent. But it had felt like he was being rejected gently, but firmly.

The man might not have seemed it, but perhaps he was a bit mean-spirited. Or maybe he, as one with more experience, had been trying to teach Haruhiro something?

"A tavern, huh..." Haruhiro looked skyward, narrowing his eyes at the glare of the sun. He wasn't sure, but it felt too early to be visiting a tavern.

Walking down Flower Garden Street for lack of any better option, he looked about for anyone who might be a volunteer soldier. He passed a few, but they all either glared at him as their eyes met, had blatantly frightening faces, or looked like ruffians, not the kind of people he could bring himself to call out to.

"I'm already getting tired of this..."

As he exited Flower Garden Street, Haruhiro crouched down at the side of the road. There was a flowerbed and a number of large buildings that looked to be boarding houses. He stayed there unmoving for a while.

Maybe if he stayed like this, someone would come up and see if he was all right. He wasn't doing it with that sort of ulterior motive, though. Well, maybe he was, just a little.

"...Maybe I've been a little naïve."

But I can't help that, can I? I mean, I don't even know where I am. I mean, not remembering anything but my name? It makes no sense! Then I suddenly became a volunteer soldier trainee or something. Like, what even is that? While I stood around, all the capable-looking people took off. I can't rely on any of the ones who stayed. I can't rely on myself either. Despite that, I somehow got stuck having to gather information all by myself. And that's not going well at all.

"Of course I'd lose my nerve after all that..."

What's wrong with losing my nerve? It wouldn't be strange at all for me to give in to despair. I know. I'll go eat another skewer. I'll eat as much as I can by myself. Not just meat skewers; I saw plenty of other tasty food around the market. I'll try every last one of them. When night comes, I'll hit a bar. There's got to be a place somewhere with girls to pour my drinks for me. Any kind of booze, I'll drink it. I'll play around. I'll just screw around until the money runs out.

Haruhiro stood up. "Not that I'd actually do that."

He couldn't bring himself to be optimistic, but giving in to desperation was just as hard.

He went back through Flower Garden Street to the marketplace.

Well, now what? Back to the front of the office? I have practically nothing to show for my effort, but it's been a while. Everyone's got to be hungry. If I want to get them fed, we'll have to go to the Yorozu Deposit Company and get their money converted there.

When he thought about it, what he'd learned about the Yorozu was valuable info. He had met Shinohara, too. Looking for Sherry's Tavern as a group once they'd eaten was an option. Besides, it wasn't like Haruhiro needed to do all the work by himself.

Yeah. Yeah, that's right! Everyone's got a stake in this.

On that note, he decided to return to the office in high spirits, but...how odd. Though he was heading in the right direction judging by the location of Tenboro Tower, no matter how many corners he turned, he didn't see the office.

"...Am I lost?"

I don't want to, but I kind of have to admit it. What else can I do? Haruhiro headed towards Tenboro Tower. *Once I get to the plaza, I'll carefully check my route. The road I first came to the plaza through was, if I recall, that one. If I go down it, I can get back to the office—I think. Probably.*

"No, hold on, was it really that road...? Or the one over there? Maybe I'm wrong. Am I wrong? Which one was it again? I-I'm not sure anymore. This is bad..."

"Haruhiro!" someone called out.

"Huh?" He hadn't imagined anyone would call his name, so he was pretty shocked.

The voice's owner looked like he had a halo of light behind him. That was an optical illusion, of course, but the smile of the man who waved to him and rushed over was truly radiant.

"Manato...!" Haruhiro cried, rushing over to the man. "Manato! I'm trying to make my way back to the office, but I can't find it! Meeting you here feels like stumbling across the Buddha in Hell!"

"You're exaggerating," Manato said, looking around. "Haruhiro, are you alone? Are there any others?"

"Yeah. Ranta, Shihoru and Yume are in front of the office...or should be. Shihoru started crying, see? After that, we agreed that I was going to go gather information while they waited there."

"Oh, so that's it. So, you figured out a bunch of stuff and you're on the way back now?"

"Well..." Haruhiro scratched his neck nervously. He wanted to show off a little, but if he lied now, the truth would come out in no time, so there probably wasn't much point.

"I don't know that anything I figured out counts as figuring stuff out. What was there...the Yorozu Deposit Company, maybe...?"

"Yorozu? Deposit Company? I don't know about those yet."

"No way. Seriously? It's a place where you can deposit your money or have it converted. It seemed kinda important. Oh, also, there was a good meat skewer place in the market...nah, that one's not so important."

"I took a peek at the marketplace a bit myself. So there are meat skewers there, huh? If they're as good as you say, I'd like to try one."

"I'll show you the place. I remember exactly where it was...though

I forgot the way back to the office."

"Okay, should we go together, then?" Manato said as if it was the most natural thing in the world. "I was just thinking of heading back to the office."

"Huh...?" Haruhiro was stunned silent.

Sure, Manato had said, "See you all later," before leaving the office. But hadn't that just been an ordinary turn of phrase, a polite way of saying goodbye? That was how Haruhiro had interpreted it. Had he been wrong? Had Manato meant to come back to the office after gathering information all along?

Something warm swelled in his chest.

Manato said, "Hm?" He cocked his head to the side a little. "Is something wrong?"

"N-nothing at all, actually!" Haruhiro said, slapping Manato on the back. "L-let's go. To the office. I don't care about Ranta, but I'm sure Shihoru and Yume are feeling alone and helpless."

"Yeah." Manato nodded and started walking.

As he followed after him, Haruhiro was glad he had met up with Manato again.

Manato strode along, showing no sign he wasn't sure of where he was going, down a path completely different from the one Haruhiro had been betting on.

Apparently Haruhiro hadn't remembered the way back properly.

Grimgar of Fantasy and Ash

4. The Joys of Guild Life

Haruhiro was now standing alone in one corner of an area called West Town.

"This ought to be the place..."

West Town was where the poor and destitute lived. A slum town, apparently. The buildings were all old and rundown or crumbling. It was all very shabby. Most of the people you would meet there were miserable wretches. Honestly, it wasn't the kind of place you wanted to walk around alone.

Why did I go and choose this place? I shouldn't have. But I've made my choice now, so it's too late.

Haruhiro was trying to walk around a building that was like a complexly interwoven amalgamation of various other stone and wooden buildings, but it was impossible to do so. When he went down the narrow alleys, he would be obstructed by wooden or stone walls and there was no way to get around to the back of the building.

However, as he tried, he ran into a ridiculously low doorway at the end of one alley. It was a rusty door and a hand with a keyhole in the palm had been carved into it.

Suspicious. So this is the entrance, huh?

"H-Helloooo?" he tried calling out, but there was no response, so he tried knocking. It made his hand hurt. He decided to try at least turning the handle and pulling. It didn't budge.

"Is this the wrong place? What the hell..."

As he muttered to himself, turning to leave, a low voice echoed through the alley. "State your business," it said.

Where had the voice come from? He couldn't tell. He was the only one in the alley and the door was still closed. But he didn't think he was just hearing things. There had definitely been a voice.

"Um, well...I was hoping you'd let me join the guild."

"Enter," the voice said and the door clicked.

Had it just been unlocked? Haruhiro put his hand on the knob and turned. He tried pulling. It was heavy, but it opened.

Beyond the door was a cramped, dusty hallway. There were shelves on either side of the hall, packed full with rope, metal clasps, wheels, and assorted other things he couldn't make any sense of. Closing the trick door behind him, Haruhiro saw there was a bright light coming from deep inside. Its source was a wall lamp and the hall turned there. The hall got even narrower as he went.

Turning his body diagonally, he managed to progress down the hall and finally come out into a room. It was dimly lit and he couldn't tell how big it was. There was a desk in the room and a woman was sitting on it cross-legged. She was playing with a knife. Her hair was long—long enough to cover half her face—but she didn't seem as eager to cover up her skin. The woman's arms, chest, and thighs were all boldly exposed.

"You want to join our thieves' guild?"

"Y-yes," he said, gulping despite himself. *I probably shouldn't stare too much.* He averted his eyes, just to be safe. "That was...my intent."

"From the look of you, you're a volunteer soldier trainee. The second one today."

"Huh? Second one?"

"Well, that doesn't really matter. If you're joining us, you'll be going through the seven-day training by yourself, anyway. It's one-on-one. I'll be responsible for you. An honor, no?"

"Huh? Well, sure..." Haruhiro looked up at the woman. He figured it would be rude to stare at her chest or legs, so he looked at her face. *I wonder how old she is. She's probably not that young. Thirty or so? That sounds about right.*

For Haruhiro, who was sixteen, she seemed pretty old, even though that wasn't nice to say. But she was beautiful. And dangerously sexy. "...I-it's an honor. Yeah."

"If you're dissatisfied, I can leave you to someone else, you know."

"N-no! Please, do take me!"

"But let me warn you." The woman stabbed her knife into the desk and licked her lips. "I'm a harsh mistress, you know? If you can't keep up, you'll be *punished,* okay?"

"...Go easy on me, please."

The woman chuckled, brushing her hair to the side. "Do you know the code of the thieves' guild?"

Here in the frontier, there were organizations called guilds. Guilds were basically trade unions for blacksmiths, carpenters, masons, chefs, and so on. It went as far as there being guilds for fighters, mages, priests and paladins, hunters, dark knights, and even thieves.

A guild was a benefit society for people in the same trade, an association to defend their rights, and an organization where they could train together.

In order to take up work in this area, Haruhiro needed to join a guild. If anyone tried to work without being part of a guild, the guilds would always get in their way. Because everyone knew that, no one would hire a person not attached to a guild.

He could only join one, which felt kind of restricting, but the guilds put serious effort into developing the skills of their junior members. If he joined a guild, they would teach him the basics of his job. Or to put it another way, for as long as he didn't join a guild, he could never learn the skills associated with that job.

Of course, the guilds didn't let anyone in for free.

What was more, once he joined, he would have to follow set regulations—a code—or face punishment.

Incidentally, this was all stuff he had learned from Manato.

Manato had told him about the unusual code that the thieves guild had. Partly because of that, Haruhiro had chosen this guild from the many options available.

"There isn't one, right? That's what I hear."

"Exactly." The woman pulled the knife out of the desk, giving it a twirl. "Well, there is honor among thieves, though. Like not running jobs on another member's turf, not stealing from our own, and so on. If we apply that to a volunteer soldier, it'd mean you should keep a one-thief limit per party and not steal from your fellow thieves or volunteer soldiers, I guess. I'll get into it later. If you become a thief, that is."

"I want to...is what I'm thinking."

"This isn't just about what you 'want,'" the woman said[...] out her hand palm up. "I'm sure you know this, but you[...] have something to give me first. The guilds don't let *anyone* in for free."

Haruhiro pulled out the pouch he had forced into his pocket, pulling the string to open it. According to Manato, this was the same for every guild. What's more, they had agreed to fix prices, so it cost the same no matter which you joined. New members were made to take seven days of lessons for beginners and be thoroughly drilled on the basics of their job. That was true across all guilds, as well.

Haruhiro pulled silver coins from his pouch. *One, two, three— really, this feels...expensive to me. Not like there's any other choice, though. Without any knowledge or skills, there's no way I could make it as a volunteer soldier. I've been told that, and I can't say I disagree. Even so, it's not cheap. Four, five, six, seven...eight silver coins.*

Eight Silver was 800 copper. He could eat 200 meat skewers with that money. Was it really okay to pay this much?

He had no choice. After hearing what Manato had to say, they'd all agreed. Every one of them should be joining a guild right now.

He took a deep breath and laid out eight silver coins on the woman's palm.

The woman clutched the coins and gave him a charming smile.

"Payment received. After this, you'll technically have to take your oath, but our guild members are freedom-loving, libertine, and take responsibility for themselves. Now you're one of us. Pretty easy, huh?"

"...Sure was. Come to think of it, I'm not sure I've even given you my name yet."

"We thieves go by a trade name. Your real name doesn't matter. You're just a new face here now. Once your seven days of training are over, as your mentor, I'll christen you with a suitable trade name. If you want an impressive one, you'd better work for it."

"Uh, then... should I call you Sensei?

"Oh, *my*." The woman leaned forward, placing her hand under Haruhiro's jaw.

Wow... Her boobs are absurdly huge. Haruhiro was nearly at risk of having to hunch over so she didn't notice his reaction.

"You'd call me Sensei? That's not bad at all." The woman grinned, stroking underneath Haruhiro's chin. "I'm Barbara. I think we're going to have *fun* these next seven days."

5. Meetup

Whether or not they actually had fun, he would never be able to tell anyone about those seven days.

The freewheeling nature of the thieves' guild meant he was free to quit anytime he wanted. He could rejoin later for eight silver, but only those who had attained the rank of mentor could teach others about thief methods, ambush tactics, the killing arts, and other secret skills of the guild.

What happened during training was, as a general rule, not to be disclosed to outsiders. That was why he couldn't talk about it.

The work name given to him by his mentor was one only to be used in the world of thieves. There was no need to tell it to ordinary people. Not that he'd have *wanted* to.

...Because it's Old Cat. My work name is Old Cat.

According to Barbara-sensei, his sleepy eyes made him look like a tired, old cat.

He couldn't deny that there was some resemblance, but it was kind of an awful name. Why couldn't he have been Panther or Jaguar or Hawk? There had to have been a cooler name she could have given him. Honestly, he was starting to feel like he'd have been satisfied with pretty much anything but Old Cat.

In any case, after seven days of training, complete with room and board, Haruhiro was now a competent thief...

...*Not.*

Barbara-sensei had taught him thief morals, thief philosophy, the importance of ambush tactics, and two skills: Picking, which was a thief's most basic skill, and Slap, which was the most basic of basic techniques in the art of fighting and killing.

Still, he hadn't mastered any of it.

Haruhiro would have to gradually improve those skills through experimentation. And to pick up more skills in the future, he would have to return to the guild and learn them from his mentor. Of course, that would cost something and of course, he would have to stay overnight for several days of lessons.

In other words, Haruhiro had learned two skills, but his proficiency with them was much too low for him to use them reliably.

As a gift to celebrate the end of his training, he had been given an old thief cloak, a well-used dagger, an equally well-used set of thief tools, and a second-hand pair of thief boots, all of which he was wearing right now. He probably looked at least somewhat thief-like thanks to this, but he couldn't really move like one just yet.

After Barbara-sensei's harsh training, he'd learned that the path of the thief wasn't easy. Quite the opposite, in fact, and he was a new thief just taking his first steps down that path. That was Haruhiro's situation right now.

Is this going to be all right...? he wondered.

Old Cat headed on to his destination with a sigh.

It was still before noon, so the market wasn't all that crowded. There were only two customers in front of Dory's Skewers. One was a curly-haired man in what looked like leather armor with a longsword and the other was wearing a bow and quiver of arrows over her back with a large machete at her hip. She had her hair in braids.

"Ranta, Yume!"

"Oh?" Ranta said, turning around.

Yume did the same, still gnawing hungrily at a skewer of meat. "Huwha?"

Yume's relaxed expression was a sight for sore eyes to Haruhiro. Even Ranta's curly hair was a welcome sight.

Thinking back, the training had been pretty difficult.

Barbara-sensei was always sexy, but she was also a total sadist sometimes. She'd never let up on him. At night, as he'd slept on the hard floor of what he liked to call his solitary confinement cell in the thieves' guild, wrapped only in a dirty blanket, he had imagined the hard time the others must be having, too. The thoughts may not have made him feel he needed to try his hardest, but they had helped console him a little.

Honestly, it had been pretty bad for him. There were a few times when he had thought he couldn't do it or couldn't take anymore and had considered running away. But he'd been terrified of Barbara-sensei and that had kept him from ever going through with it.

"Ranta...! Yume...!" Haruhiro ran over and went to give them both a high-five.

Ranta returned the high-five with a confused "Yeah!" but Yume had a look on her face like she had no clue what to do and she just left his hand hanging there pathetically.

Had he gotten carried away? It was a bit awkward. *Oh, well.*

Haruhiro cleared his throat a bit. "Hey. How're you doing? Where's everyone else?"

"We're getting along pretty well for now," Ranta said, looking around. "Nobody but us has made it back yet, I guess?"

"Yuhme ish..." Yume started trying to talk with her mouth still full, but she choked on some of her meat and started coughing. "...Urkh."

Haruhiro peeked at Yume's face. "Y-you gonna be okay there, Yume?"

"Yeah. Somehow, it looks like Yume'll be fine. She will be, but it still hurts a bit."

"It's not good to talk with your mouth full. You should try to stay calm while you eat."

"Never been sure why, but Yume always gets confused and rushed when eating, y'know?" Yume said.

"I see..."

"Master was always sayin' the same thing," she continued. "'Yume, you really should eat slower.' No, he wouldn'ta said it like 'You really should,' Master mighta said it like 'Eat slower' instead."

"Listen," Ranta gave her a doubtful sideways glance. "Can you even *use* that bow and arrow? I wouldn't know, but aren't you sort of a really poor fit for the whole being-a-hunter thing?"

"About archery, yeah..." Yume tilted her head, one cheek rising in a grin. "Master said Yume may be hopeless at it. Yume was pretty awful, no matter how much practicin' she did."

"If a hunter can't use a bow and arrow, isn't that kind of a non-starter? Like, they don't fit the image..."

"Yume wants a wolf dog, though, so hunter it is."

"A *wolf dog*, huh," Haruhiro said aloud, scratching at his neck. Experienced hunters could tame a wolf dog and communicate with it, apparently. Not just any dog, a wolf dog. Important difference. Haruhiro did see the appeal, so he could understand how Yume felt.

"A thief and a useless hunter, is it?" Ranta spat the words out in contempt. "You guys arc killing me, honestly."

"...You're the last guy I want to hear that out of, Curly," Haruhiro said.

"Don't call me Curly!"

"...Excuse me," someone interjected.

"Eek...?!" Ranta jumped up with a start, turning around.

Behind Ranta, wearing a pointed black hat and an outfit of the same color stood a petite girl. The hat was wide-brimmed and she was leaning on the staff she carried and looking down, so they couldn't see her face. Still, Haruhiro could tell at once.

"Shihoru?"

The girl nodded silently. It really was Shihoru.

"Come on..." Ranta's eyes were bulging as he tried to calm himself. "D-don't scare me like that. Calling out to me suddenly from behind. You're supposed to be a mage, aren't you? You seem more like a thief."

"...I-I'm sorry. Y-You didn't notice me...and I wasn't sure how to get your attention, so..."

"You could have just called out like a normal person! With a hey, or a yo, or a hi."

"...I'm sorry. I'm sorry for not being able to do things like a normal person..."

"Don't apologize for every little thing! It makes me look like the bad guy!"

"You kinda *are* the bad guy," Haruhiro interposed himself between Ranta and Shihoru. "If I had to choose a bad guy here, it'd be you. It's nothing to get so bent out of shape over."

"Don't try to play the good guy, Haruhiro. Even if she's got a nice, big pair of boobs she's hiding, okay?"

"Huh? Hiding...?" Without thinking about it, Haruhiro glanced towards Shihoru's chest area.

"...!"

Shihoru quickly covered her chest with her arm, so he couldn't verify one way or the other, but—*Wait, what the heck am I doing? It is not okay to look. Now my face is all hot.* Haruhiro hung his head.

"...Sorry," he mumbled.

"It's fine..."

"You can try to hide it!" Ranta said, jabbing a finger in Shihoru's direction. "But there's no deceiving my eyes. I can see through most padding and push-up bras, too!"

Haruhiro looked at Ranta with disdain. "...What kind of skill is that?"

"It's not a skill! It's a natural gift!"

"Aww..." Yume said, poking at her own chest. "Shihoru's got big ones, huh. Must be nice. Yume's are tiny, y'know. If Yume were thin, it'd be okay, but she's pretty pudgy and her boobs are tiny. Kinda depressing, don'tcha think?"

"...I'm not, uh..." Shihoru shrunk into herself as if she were trying to disappear. "...I'm just f-fat, that's all it is."

"Are you? You don't look fat to Yume, y'know."

"I-I just...look thinner in clothes..."

Ranta let out a nasal laugh. "Shihoru. You're the type girls hate, I bet."

"Huh…?"

"Calling yourself fat when you aren't. That's the fastest way to get other girls to hate you!"

"…I-I'm not doing that…" Shihoru's shoulders started to tremble. "…I-I really am fat, okay?"

"Wuh…?" Ranta said, backing off a bit. "No, wait, i-it's nothing to cry about, okay?"

"…I-I'm not crying."

"Yes you are! There are clearly tears forming in your eyes! Come on!"

"Shihoru, Shihoru." Yume said, holding her tight. "It's all right, okay? Yume doesn't hate you. Yume still doesn't know you that well though, y'know."

Haruhiro smiled wryly. "You're not really reassuring her there, Yume."

"Oh? Y'think? Well, Shihoru's body feels great. She looks thin, but when you hold her, she's just a bit squishy, y'know?"

"…D-don't touch me so much. I-It's embarrassing…"

"G-girls…!" Ranta was panting heavily. Way too heavily. "Damn, that's a feast for the eyes! And in a public place, too! You sure that's okay? Gimme more!"

"I see you're all having a good time," interjected another voice.

Haruhiro looked to where the voice came from. "Manato!"

Manato wore a hooded outfit with blue lines. In his hands, he was holding a straight stick. It was a short staff.

"Am I the last one to arrive?" Manato smiled, looking to each of them. "I'm the priest, Haruhiro's our thief, Yume's our hunter, and Shihoru is our mage. We have Ranta-kun as a warrior, too. All five of us are here, I see."

"Listen, pal," Ranta said with a frown. "Could you cut it out with the -kun and -san stuff? It takes too long to say every time. Besides, you're already calling Haruhiro by just his name."

"Okay, Ranta it is then."

"Y'know, now that you're dropping it, that pisses me off, too! Call me Ranta-sama!"

"Ha ha. I don't want to do that."

"Don't laugh off my demands so easily!"

"You can call Yume just Yume, too," said Yume.

"...Ah. Just Shihoru for me as well, if you don't mind."

"You sure? Okay, I'll do that then. Yume. Shihoru."

Yume said "Heeeere!" and raised her hand.

Shihoru gave a quiet response, too, but they couldn't quite hear it. She seemed pretty embarrassed.

"Manato," Haruhiro said, swinging his right hand.

Manato shifted his staff to his left hand and brought his right up as well. Their palms slapped together. It made a satisfying clap.

Haruhiro punched Manato in the shoulder. "Good job, Manato. Priests go through—what was it? Basic training? I think?"

"Yeah. How did your training at the thieves' guild go?"

"Huh? Oh, piece of cake," he tried to put up a strong front, but his face twitched as he did, so he quickly backpedaled. "...That was a lie. It was pretty harsh. My teacher was nuts. I mean, she's beautiful, but super scary."

"She was beautiful, huh? I'm jealous. My master was a rugged man.

He was harsh, and loud. My ears always hurt."

"Your ears hurt? Manato, just how much did you get yelled at?"

"I don't even remember. I was getting yelled at so often I started to think that maybe I was born just to be yelled at."

Haruhiro had gotten scolded pretty often by Barbara-sensei and it had left him feeling down. Not because it had destroyed his self-confidence, though. He had never had the chance to build any of that. Had Manato gone through the same thing? Maybe it was the same for anyone when they first entered a guild. If so, Haruhiro didn't need to let it get to him. Maybe he didn't need to be so pessimistic about things.

I feel a bit better now. It's thanks to Manato. He got us the information on the guilds, and he consulted with us all on which each of us should join. Where would we be without Manato? I don't even want to think about it.

"Guess it's time to come clean, huh?" Ranta said with a sigh. "The thing is, I've got something I need to tell you all. It's a big announcement."

"Huh...?" Haruhiro raised his eyebrows. "What?"

Yume said "What could it be?" blinking repeatedly, and Shihoru looked at Ranta hesitantly.

Manato was eyeing Ranta's body...or rather, checking out his equipment. Was there something strange about it? Ranta had an old longsword on his hip and he was clad in hard leather armor. Well, it was kind of a warrior-y look.

"Huh?" Manato said, narrowing his eyebrows and looking down. "Warrior armor is supposed to be—"

"Here's the announcement!" Ranta said, puffing his chest out so far his head was tilted back. "I said I was going to become a warrior,

but I didn't! The whole warrior thing just wasn't me. I felt that I was brimming with a talent that'd blossom in a different dimension, an alternate dimension, so I didn't join the warriors' guild!"

"Wha…?" Manato seemed like he was about to say something, but then lost his voice. He'd gone quite pale. And who could blame him, really?

After all, according to the info Manato had gathered, the warrior and priest were the center of any party. The warrior stood on the front line, putting up a furious battle against all enemies, while the priest was a healer who treated his allies' wounds. Every party needed at least one of each. So, when Manato had chosen to be the priest and they had determined that either Haruhiro or Ranta would be the warrior, Ranta had volunteered for the position on the basis that it sounded cool. Because Ranta had wanted to do it, and had said as much, Haruhiro had decided to join the thieves' guild.

"Hm?" Ranta was unabashed. He looked at them as if wondering what was with the strange looks he was getting. "What's wrong? Be more shocked, would you? This is one super surprise."

"…We're more than surprised," Haruhiro rubbed his pulsing temple. "We're exasperated. What did you join a different guild for?"

"Like I said, it was a feeling. It was instinct, man. Instinct. A hunch. My sixth sense at work. I heard a whispering from the god within me, see. 'Don't become a warrior,' he said. 'That's not you. You're a bigger man than that.'"

"And?" It looked like Manato had regained some of his composure, though he was still grimacing a bit. "What guild did you join, Ranta?"

"Check this out!" Ranta pulled out a skull-like…well, actually, it was just a skull…necklace and thrust it towards them. Then he pointed to the breast of his armor. There was a skull emblem burned into it, too. "Glory be to the master of death, the dark god, Lord Skullhell! I went and became a dread knight!"

"A trendy light?" Shihoru asked.

"No!" Ranta shouted, spittle flying everywhere. "A dread knight! A knight of darkness! Even the name is cool! Sounds *way* more awesome than 'warrior,' doesn't it?!"

"...Could it be," Shihoru said hesitantly, "you only became a dread knight because it sounds cool and for no other reason...?"

"'Only'? Listen..." Ranta said with a sigh. "Is there anything more important than coolness? Yeah, I didn't think so. I mean, how could there be? Think about it."

This guy could use a good punching, thought Haruhiro. He didn't do it, though. Punching him wouldn't help. It was too late for that.

"...So, once you become a dread knight, you can't quit, right?" Manato said. "They'll send people to hunt you down if you try to leave the guild or something."

"Yeah, kinda. There's this rule, 'Thou shalt not betray us until Skullhell takes you.' You get what that means? 'Until Skullhell takes you' means until you die."

"So, what can a dread knight do?"

"Summon a demon!" Ranta clenched his hand into a fist, and... lowered it. "Can't do it now, though. I can't do it during the day when the god of light, Lumiaris's, power is strong yet."

"So, it's just at night..."

"Only for now! As I accumulate vice, the demon's power goes up."

"So what can that demon do?"

"It whispers to me! Telling me there's enemies nearby. Oh, and sometimes it'll let loose a demon joke!"

"Huh..."

"Don't 'huh' at me! I'm a knight of darkness! A dread knight! It's a perfect fit for me!"

"Sure enough," Manato nodded with a half-grin. "It's a perfect match for you, Ranta."

"I know, right?" Ranta said proudly. Apparently sarcasm was lost on him.

What a blissful idiot. He might have been fine with his choice, but it was absolutely not okay with anyone else there. Had Haruhiro and the others been stupid to rely on Ranta? Maybe.

Haruhiro's shoulders slumped. "...No, I don't know..."

Grimgar of Fantasy and Ash

6. Lost and Found Warrior

Well, what was done was done and they'd have to live with it. Haruhiro could have left the thieves' guild to join the warriors' guild, but realistically, that wasn't going to be possible. He couldn't make the others wait seven days. Besides which, he didn't have the money. Volunteer soldier trainees were given ten silver for joining. And eight of that silver was earmarked for joining a guild, so in the end, trainees only had two silver to spend freely.

Even then, "freely" only meant so much. Once the seven days of introductory lessons and the room and board that came with them ended, they had to deal with the daily costs of living. If they were frugal, they could feed themselves on ten copper a day. But unless they felt like roughing it, they were going to have to find rooms to rent. They hadn't properly researched the market price for rooms yet, but it looked like it ordinarily cost forty to fifty copper per room per day.

Basically, that meant that—even if they did decide to camp out to save money—they would need to spend ten copper per day. Two silver was 200 copper, so they could only keep themselves fed for twenty days.

Haruhiro and the others needed to make money. Before they could buy their badges from Bri-chan and become fully fledged volunteer soldiers, they would first need to figure out how to survive until then.

How could they make money?

They had to work for it.

They were still trainees, but Haruhiro and the others left through the north gate to go work as volunteer soldiers. Not far outside, there was a big man wearing chainmail crouching in the brush to the side of the road.

"...Moguzo?"

When Haruhiro called out to him, the big guy languidly turned towards them and blinked a few times. He was mumbling, as if trying to say something, but the words weren't coming out. Haruhiro looked to Manato.

"Huh?" Yume said, looking up to the sky full of fluffy clouds. "Moguzo-kun got taken away by Kuzuyama, didn't he?"

Haruhiro said "Not Kuzuyama, Kuzuoka," correcting her off-handedly before walking over to Moguzo. "What's up, Moguzo? What are you doing here? And, wait, why are you by yourself?"

Moguzo furrowed his eyebrows, nodding slowly.

"I know," Ranta said, with an attempted snap of his fingers that failed to produce a sound. "Kuzuoka threw you out, I'll bet. He was fine letting you in the party, but then you proved yourself such a slow-witted dunce that he decided he was better off without you."

"Ranta..." Haruhiro was about to tell him off, but decided against it. Telling Ranta anything was an exercise in futility.

"...My money," Moguzo said, hanging his head. "...They took all of it. Told me they'd taught me enough, so I had to pay up..."

"That's terrible..." Shihoru said quietly.

"See? Told you so," Ranta said with a snort, looking pleased with himself. "That's why I tried to stop you back then. I mean, it's Kuzuoka. The guy had 'scumbag' written all over him."

"You act pretty scummy yourself, though..."

"Oh, shove it, Haruhiro! How am I scummy? Give me one concrete example!"

"Can I? Well, let's see, for starters—"

"Stop! Come on, are you keeping a mental list of people's scummy points or something? That's scummy! The act of a scummy person! You, sir, are a bona-fide scumbag!"

"Whoa...when a scummy guy starts trying to call you scummy, it really kills the mood..."

"Moguzo-kun," Manato crouched down next to Moguzo and put a hand on his shoulder. "You joined the warriors' guild, right?"

Looking closer, Moguzo wasn't just wearing chainmail armor; he also had leather gloves and boots and a bastard sword in a sheathe slung diagonally over his back. They were all secondhand, no doubt, but he looked every bit the part of a warrior. It all suited him pretty well, especially with his large body.

"I did at least..." Moguzo peeked in Manato's direction. "...manage to become a warrior, yeah..."

"Oh, you did?" Haruhiro clapped. "Well, thanks to a certain scumbag, our party doesn't have a warrior at the moment, so—"

"By a scumbag's fault, you must mean your fault, right, Haruhiro?"

Haruhiro ignored Ranta, looking to Yume and Shihoru. "What

do you two think?"

"Oh..." Shihoru nodded. "I think that would be good."

"What'd be good?" said Yume, failing to understand.

"Well, we're short a warrior, aren't we? So, Moguzo's a warrior and currently—how should I put it—free? He's perfect for us, is what I was thinking."

Yume was impressed by the idea, letting out an "Ohh" and leaning in to peek at Moguzo's face. "Moguzo, do you want to join Yume and her friends' party?"

"...Are you sure? Is it okay if I join?"

"I want you to join," Manato said to Moguzo with a smile. "That's only if you're all right with it, of course."

Haruhiro glanced sideways at Ranta. If anyone was going to complain, it would be him. What happened surprised him. Ranta playfully threw his arms around Moguzo's neck from behind.

"You're hopeless, you know that? I'll take good care of you, so be my shield, Moguzo! Do it like you're ready to die for me!"

"...Ah, now it makes sense."

"*What,* Haruhiro? I haven't said anything wrong, you know? A warrior's job is to fight furiously on the front line in battle, isn't it? That means standing up front and drawing the enemy's fire. That's why they wear hard chainmail and other metal armors with high defense to protect themselves, got it?"

"Ranta's got it right," Manato looked at Moguzo with a serious expression. "I'm not trying to scare you off here, but I think warriors have the hardest job of all. Still, we'll all support you the best we can and if anything happens, I'll heal you up with my light magic right away, so you don't need to worry about that.

"Y-Yeah... I'll do my best. But..." Moguzo rubbed his belly. "I have no money..."

"I'll lend you what you need. I think we can scrape by for now. And once we're earning, we may not need to worry about it anymore."

"Let me tell you, though!" Ranta said, mussing Moguzo's hair with a big grin on his face. "I won't lend him one red cent. I'm a firm believer in borrowing money but never returning or lending it!"

"Honestly," Haruhiro was taken aback. "You're a real natural when it comes to being the worst, you know that..."

Ranta tut-tutted him, waving a finger. "Haruhiro."

"What?"

"What happens when you multiply a negative by a negative? It becomes a positive, right?"

"So what?"

"That's me!"

"I don't get it..."

"Moron. I chose to be a dread knight instead of a warrior, yeah? That's why Moguzo the warrior is able to join our party, yeah? It worked out perfectly, yeah? Everyone should be thanking me, yeah?"

"I envy you," Manato laughed. "Being able to see it all in such a positive light. That's not something you can do just because you try to. It's a talent."

"I know, right?! That's my man, Manato! I knew I kept you around for some reason. Now this scumbag Haruhiro, on the other hand..."

"Whatever..." Haruhiro would have liked to argue back but knew it would just wear him out more. He extended a hand to Moguzo. "Let's go, Moguzo. To make some money!"

"...Y-Yeah." Moguzo took Haruhiro's hand.

Haruhiro pulled his hand, trying to get him up on his feet, but he didn't budge an inch.

"...Uh, Moguzo, you're gonna have to stand on your own. It's a little too much for me..."

Moguzo said, "Oh, s-sorry," and languidly rose to his feet.

Is this really going to work out? Haruhiro wondered for a second.

7. Slow Start

South of Alterna rose the Tenryu Mountain Range, a line of incredibly high and inaccessible mountains. This land called Grimgar was bisected by the mountain range. The far side to the south was called the homeland while here on the north side was called the frontier.

Well, the frontier was just what humans called it. To be more specific, the Kingdom of Arabakia—which ruled over the homeland Alterna and the area around it—was treating the area north of the mountains as the frontier.

Incidentally, the frontier hadn't been a frontier around 150 years ago. Which is to say, there had been many human countries at that time. There were non-human races too, but humans were the most powerful. But with the coming of a being with terrifying magical powers called the No-Life King, everything had changed.

The No-Life King had created a new race, the undead. And with him as their leader, they had done more than just expand their power. In addition to martial and magical prowess, he had likely been a capable politician as well, because he had allowed the foremost members of each race to name themselves kings and with them he had formed an Alliance of Kings.

They had declared war on the human race. The humans had been easily defeated, either being wiped out or forced south of the Tenryu Mountains. After that, at the recommendation of his fellow kings, the No-Life King had become Emperor and founded the Undying Empire. Humans couldn't set foot north of the Tenryu Mountains.

And then the No-Life King, the Undying Emperor, had contradicted his name and somehow died 100 years ago. Having lost the emperor who held it together, the Undying Empire had splintered. The Kingdom of Arabakia had taken that opportunity to establish the fortress city Alterna and the rest was history.

Incidentally, this was all stuff they had heard from Manato.

The area between Alterna and the Tenryu Mountains to the south was dotted with farms and villages while the area to the north was mostly fields and forests.

"So, like Yume was sayin'," the hunter, Yume, was explaining as she patted the grass, "there's deer and there's fox, yeah? Since it's spring, you'll get a bear comin' out every once in a while, too. Oh, and there're chimos. They're round and fluffy with beady little eyes and long, thin tails. They've got little ears and paws and they bounce everywhere they go, see? They make for pretty good prey. Oh, and there're pit rats. They're big as cats, they've got hard fur, and they're darn ferocious, I hear."

"Oh, yeah?" Ranta shaded his eyes with his hands, making a show of looking around. "From the look of it, there ain't nothing around here, though."

Yume let out a little groan and frowned. "When my master from the guild took me outside for lessons, I saw them here and there. Master would nock an arrow and—whoosh—take one down."

"Maybe over there," Manato gestured towards the woods that were up ahead and to the right. "It feels more likely there will be things hiding where there are trees, don't you think?"

"Yeah," Haruhiro nodded. "Maybe. If I were an animal, I'd be scared to stay out in the field where there wasn't tall grass or trees to hide me."

Ranta laughed. "They're all terrified of me, aren't they...?"

"Fine, it's your fault we have no prey then, Ranta."

"Shut up, Haruhiro! Say it's *thanks* to me! Say with dignity that it's thanks to me!"

"Shut up, would you? If you shout like that, you'll scare off any animals that are still around."

"It's thanks to me!"

"I am so sick of this...he doesn't hear a thing anyone says..."

"Um..." Shihoru, who had been keeping quiet the whole time, opened her mouth for the first time in a while.

"Can we ki— take down animals?"

Everyone stopped walking.

Now that she mentioned it, a volunteer soldier's job was to slay monsters and members of hostile races, not to hunt for food and things they might be able to sell.

"Yume thinks..." Yume screwed up her face, having a hard time saying what she wanted to. "Yume learned from Master how to show appreciation to an animal after taking its life, you know. But Yume likes animals and Yume really doesn't want to kill them. They're cute.

Yume'd feel bad about it, you know."

Ranta scoffed. "Don't be a softie. What are you, a prim and proper young lady? Because every living thing is eventually going to die and be embraced by Lord Skullhell. If something needs to die so we can survive, there's nothing weird about that at all."

"If that's true..." Yume suddenly took aim and nocked an arrow. She was aimed squarely at Ranta. "...it'd be okay if you had to die for Yume and everyone's sake, Ranta."

"Do—!" Ranta leapt backwards. "D-Do-Do-Do-Do-Do-Don't be stupid, Tiny Tits! Killing me won't do any good, you know?! It won't! It seriously won't! I mean it! S-stop it, please!"

"Yume would feel better after doing it. You did call Yume's breasts tiny, after all."

"Y-y-you called yourself that before, didn't you?! You said your tits were tiny!"

"Saying it yourself and getting called it by someone else are different. Especially when it's from a boy. It hurts, you know?"

"I-I-I'm sorry! I-I apologize! I apologize, okay?! Look, I'm begging you!" Ranta did a jumping kowtow. "See?! My bad! Forgive me! Please! Yume, they're not tiny! Those things are huge! Explosively huge! They're almost into marvel-of-nature territory!"

"Man..." Haruhiro looked not so much down at as down on Ranta. "You haven't repented in the least, I'll bet."

"I-I have, okay! How haven't I?! How can you say I haven't?! On what basis?!"

Yume sighed, returning her arrow to its quiver and putting down the bow. "...Waste of an arrow."

"Whew," Ranta stood up and made a show of wiping the sweat

from his brow. "You know what? Either way? Even if you'd shot, I think you'd have missed. Just saying. For the record. Hey? Yume? Stop with the machete. D-don't pull it out! That's not funny! If you stick me with that, it'll hurt! I'll die! I'll seriously die!"

"So about our prey," said Manato with a somewhat forced smile. "From what I hear, even close to Alterna, there are mud goblins, ghouls, and other targets that even trainees can probably handle. Though that's just what I hear so I don't know for sure."

"Goblins and ghouls..." Haruhiro thought hard. The names sounded familiar to him. He might just have been imagining it, but he had a vague sense that they were humanoid creatures.

"...Okay, then," Shihoru spoke more forcefully than she usually did. "Why don't we focus on those mud poplis and cools?"

When Haruhiro mildly suggested, "You mean 'mud goblins and ghouls'..." to correct her, Shihoru's face turned a bright shade of red and she shrank into herself.

"Sure, whatever works," agreed Ranta, not seeming to care.

Yume said, "That's better," seeming happy with the choice.

Moguzo said, "O-okay" with a nod.

"I guess we'll try the woods for now." The priest, Manato, took the lead. Haruhiro and the others followed him towards the nearby woods.

The woods were unrelentingly...*woodsy*. There were broad-leafed trees they didn't know the names of as well as undergrowth so thick they couldn't even see game trails. There wasn't much hard ground. It was all strangely soft or slightly squishy. The footing was poor, which made it hard to walk.

They could hear the birds singing. When the wind blew past, the rustling of leaves was everywhere.

"Muddy gobpuddings and gulls," Yume whispered. "Maybe they hang around the water a lot."

As if it had become his duty, Haruhiro corrected her: "Mud goblins and ghouls, you mean." Then he continued, "Water, huh. Where would that be? A swamp, or a spring? Or maybe a marsh?"

"Let's go look," said Manato.

Manato's taken the role of leading us, thought Haruhiro, *but considering this is the woods, it feels like that ought to be Yume's job instead. Well, I guess it's okay. Is it really okay? Whatever, it's okay.*

But, search as they might, they couldn't seem to find a watering hole. They hadn't run into any living thing other than insects either. They could always hear the birds singing but where were they?

Ranta made an exaggerated gulping sound as he swallowed his spit. "...From the look of this place, are you sure this isn't the Dead Woods or something?"

"It's gotta be Ranta's fault," Yume puffed up her cheeks and glared at Ranta. After the Tiny Tits Incident, she absolutely loathed him, it seemed. "All the critters're runnin' away because Ranta's bein' so noisy, don'tcha think?"

"I'm being quiet! I haven't said anything for a while!"

"Just by bein' there, your existence itself is loud and annoyin.'"

"How nice of you to say! Yeah, well, just by being there, your tits are already tiny!"

"...Mrgh."

"Ah, my bad. That was uncalled for. Shot off my mouth without thinking. Went and spoke the unvarnished truth. Yowch!" Ranta suddenly jumped up. "—Wha?! Wh-what?! Wh-whoa?!"

"Huh?" Haruhiro blinked. Ranta was lifting his legs up and down like some sort of dance. There was something at his feet and it was trying to cling to his leg, chomping and scratching at him. It was the size of a cat and its body was covered in needle-like hair.

"A pit rat," said Yume, looking around. "Pit rats are supposed to attack in packs so there may be more around here."

Shihoru let out a shriek then threw herself into Moguzo. No, she didn't deliberately throw herself into Moguzo; she had tried to get away from something and collided with him as she did so, apparently.

"They're here...!" Manato swung his short staff around. "Urkh! They're too quick!"

"Hey!" Ranta was still backing away while dancing. "H-help me out here, guys! Helping me should be first priority! H-help! Somebody heeeelp!"

"Fight, dread knight!" Haruhiro drew his dagger, but he didn't know how many pit rats there were and they were skittering around all over the place. The deadly fighting techniques he'd learned in the thieves' guild were meant for humans or other races with humanoid bodies so he honestly had no idea what to do. For a start, he tried swinging his dagger down at the pit rats but as he might have expected, he didn't even graze one. "Animals are fast...!"

With a shout, Moguzo used both hands to lift his bastard sword overhead for a swing. Ranta was in the direction he was swinging, too.

With a cry, Ranta leapt aside just as Moguzo's sword exploded into the spot he'd been standing moments before.

It was the ground. The bastard sword had slammed into the ground, kicking up dirt. But that was all it had done.

"M-Moguzo, damn it! Are you trying to kill me?!" Ranta finally drew his longsword. Though drawing it was all he did. He still kept running away from the pit rats. "Dammit! Dammit, dammit! My allies are trying to kill me, I'm still being targeted, nothing is going my way...!"

This dagger isn't going to cut it. Haruhiro tried throwing a kick at the pit rats, but they easily dodged it. "Moguzo was trying to help you! Be grateful!"

"He didn't help at all!" Ranta kicked off from the ground, swinging down his longsword with a battle cry. "Hatred! Wha? My dread knight skill! It missed...?!"

"Don't use skills recklessly!" Haruhiro chose one pit rat to focus his attacks on. *I'll chase it. No luck! It ran away behind that tree.*

"Ugh, jeez...!"

"Marc em Parc," Shihoru drew elemental sigils with her staff while chanting. It was Magic Missile. A fist-sized bead of light shot out the end of her staff— and impacted the back of Ranta's head for some reason.

"Gwah?!"

"Huh?!" Shihoru opened her eyes. It seemed she'd fired with them closed. Because of that, she'd fired in the wrong direction. "...I-I'm sorry! I..."

"You bitch! I'm gonna kill you! Actually, no, just let me grope you...!" Ranta rubbed the back of his head, getting ready to assault Shihoru.

Without a moment's hesitation, Manato used his short staff to trip him. Ranta stumbled forward with a confused grunt.

"What are you *doing?!*" Manato shouted at Ranta while trying to whack a pit rat. To Haruhiro's eyes, it looked like he was using his short staff well, but he still couldn't land a blow on the pit rat.

"I-if we could just get a little!" Yume was swinging her machete around wildly. Possibly because of that, the pit rats weren't going anywhere near her. "If we could just get a little damage in! Master said most animals'll run off if you can do that, so everyone do your best!"

Moguzo whacked a tree hard with his bastard sword, causing a cascade of leaves and insects to fall on him. He stood there, covered in leaves and bugs, roaring in confusion.

"This is going nowhere!" Haruhiro resolved himself to do something, dropping to one knee and lowering his posture. Not running. Not moving. Just waiting for the pit rats.

In front of me. One's coming. A pit rat. Haruhiro stuck out his left arm. *Go on. Take the bait. Try and bite me. This is bad. They're only the size of a cat, but they're damn scary. Fast, too. But I have to be patient. Patience is—* And at that point he felt a sharp pain in his right shin. "*Yowwwch...?!*"

Another pit rat had come up from behind and sunk its teeth into Haruhiro's right shin. When he reacted by trying to shake it off, the pit rat coming at him from the front bit his left arm. "Ouch!"

"Haruhiro...!" Manato rushed over to him, taking a sharp swing with his short staff. "Don't move...!" With a thud and a squeal, his right shin and left arm were suddenly released.

The pit rats were running off. At an incredible speed, too. In no time flat, all of them, even the one struck by Manato's short staff, scampered off, and there was no trace of them.

"Are you okay, Haruhiro?" Manato kneeled down next to him, inspecting his wounds.

"Uh, yeah, I guess..." His injuries weren't serious. *If I roll up my pant leg and sleeve, I'll bet there are probably a bunch of little fang-shaped holes where the pit rats bit me, though. And I'm bleeding a bit, too. But, if that's all, oh well. It does hurt a bit, though.*

"Let me heal you." Manato brought the five fingers of his right hand to his forehead, pushing on his brow with the middle finger and making a hexagram gesture. "O Light, may Lumiaris' divine protection be upon you... Cure."

Light shone out from Manato's palm. The warm light sealed up Haruhiro's wounds in an instant. Three seconds for his right shin, three seconds for his left arm, and the healing was complete.

"Awesome..." Haruhiro tried touching the spots where the wounds had been. There was blood there but no other trace of the former injury. It didn't hurt or itch in the least. "Thank you, Manato. You ended up driving off the rats in the end, too."

"Thanks to you acting as live bait, Haruhiro."

"Nah, the plan was to use my arm as bait, then handle them myself..."

"Sure...but, you know, all's well that ends well."

"This didn't end well at all!" Ranta was acting like a child throwing a tantrum, thrashing his legs about as he sat on the ground. "What's good about this? We suddenly got attacked by weird things! All we did was drive them off. We won't make a single cent from it. And hold on, I'm wounded here, too. It hurts! Heal me already!"

"Oh, sorry." Manato hurried over to Ranta.

"You don't need to apologize to Ranta..." Haruhiro muttered to himself as he looked around the area. Maybe Moguzo had swung his bastard sword around too much because he was sitting exhausted on the ground.

Shihoru was leaning against a tree as if trying to hide behind it. Her misfire with the Magic Missile must have been bothering her.

Yume was the only one still looking cheerful, her eyes darting around restlessly, and she burst into a big grin when her eyes met with Haruhiro's. Haruhiro smiled back without really intending to, but this was hardly the time for smiling at each other, he felt. *Maybe it is, though. Who knows?*

"...He's right, all we did manage was to drive them off," Haruhiro sighed. "Maybe the woods are too dangerous? Like, it could be too soon for us...?"

"Yes! I live again...!" His healing apparently finished, Ranta jumped up and swung his arm around in circles. "Okay, okay, let's get going already, people!"

"...G-go?" Moguzo blinked. "Wh-where?"

"Are you stupid? To find some mud gobs or ghouls, obviously! You've got to be kidding me if you think we're going to just go home with nothing to show for it after getting scratched up by those pit-whatever-you-call-'ems! We can't back down now!"

"I suppose not..." Manato thought for a moment, then nodded. "I think Ranta's right. There's some risk involved. Those pit rats are carnivores, right?"

"Pit rats, yeah," Yume answered. "They might be omnivores. But when they hunt in packs like you saw earlier, I've heard sometimes they'll attack humans."

"Well, they did actually attack us..." Haruhiro said.

"So they're omnivores." Manato looked downwards, stroking his chin. "Anyway, if predators like them live in these woods, there must be prey, too, don't you think?"

"Well, duh," Ranta snorted derisively. "Did you just figure that out *now*, Manato? I've been thinking it for ages now. That if predators like them live in these woods, there must be prey, too."

Haruhiro gave Ranta the side-eye. "...Man, you're just repeating what Manato said word-for-word."

"Shove it, Sleepy-Eyes! Why don't you go take a nap?"

"I already told you, I was *born* with these eyes and they don't mean I'm sleepy! Didn't I tell you that?!"

"Haruhiro." Manato had a smile on his face. "Generally, you're best off just ignoring whatever Ranta says."

"Heyyyyy!" Ranta jabbed a finger in Manato's direction. "Don't go off-handedly saying horrible things like that! I'll bet you play the good guy, but you're really a black-hearted schemer-type, aren't you?!"

Manato replied with a "Who can really say?" Then, after dodging the question, he took a deep breath. "Anyway, if there are no objections, let's keep doing the best we can here in these woods."

No one objected. Haruhiro and the others searched deeper in the woods, keeping an eye out for pit rats.

They prowled the forest until the sun started going down, but they only saw one deer. Yume took aim at it, but it ran off before she could hit it.

They saw birds a number of times. They were attacked by another pack of pit rats, but they fended them off. That was it. If it got dark out, they'd be in serious trouble, so Haruhiro and the others left the woods on weary legs.

"...What now?" Ranta asked in a dull voice. It was little surprise he was out of energy.

"There's not much we can do," Haruhiro said, desperately

suppressing a sigh. If he sighed now, he was sure something inside him would snap. "...We've got to head back. To Alterna."

"Boys in pain, all in vain, huh..." muttered Yume.

Haruhiro said, "Who're the boys in pain?" in order to correct her usage of the saying, but then realized they did have four boys in pain here, and couldn't suppress a sigh.

"S-still!" Shihoru started to say something, but then hung her head as if she'd run out of steam. "...A-actually, it's nothing."

Someone's stomach rumbled. It was Moguzo.

"...I'm hungry."

"Once we get back," Manato looked to each of them. "Let's hit the market and get dinner somewhere first. I know a cheap place where we can stay the night. It's a lodging house for volunteer soldiers in the west of town. You can stay free if you have your badge, but they charge money to trainees. Still, it's cut-rate. If we rent just one room for the guys and one for the girls, twenty copper will cover all of us."

Ranta scoffed. "Maybe we oughta camp out. Since we didn't bring in a single copper coin."

"No, we should save that as a last resort," Manato said firmly. "They may be shared, but the lodging house has baths and toilets. I think the difference between having those things and not having them is pretty big. Especially for the girls."

Shihoru clutched her staff tight, nodding repeatedly without a word. Yume agreed, saying, "He's right."

"You won't die from not having a washroom or bath," Ranta muttered, but he was the one most likely to get annoyed and start complaining if they had to do without.

"I'm with Manato on this." Haruhiro raised his hand, and Shihoru,

Yume, and then Moguzo followed suit. Ranta clicked his tongue disapprovingly but didn't oppose them any further.

And so, their first real day as volunteer soldier trainees quietly came to a fruitless end.

Grimgar of Fantasy and Ash

8. Stubborn

Yume was crouched down, leaning against a thick tree. Haruhiro crept up and tapped her lightly on the shoulder. She turned around, covering her mouth with her hand as she caught herself starting to talk.

"How did it go?" Haruhiro asked quietly. Yume nodded in response, making hand and finger gestures. Maybe she was trying to communicate something, but he couldn't make sense of it at all. Since deciphering it seemed too difficult for him, Haruhiro leaned out from the shadow of the tree to look.

It was there.

This was the afternoon of what was, effectively, their second day as volunteer soldier trainees.

Haruhiro and the others had come back to the same woods as yesterday and they had finally found a spring. And that was where it was.

It was about the size of a human child and scrawny. Its skin was yellowish, wrinkly, and caked with mud. The little tufts of hair growing on it looked like seaweed and it had pointy ears. It was facing away from them at the moment, so he couldn't see its face. It didn't seem to be wearing any sort of clothes, though there was a string around its neck.

It was a mud goblin.

It was crouched over, drinking from the spring. They could hear the unpleasant slurping sounds it was making.

Haruhiro took a deep breath and looked behind him, trying his best not to make any noise. The other four—Manato, Ranta, Shihoru, and Moguzo—had their heads poking out from some trees not far away and they were looking to him. When Haruhiro gave a big nod, they all nodded back.

We finally found some prey, he thought. *Let's do it. We're doing this. We have to. What's the signal? We never did decide on one. How am I supposed to let everyone know?*

Haruhiro decided to try raising his right hand.

This is bad. I'm getting tense. Or, rather, I've been pretty tense all along. Listen. Just do it. Yeah. Let's kill this thing.

When Haruhiro made a downward swinging motion with his hand, Ranta charged headlong forwards with a battle cry. Haruhiro couldn't help but think he was an idiot. When he looked back to the mud goblin, it had jumped up surprised and just finished looking their way.

"I-it's running away...?!" Haruhiro yelped.

"There!" Yume loosed an arrow. It missed. The mud goblin had tried to flee off to their right, but the arrow stabbed into the ground in front of it. It let out a cry of surprise and faltered.

"Nice one, Yume!" Haruhiro unsheathed his dagger and rushed in.

What the hell? I'm here first. This doesn't feel very thief-y, but I'll have to do it. Don't want to let it escape.

Mud goblins. Mud gobs. They have nice, round eyes. But they're ugly. It has a face like an old lady who hasn't bathed once in her entire life. Its teeth are all black, too. And its tongue is purplish. It's not wearing anything other than the string around its neck. Well, it's buck naked. And unsteady on its feet.

The mud gob saw Haruhiro and started shouting noisily.

I don't get why, but it's coming at me. Seriously? It wants to fight? Come on, there are six of us. Well, it doesn't know that. The hands. Its hands. Target its wrists.

Haruhiro took a slash at its left wrist.

"Slap...!"

With a surprised squeak, the gob leapt back diagonally, landing in the spring. Did he miss? No, the mud gob had a thin scratch on its left wrist that was bleeding dark red blood.

Looks like I did scratch him. It's a shallow wound, though.

Kicking up water, the mud gob jumped out of the spring and came out swinging at Haruhiro.

Is it coming? It's coming at me? You're kidding me? Stay away from me, you idiot.

"Urgh!"

Haruhiro reacted at once by falling to the left, somehow getting out of the way of the mud gob's charge.

"Hatred!" Ranta got in close, swinging his longsword down hard at it, but anyone could tell it was a sloppy strike. It missed, of course.

"Whuh? Whoa...!"

The mud gob cried out and gave Ranta a good hard kick, sending him flying. While Ranta was on his backside, the mud gob tried to get on top of him. Then, just in the nick of time, Manato stuck out his short staff, landing a blow on the mud gob's shoulder. The mud gob cried out in pain, hopping away from them.

"M-Marc e—" Shihoru started to chant and draw elemental sigils with her staff, but Ranta shouted, "Hey, your eyes are closed again!" Shihoru shrank back.

"...S-sorry!"

"Moguzo, get in front of the mud gob!" Manato barked orders. "Everyone else, surround it! Don't let it get away!"

"Yeah." Moguzo ran toward the mud gob with heavy steps, stabbing the blade of his bastard sword at it.

Ranta said, "F-fine, guess I'll have to, huh!" as he rose to his feet and moved to the right side of the mud gob. Manato was on the left. Haruhiro and Yume, with her machete, positioned themselves behind it. Shihoru had her eyes wide open and was aiming her staff towards the mud gob from far away. The mud gob looked around, taking steps in every direction and crying out loudly, like it wanted to run away but couldn't, maybe. That was just how Manato had wanted it.

"Moguzo!" Ranta tried to stick the mud gob with his longsword. "Pile on the pressure! Pressure! More pressure!"

With a great roar, Moguzo raised his bastard sword and swung. And swung. And swung. The mud gob dodged. As it nimbly ducked and weaved, Ranta shouted, "Hey!" and took a stab at it with his longsword. The mud gob picked up a dry branch and threw it at Ranta with a shout.

"Whoa?!" Ranta took a step back, just managing to strike down the branch with the base of his longsword. Their encirclement broke down. The mud gob might have tried to flee, but Manato's short staff flashed immediately. The mud gob took a blow to the tip of its right shoulder and howled in pain. Despite that, it turned towards Manato in an instant, screaming as fiercely as it could. Honestly, Haruhiro was startled. Even Manato looked like he'd backed off a bit.

After all, it was scared. The mud gob was desperate. It didn't want to die. It wouldn't just let them kill it. It was going to kill them first.

Kill.

Kill.

Kill.

If nothing else, it would at least take them down with it. The mud gob was filled with the determination to do just that.

"G-guys!" Ranta licked his lips over and over. "Don't get cold feet on me now! It's kill or be killed! I'm gonna murder this thing and accumulate vice…!"

"Stay cautious…!" Manato said as he smacked the mud gob with his short staff again. Even though it took a solid hit that sent blood splattering, the mud gob glared at Manato and grunted as if to say, "So what?"

"Gobsy's a real tough guy, huh…" Yume said, her voice wavering a little.

Tell me about it, thought Haruhiro. *It had taken a blow to the head that was hard enough to send blood flying, but it was still fine.*

"Umph! Umph!" Moguzo swung his bastard sword two, three times, forcing the mud gob to back away. When it did, that meant it was forced closer to Haruhiro and Yume.

"This one's ours, Haru-kun!" Yume said, and though it did make him think, *Hey, wait, since when do you call me Haru-kun?* she was right, they were going to have to take it out.

When he shouted and went to take a stab at it with his dagger, it turned to face him. As the mud gob roared in his face, Haruhiro struggled against his urge to step backwards. He took one swing with his dagger, then another. It connected. He felt it strike something hard. The mud gob's right arm, between the elbow and wrist. Surprised, Haruhiro pulled his dagger back. This was the first time he'd cut anything other than the scarecrow-like practice dummies. It was kind of sickening.

Wailing madly, the mud gob whirled around, splashing blood everywhere as it tried to intimidate Haruhiro and the rest.

It was six-on-one. Haruhiro and the others had the mud gob surrounded. They could attack from any direction, yet no one did.

Everyone was breathing heavily. Aside from Moguzo with his heavy sword, none of them had moved around enough that they should have needed to.

"What's with this...?" Haruhiro tried to get his breathing under control. But he just couldn't.

What is this? he thought. *Is the mud gob strong? Or are we just weak? Too weak? Can we really get by like this? Not a chance. If you just think about it, there's no way we can. We aren't cut out for this. I'm not cut out for fighting. It's scary. I can't do this. Why am I doing this? Shouldn't I stop? But what would I do then? What would happen to me?*

"Lives are at stake here...!" Manato shouted. "There are lives at stake here! Ours and its! The goblin is serious! It doesn't get any more deadly serious than this! There's no way it's going to be easy! Because no person—no living being—wants to die!"

"Marc em Parc...!" Shihoru fired a bead of light from her staff. The bead of light flew between Moguzo and Manato, striking the mud gob square in the face. It howled in pain and confusion.

"Now!" Manato commanded, striking the mud gob.

Ranta brought down his longsword and buried it in the mud gob's shoulder. "—That's hard! Was that bone?!"

"Hungh...!" Moguzo swung with all his might, slamming his bastard sword into the top of the mud gob's head.

What power. One half, maybe a third, of its head caved in.

We did it.

The mud gob collapsed and Ranta pumped his fist with a "Hell, yeah!"

Haruhiro began to sigh, but halfway through, it turned to a gulp.

The mud gob was getting back up and quite nimbly at that.

"...You've gotta be kiddin' me!" Yume stared in disbelief. Haruhiro was sure he had to be mistaken somehow. Though it didn't look like a mistake.

The mud gob started running. It probably was trying to get away.

Manato said "Wha...?!" looking flabbergasted, but still went for a leg sweep with his short staff. Surprisingly, the mud gob managed to jump and avoid it. Then it came right towards Haruhiro. Was it trying to get past him?

"That's pushing your luck!" Haruhiro caught the mud gob's right leg with his foot. Apparently it couldn't dodge this time so the mud gob tripped and fell over.

As Moguzo bellowed, ready to slam his bastard sword into the mud gob, Ranta cut ahead of him. "Out of my way, Moguzo! I'll strike the killing blow...!"

Haruhiro looked away despite himself.

There was an unpleasant noise and Ranta laughed maniacally. "Lord Skullhell! Did you see that?! To accumulate vice, a dread knight takes life from a living being and offers a part of its body at the guild altar, see? The ears are a bit big so maybe a claw will do—wait, whoa?!"

"Huh..." Haruhiro looked over at Ranta and was horrified.

The mud gob was moving. It was crawling, trying to get somewhere.

Shihoru let out a sob, on the verge of bursting into tears.

"Guess it doesn't want to die, huh..." Yume said solemnly, putting her hands together in prayer. "Rest in peace..."

"No..." Haruhiro hesitated a moment, then corrected her. "It's not dead yet..."

"We have to finish it," Manato raised his staff to swing. "otherwise... we'll only prolong its suffering."

Haruhiro didn't want to watch, but he felt obligated to see this through to the end.

Manato landed a painful blow on the mud gob and, once he confirmed it had stopped breathing, he closed his eyes and made the sign of the hexagram. Haruhiro thought he might say something to it, but Manato didn't speak. Perhaps he didn't want to make excuses for what he had done.

"Ahh!" Ranta pointed at Manato. "M-Manato, you jerk! You finished it off! I told you, if I'm not the one to do it, I can't accumulate vice...!"

"Oh," Manato said with a forced smile, scratching his head. "Sorry, slipped my mind."

"Don't tell me your hand slipped!"

"No, I didn't say my hand slipped. I said it slipped my mind."

"Like I care, one way or the other! I want a do-over, you hear me?

A do-over! How?! We can't do it! Argh! That...that should have been my first vice, and now it's gone!" Ranta fell to all-fours, punching the ground in frustration. Then he added, "Eh, whatever."

Haruhiro blinked. "Wh-whatever...?"

"It's done now. Nothing we can do about it." Ranta stood up and went over to crouch beside the mud gob. "Yuck. This is pretty grotesque. Our loot is...this, I guess? There's something hanging from the string around its neck. What is this?"

"Where?" Haruhiro crouched down next to Ranta. Trying his best not to look at the mud gob itself, he looked closely at the string around its neck. Ranta was right. There were definitely things on the string. One was an animal fang or something that had a hole drilled through it. The other was pretty dirty, but it was a coin.

"...Isn't that a silver coin? It's got a hole in it, though."

"Hey!" Ranta went to yank the string off, but quickly drew his hand back. "...Haruhiro, you do it. This thing's filthy."

"Fine, I guess..." Haruhiro cut the string with his dagger and pulled the fang and coin off.

Looks like it really is a silver coin. Well, it's got a hole in it, though.

"Can we... sell this? Actually, I'm impressed it managed to put a hole in it. That seems like a lot of work."

"Well, whatever the case," Manato placed a hand on Haruhiro's shoulder, "this is our first win."

Ranta threw his chest out with pride. "And it's all thanks to me!"

"Yeah, sure," Yume said coldly.

Ranta clicked his tongue, glaring at Yume. "...You're still holding a grudge against me? For a girl with such tiny breasts, you're pretty vindictive, you know that?"

"There's no connection between breast size and bein' vindictive!"

"Well, if there isn't one, then forget about it already! It's water under the bridge! Let me say, though, vindictiveness has long been known to cause booblessness!"

"Don't call me boobless! If they're just tiny, that's not so bad at least!"

"Boobless! Boobless! Boobless! Boobless! Hello, Miss Boobless! Goodbye, Boooooobless!"

"Argh!" Yume's face turned bright red and her cheeks puffed up. She nocked an arrow and took aim at Ranta. "Yume's gonna shoot and she's got a feelin' this arrow won't miss!"

"S-stop—You—Augh—Sorry?!" Ranta spun around and fell to his hands and knees before her. It was a spinning kowtow. "I-it won't happen again?! Okay?! F-forgive me!"

"Why are you sayin' 'forgive me' like it's an order? That oughta be 'Please forgive me, Yume-sama, I beg of you'!"

"Y-Yume-sama! I'm sorry! I beg your forgiveness! I'll do anything, please!"

"Well, if you insist," Yume's cheeks were still puffed up, but she loosened up on her bowstring faster than anyone expected, gesturing towards the spring with her chin. "Jump in."

"Huh...?"

"Go dive in the spring. If you do, Yume will let it go for today."

"Idio—You—No wa—Who do you think would do that?"

Yume drew back her bowstring again. "If that's how you want it, fine. Yume'll just shoot you."

"I'll dive."

"Good luck with that," Haruhiro said, slapping Ranta on the

shoulder.

"Be careful, okay?" Manato said.

"You don't have to tell me that!"

As Ranta stood on the edge of the spring, ready to dive, Haruhiro heard Shihoru mutter, "Serves you right," under her breath.

Ranta muttered, "Here goes," and dived immediately after that, so he probably missed the comment.

"Y-you're going to catch a cold," Moguzo said.

Grimgar of Fantasy and Ash

9. Heavy Resolve

There were a number of pawn shops in Alterna's marketplace, but none of them would pay more than thirty copper for a silver coin with a hole in it. It was hard to accept that one hole should reduce it to a third of its original value, but, in a happy surprise, the fang was worth one silver.

It turned out that there were three kinds of wolves in the frontier of Grimgar: forest wolves, also known as grey wolves; white wolves, which were servants of the White God Elhit and finally black wolves, which served Elhit's enemy, the Black God Rigel. That fang had come from a black wolf, apparently. Black wolf fangs were believed to hold magical power and they were often used as an ingredient in talismans.

With that, their earnings for the day came to one silver and thirty copper. Twenty copper went to rooms for the night and then they split the remaining one silver and ten copper evenly amongst themselves. There was two copper left at the end, so Manato held onto it to be added to the pile next time they divvied up their earnings.

Each of them got food at the stalls in the market, and when they reached the dilapidated lodging house for volunteer soldiers in the west of town, they finally felt like they'd made it home.

Even though anyone with a Corps Badge could use it, the lodging house was largely empty. The four guys washed themselves off in a bathing room that looked like someone had just laid down some stone on a dirt floor. Afterward, they dropped by the girls' room to tell Yume and Shihoru the bath was ready before going back to their own room. At the time, Haruhiro was pretty sleepy. He lay down on his hay bed and closed his eyes right away.

The volunteer soldier lodging house had four-person and six-person rooms, but no matter which you chose, it was ten copper a night for trainees. As for why the four and six-person rooms cost the same, it was probably because the rooms themselves were the same size, and, while the six-person room had two more beds, it was all the more cramped for it.

The six-person rooms' beds were small, too. The beds in the four-person rooms were compact already, so even if 170 centimeters-tall Haruhiro might fit in one of the six-person room beds, 186-centimeters-tall Moguzo probably wouldn't.

There were two bunk beds stuffed with hay. Other than that, there were two wall-mounted lamps. That was the grand total of all the amenities in the lodging house's four-person rooms. They couldn't do anything but sleep here and they had no intention of trying to. They had an early morning tomorrow, so Haruhiro figured it was time to get some shut-eye.

The bed beside him creaked loudly. Apparently Moguzo had just lain down. Moguzo had the lower bunk of the bed next to Haruhiro while Ranta had the top. Haruhiro was in the top bunk of his bed while Manato would be sleeping in the one beneath him.

"Manato...? You still up?"

"Yeah, I'm awake. Something up?"

"Nah, nothing really—" It wasn't true that he had nothing he wanted to talk about. Like what Manato thought about making eighteen copper in a day.

Of the ten silver Bri-chan had given him, he had spent four copper on skewers the first day then eight silver to join the thieves' guild which had left him with one silver and ninety-six copper at that point. Once training ended, he had spent four copper on lodgings yesterday and ten on food with an income of zero. Today, he had spent twelve copper on food while making eighteen copper. His cash on hand at the moment was one silver and eighty-eight copper. As a side note, he had left sixty copper with the Yorozu Deposit Company because it was cumbersome to carry it all around. That was going to cost him a deposit fee.

Haruhiro wasn't too bad off, but Moguzo was another story.

They had split his share of the room fee between them yesterday, but Moguzo must have borrowed money from Manato for food. He had eaten a lot today. He had a big body to keep fed after all. Moguzo probably had less than nothing. He was living in debt.

When might the same happen to Haruhiro?

No...for now at least, no one other than Moguzo, who could borrow from the others in the group, would fall below zero.

If no one will lend you money, zero is the bottom. Nothing, nada, zilch.

If it came to that, what would they do?

We need to earn more. Food and lodgings cost around fifteen copper a day, so I want to make double that. Double? Is double enough? The volunteer soldier lodging house is old and squalid. Having a pit full of urine and excrement for a toilet is disgusting and while the bathing room is fine now while it's warm, when the cold season comes around, it's going to be torture. Hay beds aren't exactly comfy, either. I wish I could get a blanket or something...

He wanted to stay somewhere better than this. He didn't even have a change of underwear and he'd washed them while in the bath, so he wouldn't have any to sleep in because he'd left them out to dry overnight. It looked like he, Manato and Ranta weren't the type who needed to shave often, but Moguzo was starting to look unkempt, so he would've liked a razor, too.

A razor or a small knife. That was just another thing they'd have to buy.

We're going to be in trouble if we don't start earning more, aren't we? Actually, it was a coincidence that the mud gob happened to have a black wolf fang we were able to sell for one silver. We may have gotten luckier than usual today. So, wait, what does that mean? Today's income wasn't so bad? It was on the higher end for us?

Even if they managed to find a mud gob tomorrow and managed to take it down without incident, it might only have a silver coin with a hole in it. One of those was worth thirty copper. Split between the six of them, that was five each. They'd be in the red even if they camped out.

It's looking pretty bad for us when you think about it. He wanted to say that, but decided against it. Once he said something, it would cause problems too big to ignore. He'd have to do something before it was too late.

Well, today wasn't so bad and no one knows what the future may bring. Tomorrow may be better than today. So it's fine. For now, at least.

"It's nothing," said Haruhiro.

"Okay," replied Manato, "that's fine, then."

"Okay!" Ranta suddenly leapt down from the top bunk. "I'm going!"

"Huh?" Haruhiro sat up. "Where are you going?"

"I let it go yesterday," Ranta said with a strangely stern look on his face. "But I just can't do that today. A man's gotta do what a man's gotta do."

"Huh...? You're not making any sense here."

"You are so dense. How can you not get it? It's obvious. I'm going to the bath. The B-A-T-H."

"The bath? For what?"

"The girls are in there now, right? They're stark naked, washing their hair and bodies. And if they are, there's only one thing I ought to be doing, right...?"

"Y-you—you can't be planning—to p-peep—"

"Eh heh heh heh. Here comes Ranta!"

"Wait, you can't do that!" Haruhiro got down out of the bed, chasing after Ranta. But Ranta was incredibly quick at times like this. He wasn't able to catch him all the way to the bathing room.

The bathing room was outside. It was attached to the lodging house, but it was in an annex so it might have been more accurate to call it the bathing hut. Ranta crouched down, pressing his ear up against the door.

"You—" Haruhiro called out, but Ranta glared angrily and brought a finger to his lips. He looked ready to kill someone. Intimidated,

Haruhiro fell silent without intending to.

No, no, I can't let him intimidate me.

Haruhiro crept up, whispering, "You can't do this..." in Ranta's ear. "There are lines you just shouldn't cross."

Like I care, Ranta mouthed at him. *Even if it makes me a failure as a person, I'll become an ogre or a demon if that's what it takes to accomplish my goals.*

Okay, now you're just blowing things out of proportion...I'm just telling you to show some restraint.

Restraint? Ranta shrugged. *I don't know the meaning of the word. It's not in my dictionary, that's for sure. Heh.*

...Wh-what?

Ranta pointed to the door. *I can hear inside. Their voices. Eh heh heh heh heh.*

Haruhiro nearly pressed his ear against the door as well, but stopped short. He thought, *No. I'm curious, but I don't want to lower myself to Ranta's level.*

Ranta gave a silent but salacious laugh, staring Haruhiro in the eye. *Don't hold back, Haruhiro. You've already given in to temptation. If you hadn't, you'd have already dragged me away kicking and screaming, or shouted to let them know.*

Urkh... That had hit him where it hurt. Haruhiro held his chest, looking around the area. He nearly groaned. There was someone off in the darkness. Two someones. They were coming this way. Who was it?

Hey, waved one of them, Manato. The giant behind him was Moguzo.

It must have caught Ranta by surprise, as his eyes were wide. *Y-you guys...*

"Hey—" Haruhiro was about to call out to them, but Manato brought a finger to his lips.

Not you too, Manato, Haruhiro thought in dismay. *Is that it? Are you okay with this?*

When he looked to them questioningly, Manato silently nodded. *Moguzo, too,* he mouthed.

Haruhiro let out a silent laugh. *I give,* he thought. *My...no, our... baser instincts win this round. Honestly, we're just curious, right? We're not going to look, right? We won't go as far as peeping, right? There's a paneless window in the hut that's high enough I can't see into it, but I can see the light leaking out and the steam rising from it, and it's all very tempting but, well, it's too high to get to, right? I mean, sure, if someone were to let me up on their shoulders or use someone as a platform, it might be doable. But we're not planning to go that far, right? We won't do it, right? We seriously won't. Not a chance.*

Haruhiro leaned in and pressed his ear up against the door. He could hear them. It was faint. No, he needed to focus harder. He should be able to hear more than that. There. He could hear them now. Very clearly.

"Even when you wear that..."

Is that voice Yume's?

"...Wh-wh-what?"

That one's Shihoru.

"...they sure're big, huh?"

"...H-huh...? Huh?! Wh-what are...?"

"...Your *boobs*, Shihoru, they're big. Oh, and their shape is adorable, too."

"...A-adorable...?" Shihoru's words, by fate or chance, expressed exactly what Haruhiro was thinking. No, probably not just him. Ranta, Manato and Moguzo must all have been thinking the same thing. Big and adorable? How did that work?! They had no idea!

"...Yup, they're adorable. Mind if Yume touches them?"

"...Wha, th-that's not, ah! N-No, it tickles! Eek...!"

"...Whew, Yume *thought* they'd feel good and boy do they ever."

"...Wai—No—Ah—Nyaa..."

"...Nyaa? You're making kitty cat noises now, Shihoru."

"...P-please, Y-yume, not so hard...!"

"...Boing, boing, look at 'em bounce."

"...D-don't say th-that, it's e-embarrassing..."

"...It'd be fun if Yume's were like this. Look what Yume's stuck with."

"...I-I think you're cute though, Yume..."

"...Whaaa? That's not true at all. What about Yume is cute?"

"...W-Well, how should I put it? You aren't fat like me, you're soft..."

"...I don't think you're fat, Shihoru. Yume has more flab than you do."

"...Well, the way you look soft is t-tasty, so..."

"...Tasty? Shihoru, you say the weirdest things. Yume isn't edible."

"...Ahhh, ummm, I-I know that, It's just, well, a metaphor, you could say."

"...Want to try a bite? Go on."

"...Oh, um, but..."

"...Just sink your teeth right in. Yume wouldn't mind if you take juuuust a little from right here."

Wh-why would she do that...?! Haruhiro pulled his ear away from the door and shook his head. *No, no, no. Wh-wh-what are Yume and Shihoru doing? What's going on in there? This is crazy. My imagination is running wild. Is that what girls are like? I don't know. How could I know?*

When he looked, Manato, Moguzo, and even Ranta had backed away from the door, as well.

That figures. Of course they would. It was too much for us to handle... what a mystery. Every mystery leads to another and now our heads are a mess.

Haruhiro looked Manato in the eyes, trying to send the message: *Let's go back to our own room.* But Manato turned his eyes in another direction. Following his glance, Haruhiro saw Ranta looking up at the night sky.

No, that wasn't what he was looking at. Not the sky. It was the window.

Ranta stared at that window with the eyes of a ravenous beast. He stood up straight, walking over beneath the window. He reached out for it, stretching. He couldn't reach. Ranta turned to them. He had the face of a demon.

...Don't you guys want to see? Are you seriously okay not doing it? You want to pass up this golden opportunity? Can you say for sure that you won't regret it? Well? Can you?

Th-that's... Haruhiro ground his teeth. *That's not...*

I might regret it, Manato was candid. *I can't say for certain that I won't. Still, what good can come of us going any further? What do you think will happen?*

Ranta scowled. *What do you mean by that...?*

Think for a second. We're excited enough as is. Any more is dangerous.

If we push ourselves too far, then what? We go back to the room...our room. A room with four guys. I don't want to go through that. It's not too late to turn back now.

Haruhiro shuddered. *That's Manato for you. He can see it would be bad...no, a tragedy. But, right now, if we stop here, we can hold on to this as a good memory—I think. I'm sure we can. We should be able to. It's probably possible, I guess.*

This was the line. If they stepped over it, there would be no going back. If possible, he wanted all of them to come back from it.

He crossed the line, but I did nothing. If only I had acted differently back then. He wanted to avoid anything happening that might make him feel that way later.

Let's go back. Haruhiro grabbed Ranta by the arm. He was ready to drag him away by force if necessary. Yet an unexpected ambush awaited him.

Moguzo stood up slowly, walked over to beneath the window, then leaned forward, putting his hands against the wall. A platform. Was he trying to become a platform? Moguzo looked to Haruhiro and the others, giving them a thumbs up.

Everyone climb up. Don't worry about me.

Haruhiro looked to Ranta. Then to Manato. They looked like they'd been struck by lightning.

I can't, Haruhiro thought.

Moguzo's resolve weighed on him. It was too heavy. He couldn't shake himself free from it. He couldn't do it. There was no way he could. It was impossible to shake free.

I have to do it.

Haruhiro and Manato nodded to each other. Which of them

would go first? Haruhiro was happy to go later or last even. First up would be Ranta, it was his idea, after all.

Ranta was crying. His eyes were streaming tears. He wasn't just crying; his nose was running, too.

Without wiping his snot or tears, Ranta went over and slapped Moguzo on the back. "Come on, man! Don't make me cry like this! You're such a great guy!"

Haruhiro whispered, "Hey…" and the next moment turned and ran the other way.

Manato was well ahead of him. That was Manato for you. Quick on his feet.

"Why does Yume hear Ranta's voice…?!" shouted Yume from inside the bathing hut.

"Oh, crap!" Ranta bolted. "N-no! It wasn't me! I-it was Moguzo! Yeah, Moguzo! I didn't see or hear nothing!"

"Whuh?!" Moguzo tripped spectacularly and Shihoru shrieked.

"Ranta, you numbskull!" They heard Yume kick the wall hard from inside. "You creep! You letch! You pervert! Go far away and never come back…!"

Grimgar of Fantasy and Ash

10. Damuro

They confessed their sins to Yume and Shihoru, prostrating themselves on the ground as they apologized profusely.

Haruhiro, Manato, and Moguzo did, that is.

Ranta said, "I didn't see nothing, so quit your whining!" disgusting everyone with his aggressive lack of contrition. It went further than that, though. Yume and Shihoru began to resolutely ignore Ranta's existence.

Haruhiro couldn't say for certain if that had made their teamwork any worse or not, but it probably had no real effect.

The following day, the day after and the day after that, Haruhiro and the others earned basically nothing. And by "basically nothing," that meant their income was close to zero. Okay, let's be blunt; it was *zero*.

Haruhiro couldn't bring himself to ask his comrades about their pocketbooks, so he didn't have a full grasp of their finances. His own, however, he knew in meticulous detail.

Over the three days, he'd been fourteen copper in the red, thirteen copper in the red and twelve copper in the red for a total of thirty-nine copper in the red. If he didn't include the less-than-one-copper he owed in deposit fees, Haruhiro's total assets included one silver and forty-nine copper.

His hopes to buy daily necessities from the market, or to buy a new pair of underwear, were long since dashed. Of course, when it came to his hope of moving somewhere better than the volunteer soldier lodging house, it would be presumptuous to even dream of something that far beyond his means. He had been cutting his food expenses down one copper a day, but how low could he get them? That was the biggest concern for him right now.

The shock of going three days without income was big, so incredibly big that since coming back to the lodging house and bathing today, no one had spoken a word.

All of the others were lying on their beds. Maybe they were asleep already.

No, probably not. None of them could possibly be so dense as to be able to sleep soundly under current conditions. Well, so he thought, but Ranta was snoring.

Wow. Haruhiro was so disgusted, it went all the way back around to a sort of admiration. *Well, me too. I ought to get some shut-eye. All this thinking isn't doing me any good. Something good might happen tomorrow, anyway. Today's over now. I can't do anything about that. Tomorrow's what's important now. What will I do tomorrow? Give it my all and go hunting for prey. I have to earn something even if it's just one copper. I guess one's not enough. Yeah, that's no good. I'll earn a lot. As much as I can. Gotta do something before the money runs out.*

As he tossed and turned, he heard someone getting up in the bunk below him.

"...Manato?"

"Yeah."

"You're up? It's still night. Or rather, the night just started. Running to the washroom or something?"

"Nah," Manato had gotten out of bed, it seemed. "I'm going out for a bit. I probably don't need to say this, but I'll be coming back, so don't worry."

"Huh. You're going out...at this time of night?"

"The night's just getting started," Manato smiled slightly. "See you later. You must be tired. Don't wait up for me. Go ahead and sleep."

"Oh, okay." Haruhiro nodded. Then it occurred to him that maybe he shouldn't let Manato go alone. But by the time it did, Manato had left the room.

To assuage his anxiety, he struck up a conversation with Moguzo, who hadn't gotten to sleep yet, talking about this and that, but at some point, Haruhiro nodded off. When he woke up, Manato was back. He'd even gotten out of bed earlier than him.

"Morning, Haruhiro. I want to try going to a new place today. What do you think?"

Last night, Manato had gone to Sherry's Tavern, a place on Flower Garden Street where volunteer soldiers gathered. While he was there, some people had treated him to drinks while others had practically forced them on him. Manato didn't go into details, but it must have been pretty expensive.

"You could've taken me with you," Haruhiro tried saying.

"Haruhiro, you can drink?" Manato asked in response.

"I dunno," Haruhiro tilted his head in contemplation. "Have I drunk before? Maybe not."

"Well, as for me," Manato smiled mischievously. "It turns out I might just like it. So, maybe part of the reason I went there was that I wanted to drink."

Everyone was sick and tired of the forest by this point, so there was no resistance to Manato's proposal when he made it.

Around four km northwest of Alterna, a bit over an hour's walk away, there was a city.

Well, no, it would be more correct to say that there was what once had been a city. At least for the moment, nobody lived there. Nobody *human,* that is.

Eighty percent of the defensive wall that had once protected the city had now crumbled. More than half the buildings had collapsed, probably seventy to eighty percent. It was full of rubble with weeds growing in places. There were rusted swords and spears lying around, some of them stabbed into the ground. Even more terrifying were the skeletons scattered all over.

There was some kind of animal—they couldn't decide if it was a cat or dog—walking atop the roofs and crumbling walls, but it ran away immediately when they tried to get close. There were crows cawing everywhere. When they looked towards the source, they found one ruin had become home to tens of crows, possibly more.

Long ago, Damuro had been the second-largest city in Arabakia. It had been much larger than Alterna. However, the No-Life King's allied forces had invaded and laid waste to it, bringing it under undead control.

Things were different now. After the breakup of the Undying Empire, the goblins, who had once been a slave race with no king, revolted and drove out the undead to make the city their own. Now, Damuro was a den of goblins.

However, the southeast corner of Damuro—called the Old City—had gone unmaintained and fallen to ruins. Even so, it was not the case that there were no goblins in the Old City of Damuro. There were.

"...There's just the one...I think?"

Haruhiro had hidden behind a wall that looked like it would collapse if he put his full weight against it, spying into a house that was missing a ceiling and one wall. He was a thief, so he was gradually becoming the party's go-to person for scouting, but he hadn't learned the Sneaking or Burglary skills, so he was really just an ordinary guy who could open locks with the Lock Picking skill. He wondered if it was really wise to have him handle this.

Mud goblins, like the one they had taken down in the forest, were a breed of goblin, apparently. And the goblin here certainly did look similar to the mud goblin. But this one had yellowish-green skin and wasn't filthy. It even had clothes on and was carrying a club or something at its waist. The bag slung over its shoulder must have been a goblin pouch. The mud goblin had kept its valuables on a string around its neck, but these goblins carried bags like that one around. They had heard one of the traits of goblins was that they would put any valuable things they had in there, carrying it with them at all times.

The goblin was sitting back to the wall with its arms crossed. Its face was cast downwards, its eyes closed. It was still daylight hours, but was he taking a nap? That's what it looked like.

Haruhiro, quickly but as quietly as he could manage, headed back to where the others were standing by.

"One goblin. Looks like it's asleep."

"Good, let's kill it," Manato nodded with a grim look. "Since Moguzo's in chainmail, he can't help but make noise. So first, Haruhiro, Ranta and I will get up close. Moguzo, Yume, and Shihoru will close in after that. If we can get in close without waking the goblin, the three of us will snuff it out. If it wakes, Yume, you use your bow, and Shihoru, you use magic to target it from a distance. Moguzu, you'll charge up front. If it becomes a straight-out battle, we'll use the same formation as last time. Everyone surrounds it so it can't escape."

Everyone nodded at once. Having gone three days without an income, even Ranta was a picture of seriousness.

With Manato taking point, the three of them set out. They reached the house quickly enough, but it was everything that came after that which would take time. The house was full of rubble and they couldn't afford to step on anything. They ended up making noise a number of times and it took longer than expected. They were close enough now that with another step or two, the goblin would be in striking range.

Moguzo and the others were just outside the house. Manato looked in turn to Haruhiro, then Ranta. Ranta pointed to himself.

Haruhiro wasn't sure leaving this to Ranta was wise, but Manato waved to him, the signal for *do it*. Ranta took a deep breath and walked up to the goblin. Without raising it overhead first, he stabbed his longsword into the goblin's chest.

The goblin groaned and its eyes shot open. It spotted Haruhiro then understood what had happened to it. The goblin screamed, reaching out for Ranta's face.

Ranta leaned back so Manato shouted, "You can't do that!" at him. At the same time, he drew his short staff, clubbing and stabbing at the goblin with it repeatedly.

"Dammit...!" Ranta pushed his longsword in and twisted it.

Haruhiro was unable to do anything. If he got closer, he'd probably just get in Manato and Ranta's way. The goblin continued to writhe in agony, shouting what must have been a torrent of verbal abuse as it grew weaker and weaker. The mud gob had put up such a fight, but when caught sleeping, was this the best they could muster? Eventually, it stopped twitching.

"...Is it dead?" Ranta peeked at the goblin's face, his shoulders heaving with heavy breaths. Haruhiro imagined the goblin reviving and then tearing Ranta's nose right off with its teeth, but it didn't happen. Manato closed his eyes, making the sign of the hexagram. It looked like it was over.

Moguzo, Yume, and Shihoru entered the house.

Ranta planted a foot on the goblin's chest and yanked his longsword free. "Gotta lop off a claw or something. Vice, vice..." he muttered to himself.

Manato delicately removed the goblin's pouch that was slung over its shoulder. He opened it, pouring out the contents. Haruhiro's eyes bulged.

"Silver coins!" he shouted.

Maybe goblins liked to collect human currency. And, what was more, unlike the mud gob's coin, these ones were hole-free. There were four undamaged silver coins. Four silver. There was also a rock that was clear like glass. Also some bones. They didn't know what animal they came from, but they were finger bones or some other thin bones.

"Ohhh!" Yume's eyes went wide. "Amazin'! That's a new record, isn't it? Though it's still just our second time."

"...Four silver," Shihoru said, blinking repeatedly. She didn't know what to say, it seemed.

Moguzo had let out an impressed groan, then kept his mouth shut.

Manato looked to the sky. With a sigh, he said, "It's still not enough," shaking his head. "We have to keep this up. It happened to go easily this time, but it won't always be this way. Keep on your toes and let's find our next target."

"Oh, come on!" Ranta slapped Manato on the back. "Don't be such a square! We just had a big win. All thanks to me! What's the harm in celebrating a little?"

Manato knitted his brows for a moment but quickly went back to a smile. "I suppose you're right. I don't mind you celebrating a bit. You did a good job, Ranta."

"I know, right? Right? I'm so awesome, aren't I? Especially the way I put that gob to the sword with a cruel and merciless smile. I must've looked like a real dread knight there, huh?"

Haruhiro said, "Nah," waving his hand. "You looked just as frantic as ever, Ranta."

"You moron! I was cool as a cucumber! Where were you even looking, man?! Oh, I know! That's what it was! You couldn't see it with those sleepy-looking eyes of yours!"

"You've run that joke into the ground already, I'm not gonna give you a response every time. Sorry."

"Give me a response! You've got to respond! You're making me feel kinda pitiful here!"

Everyone laughed for a while. Afterward, they did as Manato suggested, bracing themselves for what was coming as they searched for their next target.

Their first day in Damuro's Old City went smoothly. When they considered their days so far, the way it went so smoothly scared them.

By evening, Haruhiro and the others had taken down a total of four goblins including the one they had caught sleeping. From their four goblin pouches, they had acquired a sum total of eight silver, a clear stone, a black stone, a reddish stone, assorted bones and fangs, something resembling a key, a gear, and some sort of metal fittings. When they sold it all, their loot came to a total of ten silver and forty-five copper. Split six ways, everyone received one silver and seventy-four copper, with one left over. Food and lodgings that day cost him fifteen copper so Haruhiro's total assets came to three silver and eight copper. If tomorrow went smoothly as well, he had promised himself a pair of underwear and a knife.

The next day, however, went quite poorly. When they found a group of five goblins, Ranta said they should charge in, but they took a vote, and he was overruled by the majority who wanted to avoid the fight. Unless they caught one of the creatures by surprise, a single goblin was tough and two was risky so taking on five was out of the question. Haruhiro thought backing down was the right choice there.

However, after that, they didn't spot any groups of two or fewer until the end of the day, when they were getting ready to head home and came face-to-face with a lone goblin. As a result, they made one silver that day.

Just one silver.

If he thought about it that way, Haruhiro felt like he'd be cursed, though. They could have gone into the red but instead they had made one silver. Haruhiro decided to look at it that way. The underwear and knife could wait until they were making more profit.

On their third day in the Old City of Damuro, they tried making a simple map while searching for goblins. It had been Manato's idea and he'd also procured the small notebook and pencils they'd used to make it. Manato said that if they got the lay of the land, taking notes on where goblins were, it was guaranteed to come in handy.

Either way, it was pretty fun to walk through the Old City, methodically mapping it out. Saying, *Let's go over that way next or We haven't gone this way yet, let's go,* they would naturally start to form objectives. They learned the roads, too. When they entered an unmapped area, it put them on edge, and when they were in a place they already had on their map, they could relax a little. That day, they took down three goblins and once the loot was sold, they had seventy-two coppers each.

They didn't let it go to their heads. They weren't making that much money.

However, Yume and Shihoru had said they wanted to go shopping, so Haruhiro was going around the market, too. While he was looking, he happened across a pair of cloth underwear. He haggled his hardest but even a used pair cost twenty-five copper. He had stuff to carry now, so he bought a bag to carry it all in out of necessity. There were a good number of used ones at a reasonable price, so he bought a durable-looking one made out of hemp for thirty copper. Compared to the underwear, it felt like a real bargain.

After returning to the volunteer soldier lodging house, they all talked together about what they'd bought, where they'd bought it, and what they wanted to buy next. They got really into it, so they had trouble getting to sleep afterward. Once Ranta, who had been prattling incessantly until not long ago, suddenly fell asleep, breathing softly, it wasn't long before Moguzo could be heard snoring, too. Haruhiro tried to fall asleep. He was exhausted—sleepy even—yet for some reason his consciousness was making no attempt to descend into the depths of slumber.

"Manato," he tried calling out, and, as expected, Manato was awake and responded with a "Yeah?"

Haruhiro was happy to get a response and all, but he didn't really have anything to say to him. Well, that wasn't true; they had a lot to talk about. He just couldn't come up with anything so quickly. But staying quiet too long would be weird. He had to say something.

After grasping hurriedly for something to say, "Thank you," was what came out and he was embarrassed.

"What's that for, all of a sudden?" Manato laughed. "I'm the one who ought to be grateful."

"Huh? You're grateful...? Why?"

"To everyone, for being my comrades. I'm thankful for that. I'm sure when I say it like this, it probably comes across as a lie, but I really do feel that way."

"No, I don't think you're lying, but..." Haruhiro chewed the inside of his right cheek, thinking. "How should I put this? We're always relying on you. If you hadn't been there for us, we'd have been in serious trouble. Depending how things had gone, we might not still have been alive by this point."

"That goes both ways. Without you and the others, there's no telling what might have happened to me. We aren't in a situation where you can survive on your own, you realize."

Haruhiro hesitated on whether to say this or not, but he wasn't good at hiding his feelings. He lacked the patience. "...Now, I don't want you to take this the wrong way, but I think you could have found any number of people willing to be your comrades. By asking someone to let you join their party, for instance."

"A volunteer soldier party? Honestly, the thought never really crossed my mind. You know, I'm probably not the type that can put up with having to bow his head to others. Hierarchical relationships, too. I doubt I'm any good at handling those. I don't remember what I was doing before I came here, though, so I don't know for sure."

"Ah..." *Now that he mentions it, that's true.* When Haruhiro tried to remember his past, it was like grasping at something soft and fluffy. It never retained its shape. He had forgotten that fact entirely. Maybe he just hadn't had the leeway to think about it.

"It might be the same for me," he admitted.

"Somehow..." Manato paused there, hesitating for a second. "Somehow, I feel like I'm not the sort of person that anyone should be treating as a comrade."

"That's not..."

That's not true, I think. I think, but I can't say it outright. I only know Manato as he's been since coming here. That's all Manato knows about himself, too.

Even Manato didn't know Manato. Of course, it was the same with Haruhiro. The more he thought, the less he understood. So it was better not to think about it at all. Nothing would come of thinking about it. After all, he couldn't remember anything.

He had things to do. Things he had to do in order to live. He needed to earn money.

"As for what the past Manato was like," Haruhiro said with forced cheerfulness, "it doesn't matter. No one cares. It's the current Manato that's our comrade. You're like our leader. We'd be in trouble without you here for us."

"I need the rest of you, too."

Haruhiro nodded. But Manato was in the bunk beneath him, so he wouldn't see the nod. He needed to say it out loud. But, what could he say...? While he was wondering, Manato burst out laughing.

"Still, it's just so weird. All of this. What are we even doing? Swords and sorcery. It's like we're in a game or something."

"A game, huh. You've got that—" Haruhiro blinked, then tilted his head in confusion. "A game...what is that...?"

"Huh?" Manato thought deeply for a moment, as well. "...I don't know. But that's what I said just now. 'It's like a game.' It came to mind at the time."

"Well, when you said it, I felt like you were right. But what sort of game? A game..."

Something felt off. It was on the tip of his tongue, but he just couldn't get it to come out, that sort of *off* feeling. Still, he felt like they should put an end to this conversation. They had bigger things to worry about. Haruhiro and the others would go to the Old City of Damuro again tomorrow.

He yawned. It felt like he could finally get to sleep.

Grimgar
of
Fantasy and Ash

11. Don't Go

"There's one headed your way, Ranta!" Haruhiro called out, and Ranta responded immediately.

"I already knew that!"

One of the three goblins Moguzo and Manato had lured to the front line was headed for Yume and Shihoru in the rear. Haruhiro and Ranta were the middle guard, so they were supposed to try to catch the goblins from behind or to the side, but they needed to defend the back line as well. So Ranta, who was closer to the two of them, went to face the goblin.

It had been thirteen days since they had begun fighting goblins in the Old City of Damuro, so they could pull off this sort of team play without a word to each other. Though, every once in a while, Ranta would obsess over his own fighting style or skills, shooting whatever teamwork they had going in the foot completely. Fortunately, this time he was fine.

"Ha! Anger!"

—Or not.

Ranta leapt in from outside his opponent's range, longsword outthrust, to use his most recently acquired skill. It missed spectacularly.

"—Wha?! You're no ordinary goblin, are you...?!"

"It's *clearly* just a normal goblin, man!" Haruhiro said, looking to Manato with a wink.

Moguzo and Manato could be counted on to handle their two goblins. Haruhiro ran over and got behind the goblin that was pressuring Ranta with a rusty sword.

"Dammit...!" Ranta deflected its rusty blade, glancing to Haruhiro.

Don't look at me, thought Haruhiro as he took aim.

Ranta wasn't the only one who had learned a new skill. Each of them had learned a new one from their guilds. However, they'd only just learned them so they only knew how to perform them. Haruhiro wasn't confident that he could use his skill effectively in battle, but if he didn't make an active effort to use it, he would never get past that point.

I paid good money to learn this skill, and I swear I'll master it, he vowed. "...That's easier said than done, though."

The goblin was cautious, turning often to watch its own back, hopping around nimbly and swinging its rusty sword to keep him in check. Haruhiro just couldn't line up a good strike.

If Ranta could keep it occupied, he'd be fine, but he figured it would be a mistake to count on that actually happening. Ranta wasn't the type to let the enemy's focus fall entirely on him. Neither was Haruhiro, for that matter. Both of them were too afraid to get into a serious exchange of blows, so they tried to circle around to get behind it, or at least to its side. Because of that, they went in circles around the goblin and, of course, the goblin spun in circles trying not to let them get behind it, so no one had any clue what was going on.

"Jeez! What're you two doin'?!" Yume pulled her machete and came at the goblin swinging.

It looked like she'd taken it by surprise. It froze up for a second.

Yume swung her machete as if drawing an X-shape. "Diagonal Cross!"

The goblin cried out, falling back from the sudden onslaught, but it took a shallow cut to its shoulder. Its back was to Haruhiro.

Now, thought Haruhiro, but his body had already moved on its own. In a breath, he closed the gap and thrust his dagger into the goblin's back with a twist. This was his skill: Backstab.

Perhaps because the goblin was only wearing soft leather armor, Haruhiro's dagger sunk in a good 10 cm. The goblin tried to turn around, so Haruhiro wrenched his dagger out of it, falling back. The goblin coughed up blood and, despite whatever it had been about to try next, it collapsed. It was still twitching, but Haruhiro could tell it was at death's door. If it hadn't been, it would've flailed about more violently.

"Huh...?" Haruhiro looked back and forth from his dagger to the fallen goblin. "Did I hit it in a good spot? Maybe? Or a bad spot...?"

"Whoa?! I've gotta finish it!" Ranta leapt on the goblin, slamming his longsword through its neck. "Nice! I got my vice!"

Yume arched her eyebrows. "Yume thinks this after every battle, but dread knights sure are savage, huh?"

"Don't say 'savage'! Use the more elegant term, 'atrocious'! We dread knights serve the Dark God, Lord Skullhell. We are atrocious and inhumane, cold and ruthless knights with neither blood nor tears!"

"Ohm, rel, ect..." Shihoru drew elemental sigils with her staff, beginning to chant a spell. "Vel, darsh...!"

Mages used the power of magical creatures called elementals. Shihoru had called on a shadow elemental, which looked like a mass of black seaweed. It made a signature *vwong* noise as it flew. This was the Shadow Beat spell.

Instead of Arve Magic, the magic of fire, Kanon Magic, the magic of ice, or Falz Magic, the magic of electricity, Shihoru had chosen to learn Darsh Magic, the magic of shadow. In some ways, Haruhiro felt that Shihoru's own personality had come out in that decision.

The shadow elemental hit the goblin Manato was fighting in the back of the head. But it wasn't just the goblin's head it affected; the goblin's whole body convulsed for a moment, and it let out a strange croak. Instead of heat, cold, electricity or blunt force, Shadow Beat was a spell that used hyper oscillation to deal damage.

Manato immediately followed up with a blow from his short staff then kicked the goblin to the ground. Ranta savaged the fallen goblin.

"Take this! Hatred...!"

Hitting them when they were down was Ranta's specialty. There was no need to use a skill on an already-weakened goblin that had already fallen, but that sort of reasoning had no place in Ranta's mind. Ranta tried to bisect the goblin with his longsword—and failed. The longsword struck the side of the goblin's head and bounced off its skull with a wet thud. That made Ranta lose it.

"Dammit! You're just a stupid goblin! Take this! And this! And *this...!*"

While Ranta tormented the dying goblin, Haruhiro went to take care of the remaining one that Moguzo was facing.

No, it looked like Haruhiro wouldn't need to do anything. The goblin swung its rusty sword with a cry, but Moguzo blocked it with his bastard sword. Their blades locked. Moguzo had the advantage now. He was strong and had learned a skill that let him shift from locking blades to attacking.

"Hungh...!" Moguzo wound his bastard sword around the rusty blade, slashing the goblin in the face with the tip. This was his skill: Wind. Moguzo wasn't fast, but he was pretty skillful. The goblin faltered and stepped back.

Haruhiro cried out, "Go!" and Moguzo went. He got in close, slashing diagonally with all his strength.

"Thanks...!"

Rage Blow was the most basic of basic skills taught to a warrior in beginner's training. It looked like something anyone could copy after seeing it, but it was probably difficult to find the right timing to actually land a hit with it. Whenever Moguzo used Rage Blow, he shouted, "Thanks!" so within the party, they called it the Thanks Slash. It was a cute name that belied a rather powerful strike.

Moguzo's sword entered through the goblin's shoulder and made it halfway through its chest. With a grunt, he swung his sword and the goblin was sent flying.

"Yahoo!" Ranta rushed over to the goblin, impaling it with his longsword.

Haruhiro had to agree with Yume; Ranta really *was* savage. He acted like a total barbarian, slashing off the goblin's ear with a knife and shouting.

"Gwahaha! That's three vices in a row! That makes eleven vices total! My demon's powered up! Whenever it feels like it, it'll whisper in the enemy's ear to distract it! That's awesome!"

"Whenever it feels like it...?" Haruhiro said with a sigh. "Your demon sure is useless, huh?"

"Hey! I won't let that pass, Haruhiro! Don't you go dissing Zodiac-kun or I'll curse you!"

Zodiac-kun was the name Ranta had given his demon. Well, no; Zodiack was its proper name. Zodiac-kun was more of a nickname. Either way, it was never any help.

"I mean, you can only call it out at night, anyway."

"Moron, when I reach eleven vices, its rank goes up, so I'll be able to call it at dusk and just before the sun rises!"

"Generally, we head back to Alterna by dusk, and you're asleep when the sun comes up."

"Hmm. Well, yeah, but..." Yume had her cheeks puffed up angrily, with her eyes shining. It was such a complex expression. "Unlike its owner Ranta, Zodiac-kun is just a little bit cute, you know?"

"I'm not his owner! You can't 'own' a demon like some sort of pet. If anything, Zodiac-kun is possessing me. He's a demon, after all!"

"...Which means," Shihoru looked at the ground, laughing sinisterly, "before he could curse Haruhiro, Ranta's already been cursed..."

"W-well, yeah, I suppose I am. I-I am?! Seriously? Zodiac-kun, are you cursing me? No way, right? Zodiac-kun? What's your take on this? Wait, no, it's daytime, I can't ask him..."

"Good work, everyone," Manato looked to each of them with a smile. "I'll heal your wounds, so—actually, it looks like no one's injured. Still, if you're feeling any pain, just tell me. But if everyone thinks they're fine, let's check the goblin pouches."

"Me, me, me! I'll do it! Me! Let me do it!" shouted Ranta.

In the three goblin pouches, they found seven silver coins, two stones that looked like they might be worth something, three fangs or bones they didn't know whether they could sell or not, as well as some assorted junk they figured was worthless. Depending on what price the stones went for, they had over ten silver if they were lucky, but at least eight even if they weren't.

They had left Alterna at 7:00 in the morning to arrive in the Old City of Damuro at 8:00. Judging by the angle of the sun, it was now past noon. Haruhiro and the others gave the goblins a simple burial— or rather just cleared them away—then took an afternoon break at a spot not far away. Each of them had brought bread, dried meat, or other foodstuffs in their backpacks. It was time to enjoy a nice lunch.

"Oh, gotta pray." Yume shaved off a thin slice of the dried meat with her knife, leaving it on the ground as she put her hands together and closed her eyes in prayer. "White God Elhit-chan, thank you for everythin'. Yume'll share some of her food with you, so keep lookin' out for her, okay?"

"So, about what you're doing there," Haruhiro said, tearing off a piece of bread. It came from Tattan's Bakery just outside of West Town. It was rock-hard, but it was cheap and tasted decent enough. "That's a ritual that's laid out in the rules of the hunters guild, isn't it? You have to offer a little of your food to your god, right?"

"Sure do," Yume's eyes were wide with enthusiasm and she turned to face him. "The White God Elhit-chan is this reeeeally big wolf, y'see. And there's this reeeeally big Black God called Rigel who's a wolf, too. Elhit and Rigel are on super-bad terms with each other. Because Elhit-chan watches over us hunters, we can get through our daily huntin' without any accidents."

"So, basically, it's an act of worship. Hunters worship the White God Elhit. But you're calling your god Elhit-chan and offering to share some of your food. Is that okay?"

"Nah, it's fine," Yume chuckled. "Elhit-chan is forgiving, so Yume doesn't think Elhit-chan'd get mad at her over something like that, y'know. Actually, Elhit-chan's never gotten mad at Yume."

"...Your feelings," Shihoru said while carefully holding something that looked like a doughnut. "I think your feelings are what gets through to your god. Though that's just what I think..."

Manato took a sip from a leather waterskin, then said, "Yeah," with a nod. "The words you say are important, but the feeling you put into saying them is even more important. The prayers we priests use in our light magic won't work if we say the words wrong, but I don't think your prayers to Elhit are the same."

"Yume puts a lot—a loooot—of feelin' into it." Yume spread her arms wide to show them. "Yume goes to sleep at night, yeah? Well, when she does, Elhit-chan shows up in her dreams pretty often. Yume asks, 'Can I ride on your back, Elhit-chan?' and when she does, Elhit-chan says, 'Sure,' y'see. Yume went for a ride on Elhit-chan and we run around like *whoosh*. Elhit-chan is crazy-fast. Yume says, 'This is amazing.'"

"...This story," Ranta chewed his dried meat loudly while putting on a sour face. "It's got an actual point at the end, right? I've held my tongue and listened for a long time, so if you don't have a good point, I'm gonna snap. Like, seriously."

"A point?" Yume cocked her head to the side and blinked at him repeatedly. "No. There isn't one."

"What?!" Ranta shouted and did an incredible face fault. "Are you stupid?! Don't tell long stories with no point! What'll you do if I drown to death, unable to escape from the spiral of broken expectations?!"

"Go ahead..." Shihoru muttered under her breath. "I wish you'd drown to death..."

"Ah!" Ranta pointed at Shihoru. "Ah! Ahhhh! I heard that! I heard you, Shihoru! Just now, you just told me to go die, didn't you, huh?!"

"...I only said that I wished you'd drown."

"You're even making requests about the cause of death! You're horrible! That's the lowest thing you can do as a person! You're the most rotten, horrible girl in all of history, that's what you are!"

"Don't mind him, Shihoru." Yume held Shihoru tight, patting her on the head. "The guy sayin' it is the lowest of the low, after all. You've done noooothin' wrong, Shihoru. It's Mr. Terrible here who's to blame. He's so low, he may not even be human."

"I'm human, okay?!"

"Even if you have curly hair," Haruhiro said.

"Yes! Even with my curly hair..." Ranta began to agree. Then he turned to glare at Haruhiro, pulling at his hair as he did. "Curly hair has nothing to do with it! Heck, I'd even consider making it a requirement for being human! Those without curly hair are not human! How's that?!"

"...If that's how it's going to be," Moguzo said, swallowing a hard, fist-sized bun whole, "maybe I don't want to be human."

"Yume, too."

"...Me, too."

"Same."

"Hold on." An oddly serious look fell over Manato's face. "Let's think this over calmly, okay? Let's think over whether curly hair really is the problem here. I think not. Curly hair has done us no wrong. Curly hair is not to blame here. In fact, I'd say curly hair may be the victim in all this."

"Hm?" Ranta pulled at his hair. "...The victim? This guy? So, what, then the villain is... meeeee?! Are you saying it's all my fault that curly hair turned evil?!"

"I was kidding, Ranta."

"Manato! You're always grinning, so it's hard to tell when you're joking and when you're serious! You're a black-bellied bastard wearing a smile as a mask!"

"H-he is *not!*" Shihoru stood up and shouted. Her face was bright red and she looked like steam might start rising out of her ears any second. "H-he is not black-bellied! N-not Manato-kun! He isn't black-bellied or a bastard! Y-You take that back! R-right now! Do it!"

"...Uh, sure," Ranta was taken aback. "But, do I have to really? It's not like I actually think it, you know? If I have to take abuse, isn't it fair that I get to dish some out, too?"

"T-take it back!"

"F-fine, fine. I'll do it. I'll correct myself. Manato's belly isn't black. Manato's belly is white. I see him in the bath every day, so I'd know. It's white, you know, Manato's belly. Seriously. He's pale. For a guy. Actually, even by girl standards, he'd be pale."

"Wh-white..." Shihoru looked a little dizzy. "...Manato-kun's white belly... The bath..."

"Am I pale, really?" Manato compared his skin's color against his priest robes. "I don't think I'm that pale. Haruhiro, am I pale?"

"Yeah, sorta..." Haruhiro looked from Shihoru to Manato, comparing.

Manato is pale, but Shihoru's even paler. But that's not really the point right now. I thought it might be the case, but this pretty much confirms it. Shihoru has a thing for Manato. Does he not notice it? I don't think he's dense like that, so that isn't it. Is he pretending not to notice, then? If he is, maybe he doesn't feel the same way about her. Poor Shihoru. Though I'm not sure it's my place to be feeling sorry for her.

"You could say you're pale. Yup. You're pale. Your skin's smooth, too."

"Skin...smooth..." Shihoru looked like she might collapse. "Smooth...skin..."

"Shihoru, you okay?" Yume supported her. "If you fantasize too much, it'll only cause problems. You should try to keep it under control. Shihoru? Shihoru?"

"Nyahhhh..." Shihoru's eyes were swirling and she clung on to Yume tightly.

Shoot, thought Haruhiro. *Maybe I went too far there. She was acting kind of cute there, or funny at least, so I couldn't help myself.*

Ranta scoffed at them then started eating his bread. He seemed unamused by this turn of events.

I wonder why, thought Haruhiro. *Maybe Ranta has a thing for Shihoru? It looks like Shihoru is into Manato, so maybe he's upset about that? If so, it's time for Ranta to take a good, long look at himself. For starters, buddy, you've done nothing that would make the girls love you and everything that would make them loathe you.*

"We've become a good party," Manato said quietly to himself.

"Huh?"

"We can take on up to three goblins at a time now. No one even got hurt, so I think it's safe to assume we could handle more. Yume's much better with a machete than she is with a bow. She has a lot of strength. If we think about our methods some more, we might be able to handle four."

"Oh, about that..." Haruhiro imagined it. Moguzo and Manato would both handle one, Haruhiro, Ranta, and Yume would handle the other two. If Shihoru caught one with Shadow Beat so they could finish it off quickly, he felt like they could pull it off. "Yeah, four sounds doable."

"I knew we'd be able to rely on Moguzo. After all, he's got such a big body. Just by being there, he intimidates the enemy. And with his precise swordsmanship, he can get what needs doing done."

"Ah, I'd been thinking that, too. Moguzo's talented."

Moguzo swallowed a bun. "...R-really? You think? I don't know why, b-but I like doing detailed work."

"It doesn't suit you!" Ranta yelled, taking out his frustration on him. Moguzo just shrugged.

"Y-yeah, I think so, too..."

"Hey, it's a good thing," Haruhiro said, glaring at Ranta slightly. "Moguzo isn't sloppy, unlike a certain someone."

"Oh? What, you saying that to me? Me, the guy they call the Gale-Speed Machine of Precision?"

Yume glared coldly at Ranta while patting Shihoru reassuringly on the head. "Nobody's ever called you that, Ranta."

"Ranta's amazing, too." Judging from the subdued expression on Manato's face, he wasn't joking. "Especially the way he's always ready to attack. He's not afraid of failure, so I think he's improved at using his skills faster than any of us. The rest of us, myself included, are more cautious, you could say. Without Ranta around, we might not be willing to take that next step forward."

"Yeah, I guess?" Ranta said, looking about worriedly. Had that flustered him? "Well, you know what they call me. The Whirlwind Machine of Forward Momentum, yeah?"

Haruhiro teased, "What happened to the Gale-Speed Machine of Precision?"

"As for Shihoru..." Manato paused for a breath.

He has noticed Shihoru's feelings for him, after all, Haruhiro surmised.

"...Shihoru is always aware of her surroundings. Darsh Magic has a lot of spells that can confuse or bind the target, if I recall. That lets her help us when needed. You wanted to learn Darsh Magic so you could help us, didn't you, Shihoru?"

Shihoru stared blankly for a second, but then nodded without a word.

Haruhiro was dumbfounded. *I thought she'd passed up the easy-to-understand choices like fire, ice or electricity and chose a more niche option instead because that's just what Shihoru's like. Was I wrong? It wasn't just a matter of her tastes. Shihoru put some genuine consideration into it. I'm so stupid. I don't know a thing about her.*

Manato looked to Yume. "I think Yume may well be the bravest of us all. She isn't afraid of anything. As the healer, I wish she'd be more careful, but I'm also glad that Yume might be there to help if anything happens."

"Yume is?" Yume said, pointing to herself, her face melting with glee. "You sure? Is Yume really that brave? Yume doesn't think she's ever been told that before. Though, maybe she doesn't think many things are scary. Yume hopes you'll give her a pass for being a hunter who can't use a bow."

"Everyone has weaknesses and things they can't do," Manato said, as if trying to convince himself of it as well. "When you're alone, those failings can be fatal, but we're a party. We can make up for each other's shortcomings."

"Oh, yeah." Yume nodded repeatedly. "That's right. Yume may cause trouble for all of you goin' forward, but she'll do her breastest."

Ranta snorted derisively. "You mean 'bestest,' like 'best,' not 'breastest.' Breastest sounds like, you know, you'd need some special kind of breasts."

"Breastest..." Yume touched her own breasts. "Yume wonders what kinda breasts are the breastest breasts. How distantly related are they to Yume's tiny breasts?"

It would be awkward to just leave that hanging, so Haruhiro offered, "...Maybe they're in the same family?"

Yume looked at Haruhiro with a totally serious expression on her face. "Do you think they're in the same family, Haru-kun?"

"I-I dunno. I wonder."

"Yume wonders, too. The breastest breasts. It does sound a little cute, you know."

"The br—" Moguzo started to say, but when everyone turned to look at him, sweat beaded on his forehead and he waved his hands and shook his head. "I-i-i-i-it was nothing. R-r-really, nothing."

"...Now I'm curious." said Shihoru.

With Shihoru staring at him, Moguzo cast his eyes downward, then apologized with a "S-sorry," so no one pushed him about it any further, but what had Moguzo started to say? Haruhiro was pretty curious, if not to the same degree as Shihoru.

After that, they continued to make small talk over lunch until the time came to start their afternoon work. As they were leaving, something occurred to Haruhiro.

Manato praised all of the others, but did he say a single thing about me? Maybe he just forgot. Or was it that there was nothing praiseworthy about him? *Does Manato have a low opinion of me, maybe? We talk a lot, though, I think. Maybe I'm only useful as someone to talk to?*

It worried him, but it was a little late to ask, "Hey, Manato, what about me...?" That would have been far too embarrassing.

Ah, well.

He'd probably just forgotten, or the conversation moved on before he could get to Haruhiro, that was all. It still made Haruhiro a little anxious, but that was how he decided to take it.

Focus, man. You need to focus.

"...Found some."

Haruhiro raised a hand, signaling the group to stop. They would all hide in the shadows until things were scouted out. Of course, Haruhiro would go alone to do that. There were rare occasions when Ranta wanted to come along, but honestly, Haruhiro felt it was easier for him to go alone. He only needed to worry about himself that way.

Once I save up enough money, Sneaking is one of the thief techniques I definitely want to learn. Of course, I'm doing my best not to make any noise while walking now, but there must be some trick to it. I want to know what that is. I want Barbara-sensei to teach it to me.

The goblins were in a broken-down, two-floor building made out of stone. The second floor had largely collapsed and part of the wall on the first floor had crumbled in places, as well. On the second floor, which was more like an open balcony, there was a goblin clad in solid-looking metal armor with a sword slung over its back while on the first floor there was another goblin sitting on the ground. It was a big one.

Most goblins were between 120 and 130 cm tall. If they reached 140 cm, they were pretty big for their kind. They were a race of creatures the size of human children. But this goblin was nothing like that. From a distance it was hard to tell its exact height, but it was easily one, maybe two, sizes larger than the goblin upstairs.

I've never seen a goblin like that before. Haruhiro thought. *As for equipment, is that chainmail it's wearing? It's even got a simple helmet. Can't tell what weapons it has from here.*

I've searched the area around the building, and it doesn't look like there are any more. There are two goblins. The armored goblin and the really big goblin.

Haruhiro went back to the others.

"It's dangerous. There are only two, but one of them's huge. It might be as big as I am."

"A hobgoblin." Manato's eyes widened a little. "They're a subrace of goblins with a larger build than the ordinary ones. They're stupid brutes that the goblins use like slaves, so maybe that's what that one is."

"Oh, yeah?" Ranta licked his lips. "If it's got a slave, that could be a high-ranking gob, don't you think? If it is, it's gotta have some good loot, for sure."

Haruhiro stroked his chin. "...It did have plated metal armor on. The hobgoblin was wearing chainmail, too. That and a helmet. It might have been large enough for one of us humans to wear."

"Ooh..." Moguzo groaned in approval. Since, as a warrior, Moguzo faced the enemy in straight-up battle, defensive items were important to him. But they were also expensive. New ones were well out of their price range and if they went with used goods, they'd have to search hard to find ones that fit or go to a blacksmith to have them resized. That was why all of them, Moguzo included, were still using the stuff their guilds had given them.

"Two of them, huh?" Manato lowered his eyes. He seemed uncertain.

"Hmm," Yume looked up diagonally in thought. "Yume thinks we can handle two of them, though."

"If I..." Shihoru grasped her staff tight. "...were to target one first and manage to hit it with a spell, it would be easier to handle things after that...I think."

"Yume'll try whooshing some arrows at it, too. Even if she misses, the gobbies'll get scared, so then you can go right at 'em."

Manato looked at his comrades' faces. They were all eager to fight. Perhaps his earlier praise had raised their morale because they were more fired up than usual. Haruhiro wasn't and he felt a bit left out because of that, but he didn't want to be a wet blanket. Haruhiro said, "Guess we're doing this," and Manato nodded.

"Okay, let's do it."

The plan came together in no time. Haruhiro, Yume, and Shihoru would go first, starting the attack from long range. Once the enemy noticed them, Moguzo and Manato would move up to the front. Moguzo would take the hobgob and Manato would take the armored gob. Haruhiro, Ranta, and Yume would attack from behind or to the sides while Shihoru would support them with magic from a distance.

They got in a circle, all putting their hands in the center. Manato yelled "Fighto!" and they all threw their hands up at once and shouted "Ippatsu!"

At some point, they had started doing this to get their spirits up, but why they did it remained a mystery to Haruhiro.

"...What is 'fighto ippatsu,' I wonder?" he commented.

"...I dunno." Shihoru tilted her head to the side, puzzled. "But doing it gives me this vague feeling of nostalgia."

"Yume gets that feelin', too. But she doesn't know what it is. Weird, huh?"

Haruhiro approached the two-story building with Yume and Shihoru in tow. Manato, Moguzo, and Ranta were following them too, about six or seven meters behind. Whatever the range of a bow was, magic had a range of around ten meters.

Can we get close enough to be ten meters away? thought Haruhiro. *That might be a bit difficult. More like impossible. Not using this wall. It's about fifteen meters away from the building, but if we go past it, the gobs will notice us.*

Haruhiro brought his face next to Shihoru's ear. He was about to whisper something to her, but she had a distinctive, sweet smell coming from her, and that made it hard for him to breathe.

"...Shihoru, do you have something on?"

"...Huh? What do you mean?"

"No, never mind. Sorry. Think you can hit them from here? It's a bit far, I know."

"...I'll try. I have zero confidence, though."

Shihoru brought her hand to her bosom, taking a deep breath. Yume readied her bow and nocked an arrow. The gobs weren't looking in their direction. The two popped up from behind the wall and

Shihoru began drawing elemental sigils with her staff.

"Ohm, rel, ect, vel, darsh...!"

With a *vwong*, a shadow elemental that looked like a blob of black seaweed launched from the tip of Shihoru's staff. At the same time, Yume let an arrow fly. The arrow sailed over the armored gob's head while the shadow elemental struck the hobgob in the left arm, causing it to sputter and convulse. It looked like the armored gob had noticed the arrow. He turned their way and Haruhiro cried out, "We've been spotted!"

"We're going in!" Manato gave the order at once.

The hobgob picked up a spiked club that had been left at its feet, rising unsteadily. It looked like the Shadow Beat spell had worked.

The armored gob had something in its hands. What was that? A weapon? There was something that looked like a bow mounted on the end of a sturdy stock. The armored gob turned to point it at them.

Haruhiro put a hand on Yume and Shihoru's shoulders. *Get behind cover,* he tried to say. The arrow flew before he could.

Haruhiro pushed Shihoru and Yume down, causing them to land on their backsides. Haruhiro stepped backwards with a groan. Then came the pain. In the left side of his chest. It was there. An arrow. It hurt. It hurt, it hurt, it hurt!

Haruhiro crouched. Changing position hurt. Staying still hurt. It hurt so bad, he couldn't breathe.

Shihoru let out a little scream while Yume put a hand on Haruhiro's back.

"Haru-kun...?!"

He gasped, unable to say it hurt.

Don't touch me, he thought frantically. *Just don't. It hurts. This is bad. I'm gonna die? Aren't I? Me, die? No, that won't happen. I don't think so. I don't want to die, at least. It hurts, though. It really hurts. Help. Someone. This is no good. I can't go on like this.*

"Haruhiro!"

It's Manato. Manato's here for me.

Manato suddenly tore the arrow out. It felt like something important had been torn out with it and Haruhiro coughed up blood.

I-If you do that, I'm gonna die, Manato.

Manato didn't worry about it, making the sign of the hexagram and saying a prayer.

"O Light, may Lumiaris' divine protection be upon you... Cure."

Light shot out of Manato's hands, closing up Haruhiro's wound.

I think I'm probably healed. But the pain won't go away.

Haruhiro breathed in, and in and in. It hurt too much to breathe out. With time, the pain lessened. He could breathe properly. Haruhiro tried touching the right side of his chest. It was soaked with blood, but it didn't hurt.

"M-Manato...!" Ranta shouted. "Hurry up! W-we can't keep this up...!"

Manato shouted, "You're fine now, right?!" and as soon as Haruhiro nodded, he took off running.

Oh, right. In the time while Haruhiro was being healed after getting hit, the battle had kept going. He looked over towards the building. There was an intense battle going on, with Moguzo against the hobgob, and Ranta and Yume against the armored goblin. Was Manato planning to go assist Ranta and Yume?

A bead of light from Shihoru's Magic Missile spell struck the hobgob, but it didn't even shake it. Haruhiro jumped hurriedly to his feet. With Manato going to help against the armored gob, they'd manage somehow. He needed to do something about the hobgob.

"Moguzo, hang in there...!" Haruhiro called out to Moguzo as he took up a position behind the hobgob. Its attention must have been focused solely on Moguzo in front of it, because the hobgob didn't even look at Haruhiro. It would be easy to line up a Backstab like this. Or at least, it should have been, but he just couldn't get close enough.

The hobgob's height was somewhere between Haruhiro and Moguzo. It looked like it was thicker-set than Moguzo, too. Its spiked club looked to be made out of wood, but it was pretty thick. If one of them took a good hit from that thing, even Moguzo with his chainmail wouldn't get off unharmed.

Chainmail. Right. Haruhiro thought grimly. *The hobgob's chainmail is the problem. It's not just on its upper body; it's even wearing pants made out of linked chain. Then there's the helmet on top of that. You could call it a perfect defense. Can I even do anything with my dagger?*

"Thanks...!" Moguzo let loose his special attack, the Thanks Slash.

Haruhiro was ready to applaud for a second, but then found himself agape. Moguzo's bastard sword had hit the hobgob's left shoulder and yet the hobgob merely staggered a little, not missing a beat before it counterattacked. Moguzo was almost too late in deflecting the incoming club. No, it was pushing him back. Moguzo's stance fell apart.

This is bad. Moguzo's gonna get taken out.

"Why, you...!" Haruhiro body-checked the hobgob, trying to stab it with his dagger. There was an unpleasant noise, but—no good, the blade wouldn't go through. It bounced off. Still, the hobgob stumbled forward, then turned to face Haruhiro.

The club's coming.

Haruhiro jumped out of the way.

"Whoa!!"

That's scary. It didn't even graze me. I had room to spare. But that was dangerous. It felt like my organs curled up inside me, like I was more dead than alive. Haruhiro backed away. He had no other choice.

"I-I can't do this...!" he cried.

"Ohm, rel, ect, vel, darsh...!" Shihoru chanted a spell. A shadow elemental slammed into the hobgob's flank, causing hyper-vibrations.

Moguzo brought his bastard sword down on the convulsing hobgob. "Hungh!"

A blow to the head. Sparks flew, the helmet was dented, and the hobgob staggered.

Haruhiro shouted, "N-now's our chance!" and rushed in to help. He'd give it a flying kick. The hobgob was scary, but not if he could just knock it off its feet.

Before he could jump, Manato called him.

"Haruhiro, get over here! Ranta's down...!"

"What?!" He looked over to see Ranta on the ground, bleeding from the neck. "H-his neck...?!"

Manato was trying to check Ranta's wounds which meant Yume needed to face the armored gob alone.

Damn, that's not good. Haruhiro thought.

Haruhiro charged at the armored gob which was shrieking and swinging a sharp sword at her as it chased after Yume.

"Hey, gob, over here!"

That caught its attention, but now he had to trade blows with it. Not that he could. The armored gob nimbly swung around a sword that was about the same length as Ranta's longsword.

Haruhiro ran around. It was taking all his effort just to dodge, evade, and generally run away. The armored gob was more quick-witted than any goblin they had faced before. With the skillful swordplay it was demonstrating, he started to suspect it had undergone some sort of specialist training. If he carelessly tried to parry the armored gob's blows with something as flimsy as a dagger, who knew what would happen to him? He worried whether Moguzo was all right on his own, but he couldn't afford to look over to check.

"Brush Clearer...!" Yume swung at the armored gob from behind with a powerful sideways sweep with her machete. However, it appeared to have been anticipated. The armored gob turned and easily parried the machete, knocking it from Yume's hands, then went on to follow it up with another attack.

"Not happening...!" Haruhiro sprung himself at the armored gob. He didn't want to think it, but maybe the gob had predicted this too, as it turned around, swinging down its sword at him.

Oh, crap! Haruhiro tried to catch the blow with his dagger. *No good. I can't stop it completely.*

There was a scream of metal on metal as the armored gob's sword ran down the blade and, when he couldn't stop it, even with the handguard, it bit into Haruhiro's right arm.

"Yowch...!" Haruhiro dropped his dagger. The armored gob pushed in further.

He's gonna cut me down, thought Haruhiro. This was a close call.

"Anger...!" It was Ranta.

Ranta leapt in from the side, thrusting. The armored gob crouched and got out of the way, not missing a breath before shifting to counterattack.

Ranta fell back. Right away, he retreated diagonally. "Dammit! This is bull! You're just a goddamn gob...!"

Ranta wasn't looking so good. He had gone pale and he was sweating profusely. It looked like the wound had been healed, but that didn't bring back all the blood he'd lost. Still, he had come just in the nick of time. Haruhiro had survived.

It hurts though, he thought. *My right arm. That cut went really deep. I'll pick up the dagger with my left. I can't get my right arm to move. It hurts.*

"Haruhiro!" Manato rushed in, getting ready to use his light magic right away. "O Light, may Lumiaris' divine protection be upon you... Cure."

Gritting his teeth and bearing the pain, Haruhiro checked his surroundings while Manato healed him. Moguzo was fending off the hobgob's fierce attacks somehow but he was having a really hard time of it. He was starting to look a little unsteady on his feet.

They probably couldn't count on any more support from Shihoru. She was crouched down, probably after overusing her magic. Ranta, somehow or other, was managing to slip away from the armored gob's attacks. It looked like Yume was hurt somewhere, possibly her arm.

"...Okay," Manato touched Haruhiro's right arm, then yelled to Yume. "Yume, get over here! I'll cure you!"

"Yume is fine! She can keep fightin'!"

"Just get over here! Haruhiro, trade places with Yume!"

"...On it!"

Haruhiro did what Manato had said, but he had some misgivings. *Is this going to be okay? Manato was running short of breath. Hasn't he used magic too many times in a short span?*

But Haruhiro was a thief; he didn't know much about magic. And besides, between himself and Manato, whose judgment did he trust more? Manato's, of course. Haruhiro didn't have that much self-confidence.

It'll be fine like this. It should be fine. It has to be.

Haruhiro switched places with Yume.

I want to attack the armored gob. he thought. *But I just can't get myself to do it. If I attack, I'm scared it'll get me with a counterattack. Is it the same for Ranta? The armored gob is tough. There are no openings to attack. On top of that, it put on a helmet at some point. Plated armor and a helmet. This is hopeless. Even if I get a lucky hit with my dagger, it'll bounce off. It's questionable whether Ranta's longsword would do any better. Maybe Moguzo's bastard sword? But he has his hands full fighting the hobgob, and he's probably losing that fight right now.*

We've already lost, he suddenly thought. *Yeah. We've lost. We can't win. There's nothing we can do to win this. Honestly, I must have known. Must have realized it a while ago. This is what losing looks like. We're losing? If we lose, what happens to us? We get taken out? We die? All of us?*

Haruhiro looked over to Manato. Manato was still healing Yume. No, it looked like he'd finished. They were coming over his way now.

"Haruhiro, go help Moguzo!" Manato said and Haruhiro nodded reflexively.

Is this okay? Well, I do need to help Moguzo. That's for sure.

Haruhiro tried to get behind the hobgob. That was when it happened.

"Ngahhhhhh!" The hobgob let out a bestial roar, slamming its club into Moguzo. Moguzo turned his bastard sword sideways, blocking it with a grunt of exertion, but the hobgob didn't stop. "Ngah! Ngah! Ngah!" It battered his bastard sword with its club. Again and again, harder. Its club was made out of wood, so why didn't it break?

Moguzo was unyielding. He held his bastard sword by the hilt and blade, blocking the club with it. He was managing to hold it off somehow, but the hobgob was at an overwhelming advantage.

"Ngah! Ngah! Ngah! Ngah! Ngah! Ngahhhh...!!" it hollered.

"Ungh...!" Moguzo was finally forced to take a knee. He was bleeding from the head. Had one of the club's spikes gotten him? The hobgob kicked Moguzo down, trying to get on top of him.

I can't let that happen! Haruhiro thought. *It'll be bad. Seriously, bad.*

Then next thing he knew, he was grappling the hobgob from behind. It would have been nice if he could pin its arms behind its back, but that was impossible. The hobgob thrashed around violently, trying to throw Haruhiro off as he held on for dear life. "Whoa! Ohh! Whoaaaaaaa...?!" he cried.

"You're doing fine, Haruhiro! Keep buying time like that...!" Manato was trying to treat Moguzo apparently.

And you want me to keep this up while you do that? You're kidding me, right? No way, it's not even possible.

The hobgob cried, "Ngah!" and elbowed Haruhiro as he clung to its back.

That got me in the belly. It doesn't just hurt; I'm feeling faint. Not good. If I pass out, that's the end. If it throws me off, it'll be seriously bad. I'll die. I'll absolutely die.

"Ah...!"

What he had been dreading happened. How? He had no idea.

The hobgob threw Haruhiro off its back, slammed him into the ground then kicked him around. Haruhiro couldn't breathe.

Haruhiro said "...H-help." *Help me.* Who was he hoping would save him? He didn't know. But help came.

"Smash...!" Manato's short staff struck the hobgob in the head, but the hobgob was wearing a helmet. Even so, it seemed to have had some effect. He had probably given it a mild concussion. Manato kept striking the hobgob, crying out with each blow.

"Haruhiro, get up! Run! Everyone, run away...!"

That's it, Haruhiro thought, leaping to his feet. *That's what we do. We run. Running is all we can do.*

He started to take off, but quickly stopped. "M-Manato, what about you...?!"

"I'm coming, too! Obviously! Now hurry up and go!" Even as he attacked the hobgob, Manato was trying to get away. Moguzo, who was back up after Manato healed his head injury, bellowed, "Thanks!" unleashing a Rage Blow at the hobgob. While it didn't hit, it did make it back off.

Ranta and Yume quickly turned and fled. Shihoru was trying to run, too. With a battle cry, the armored gob slashed Moguzo in the back. But thanks to his chainmail, it seemed he was fine. Haruhiro raced to catch up with Ranta, looking back over his shoulder as he went.

"Manato, that's enough! Everyone's gotten away!"

"I know!" Manato jumped backwards, giving the hobgob a two-thrust combo when it charged after him. The hobgob stopped in its tracks. Manato executed a brilliant change in direction, slipping past the armored gob's sword. In no time, he was close to catching up with Haruhiro.

It was too early to breathe easy, though. Haruhiro went to turn around. Just as he did, he saw the armored gob throw something. It spun through the air, probably hitting Manato in the back. Manato let out a grunt, nearly stumbling, so Haruhiro was sure of it.

"Manato...?!"

"I'm fine!" Manato steadied himself immediately.

He's still got a steady gait, so it doesn't sound like it's a deep wound. The hobgob and armored gob are coming after us. We've got to run. For now, we just have to run.

It was a good thing they had made a map. Thanks to the work they had done on it, they had most of the layout of the Old City of Damuro in their heads. That allowed them to avoid getting lost, and to avoid dangerous areas with lots of goblins. Haruhiro and the party ran. Even when their breath ran short, their lungs screamed and they felt like they were going to die, they kept on running, even after they had lost sight of the hobgob and armored gob for a while.

Manato was the first to stop running.

No, that wasn't it.

Manato suddenly collapsed onto the ground.

"...!" Haruhiro tried to call Manato's name, but he had lost his voice.

His back. In Manato's back, it was there—something—a blade, a curved blade, something like a throwing knife.

No one said anything. They all stared at Manato. They couldn't say anything. What could they have said?

"Urkh..." Manato tried to get up. He couldn't. He just managed to turn over onto his side. "...O-ow... I think...w-we're fine...now..."

"Manato...!" Haruhiro crouched by Manato's side. But was it okay to touch him? Or not? He didn't know.

"Manato, y-your wound, m-magic! That's right, use magic to cure it..."

"...Oh, yeah," Manato brought his right hand to his forehead. It fell limply to the ground. "...I-I c-can't...do it...I-I can't...use magic...!"

"D-don't talk!" Ranta shouted. "D-don't you talk! Just make yourself comfortable, comfortable... Wait, how are you supposed to do that?!"

Shihoru walked over unsteadily, sinking to the ground at Manato's side, across from Haruhiro. She reached out. Her finger touched the throwing knife. The moment it did, she jerked her hand back. Shihoru's face had gone ghastly pale.

Manato's face looked even worse. It wasn't blanched or livid; it was ashen.

Moguzo went rigid, standing there like he was some sort of huge ornament.

"Wh-wh-wh..." Yume messed up her hair. "...Wh-what do we do?"

"What...?" Haruhiro clawed at his chest.

What do we do? What can we do? Think. There has to be something. There can't be nothing. Tell me. Please, Manato. Manato.

Manato was wheezing, his breath unsteady.

"Y-you're gonna be okay, all right, Manato? You're gonna be okay, all right? Just, just hang in there. Hang in there, Manato, all right?"

Manato looked at Haruhiro, moving only his eyes.

"Haru...hiro."

"Wh-what? What is it? Manato, what is it?"

"...I'm... so...rry..."

"Huh? What? S-sorry? Why? For what?"

"...Damn...it...Ahh... Why...me...? Haru...hiro... I'm counting... on you..."

"Counting on me? On *me*? For what? What do you want from me? Wait, no, Manato, no."

"...I... can't... can't... see... Is every...one...there...?"

"We're here! Everyone's here! Manato! We're here! Don't go!"

"Ah... it's...too bad..."

"Don't go! Manato! You can't leave us! Don't go! Please, Manato...!"

Manato took a deep breath, then spat it out. In that moment, his eyes took on a glassy look.

Shihoru brought her hand to Manato's chest. "H-his heart's not beating!"

"G-give him CPR!" Ranta shouted.

It was an amazing flash of inspiration, Haruhiro thought. It felt like they had solved everything, telling each other what to do as they tried to resuscitate him. For minutes, then tens of minutes, they pumped on Manato's chest after pulling out the knife, and gave him mouth-to-mouth. They must have kept going for over an hour.

"...I-isn't it time we stopped?" Moguzo said, sobbing. "I-I feel bad for Manato-kun...you know."

"Fine!" Haruhiro nearly lashed out at Moguzo, but stopped himself. "...Fine, what do we do, then? Are you telling me we should just leave him? Are we just gonna abandon Manato?"

"Magic," Shihoru said, lifting her face. Her eyes were swollen and bright red from inflammation. "Maybe we can do something with magic. I mean, there's magic that heals wounds, after all."

"Yeah," Yume nodded repeatedly. "Yeah, there must be somethin' we can do. There has to be. Lessee, where was it? The priests' guild's, um, what was it...? Temple!"

"The Temple of Lumiaris, huh?" Ranta wiped his tears with the back of his hand. "That's enemy turf for a servant of Lord Skullhell like me, but now isn't the time to worry about that."

Moguzo picked up Manato. "I'll carry him."

Haruhiro nodded. "Okay, let's go."

Any time Ranta or Haruhiro offered to take over carrying Manato or to help, Moguzo said, "I'm fine," and refused. Until they made it all the way back to Alterna, and to the Temple of Lumiaris in the northern district, Moguzo really did carry Manato all by himself.

When they entered the temple, men wearing priest robes with the same blue-lines-on-white-fabric design as Manato's stopped them. One of them seemed to know Manato and told another man to go and find Master Honen.

This Master Honen, whoever he was, came at once. He was a man built like a rock and looked like he'd make a better warrior than a priest. When he opened his mouth to exclaim, "Oh, how terrible," his voice was abnormally loud, too.

Come to think of it, Manato had said his master had a big voice and his ears always hurt because of it, hadn't he?

As Haruhiro remembered that, unable to bear it anymore, he prostrated himself before Master Honen. "Please, save Manato! I'll do anything, so please! I'm begging you...!"

"You fool!" Master Honen roared. "Even the shining God of Light, Lumiaris, cannot save the dead! Manato, how could you be such a fool?! I recognized you as a youth of rare promise; that is why

I attended to your education with such love and care! How could you throw your young life away like this?!"

"Why, you...!" Ranta went to grab Master Honen, but Yume said, "Stop that!"

Ranta gave up easily. Likely because he saw the flood of tears coming from Master Honen's eyes.

Shihoru fell to the ground, sitting on the cold temple floor. Moguzo stood there unmoving, with Manato still in his arms.

"Now that this has happened," Master Honen's voice didn't waver, but his tears never stopped, "you must at least give him a proper burial. The curse of the No-Life King turns those who go unburied in the frontier into his servants. You have five days at most. Some have turned into zombies by the third day."

Haruhiro felt like laughing for some reason. It wasn't the time for laughter, and he knew that, but still. "...You mean you want us to cremate Manato?"

"Indeed. There is a crematorium outside Alterna. Once you have purified the remains with fire so they will not rise again, bury his ashes up on the hill."

"Can I ask something?"

"What?"

"I assume that costs money, too."

"If you cannot afford it, I will pay."

"No," Haruhiro sighed. It was a deep, deep sigh. He was angry. But getting mad just seemed ridiculous. "...No, thanks. It's not like we don't have any money. If we don't have enough, we'll figure something out. Manato was my—our comrade."

Grimgar of Fantasy and Ash

12. Which Way?

They dug a hole in an empty spot halfway up the hill and buried the bones wrapped in a white cloth there. Then they placed a stone on top that was just large enough that they could still carry it. On the stone, they carved his name. After that, they carved the crescent moon symbol of the volunteer soldiers, painting it red. Trainee or not, Manato was still a volunteer soldier and his grave would carry the red crescent he was entitled to. Looking around, they saw other graves with the red crescent, some with the paint beginning to peel away. Many volunteer soldiers slept here on this hill.

Haruhiro looked up to the tower on the hilltop—where he and the others had come out of—with resentment.

When was that? he thought. *It must have been less than a month ago and yet it feels like so much longer. We came out of that tower? Really? I can't see any entrance or exit to it. Where and how did we come out from it? I don't know. It doesn't matter. Nothing matters anymore.*

Fifty copper at the crematorium, fifty for the burial plot. One silver in total for the burial. A person was dead and it only cost one silver.

Haruhiro had paid it, but he wasn't sure he should have. Manato had been carrying seven silver and twenty-one copper. They had burned his clothes with him, but had several his possessions like his short staff and backpack left.

What should we do with those? Haruhiro thought. *Do we have to do something with them? I don't want to think about it. It's too much of a bother.*

Manato's dead. He's really dead. It's been less than a day.

When they brought Manato to the crematorium yesterday, the manager said they were closed for the day and to come back first thing the next morning. Unsure what to do, they had turned back to the temple where Master Honen offered to take custody of the body until the next morning. However, they couldn't bring themselves to just leave Manato behind. In the end, they had stayed up all night, surrounding Manato's body which had been left in a corner of the temple.

Right, Haruhiro thought now. *None of us have slept. Maybe I dozed off for a bit, but I haven't slept properly. That's why my thoughts are kind of hazy. Even with all of us sitting here in front of Manato's grave, it's just not sinking in.*

Even sitting was too much for Shihoru, who was exhausted from crying. She was leaned over on the ground, somehow supporting her body with both arms. Yume stared up into the cruelly blue sky, looking for birds perhaps. Moguzo had shrunk his big body into a ball, staring into space.

Say something, Ranta. Why have you been quiet all this time? If you don't talk, who will? Fine, whatever. Suit yourself.

Haruhiro tore some grass out of the ground. "It's weird, you know.

This is just weird. It is...isn't it? Guys?"

Ranta turned towards Haruhiro, but he said nothing. He looked despondent.

"You know, Manato once said," Haruhiro threw the grass away. "This is like a game. I thought the same thing, but what kind of game? I don't know. But this isn't a game, after all, is it? It's something else. Something's weird here, definitely. This is bullshit...just *bullshit.*"

What did Haruhiro want to say? What was he trying to say? What time was it now? It was well past noon. Evening might be coming soon. There was a bell in Alterna that chimed once every two hours. Once at 6:00 in the morning, twice at 8:00, three times at 10:00, and so on. How many times had it rung the last time he heard it? He couldn't remember at all.

Ranta slowly rose to his feet. "I'm out of here."

"...Where're you goin'?" Yume asked. But Ranta just gave a short laugh, apparently having given in to despair.

"Does it even matter? Anyway...just staying here forever isn't going to accomplish anything. We can't do anything for him now."

Even when Yume shouted, "You moron!" at him, Ranta didn't argue back. It wasn't like him at all.

Ranta's going to leave us, thought Haruhiro, who chased after him. Moguzo went with him. Haruhiro stopped for a moment, turning back to look. Yume was hugging Shihoru around the shoulders. She looked to him, and nodded—or perhaps shook her head, it was hard to tell from a distance. But they would be staying here a little longer; that's what he thought she was trying to tell him.

Is Shihoru gonna be okay? he wondered. *She's in shock, I'll bet. Even more than I am, probably. Because I'm pretty sure Shihoru was in love with Manato.*

Ranta looked like he planned to head back to Alterna. Haruhiro was about to ask him where he was going, but stopped short. It didn't really matter.

Before they reached Flower Garden Street in the north quarter, the bell rang seven times.

It's already 6:00 in the evening. Small wonder there are so many people out.

Ranta entered a large tavern. There was a sign out front identifying it as Sherry's Tavern. Haruhiro knew the name and that it was a hangout for volunteer soldiers, but he had only ever seen it from the outside.

Manato came here to gather information sometimes, right? I left it all to him. For anything and everything, it was always Manato. I didn't do a thing. Just followed after Manato, doing whatever he told me to do.

Lamps hanging from the ceiling dimly illuminated the spacious tavern. Sherry's Tavern really was a large place. There was more than just the one floor. It had a second level as well and there was an open ceiling over about half of the establishment. It wasn't crowded yet, with less than half the tables occupied, but even so, there were probably over a hundred people there. Many voices could be heard talking and laughing at all times, occasionally punctuated by angry shouts, and the spirited voices of the waitresses could be heard all over the room. Ranta found an open table in one corner of the first floor and sat down. Haruhiro and Moguzo sat down with him. When one of the girls came over, Ranta immediately said, "Three beers," ordering for the other two without ever asking them.

"...I don't really want to drink alcohol," said Moguzo.

"What do you want then? Milk?" Ranta crossed his arms, kicking the ground. "You sound like an idiot. This is a tavern. If you're gonna drink at a tavern, it's gotta be alcoholic."

"B-but..." Moguzo sat hunched over, shrinking his head into his shoulders. "Should we be drinking at a time like this...?"

"You dolt. Now is exactly when we ought to drink." Ranta sniffled and rubbed his eyes. "...Manato came here to drink a few times, didn't he? But, well, you know what happened to the guy. So, we should drink in his place...no, that isn't what I'm thinking. That's not quite it, but..."

"Yeah..." Haruhiro rested his elbows on the table, hanging his head. "...Yeah. You're right."

Once the beer came and they'd paid their waitress, the three shared a toast. Maybe it was just because they were parched, but the bitter beer tasted great. Was this the same beer Manato had drank? Had he liked it?

Probably because of the alcohol, Haruhiro's face grew hot and his thoughts hazy. Ranta and Moguzo were red-faced, too. Ranta slammed down his ceramic beer mug on the table.

"...This is the worst. The worst, I'm telling you. Seriously, seriously, seriously! I can't keep doing this. I've had all I can take. I'm not joking. It's not like I was doing this stuff because I wanted to to begin with. How'm I s'posed to keep doing it when it means having to go through this? It's the same for you two, right? To hell with being a warrior, to hell with being a thief, to hell with being a dread knight. To hell...to hell with being a priest. I'm done. It's over. I'm out. I'm done with all of this. From today on, I quit!"

"If you quit..." Haruhiro ground his teeth. "...if you quit, what're you going to do?"

"I'm not going to do anything. Who cares, really? Is there some rule saying I've gotta do stuff? Who decided that? Even if there is a rule, I'm not gonna follow it, okay?!"

"This isn't about following a rule or not. We've struggled to come this far as a group because we didn't have any other choice!"

"That's not my problem!"

"Yes, it is your problem! Think for a second!"

"I can't think about this stuff. It's all stupid!

"U-um," Moguzo interjected. "S-stop it, both of you. Don't fight, okay?"

"Shove it!" Ranta violently pushed Moguzo aside. "Besides, even if I did keep going, how the hell are we supposed to do anything?! What do we do from here on out?! He's gone, don't you get it?!"

"I know that!" cried Haruhiro. "Even without you telling me, I know that much at least!"

"Oh, you do? Well, then tell me this! How are you, the guy who kept getting injured and needing him to help you, going to keep going?! Huh?! How about it?!"

"That's—"

"For starters, you were constantly getting injured and that made him use too much magic! That's how things ended up like they did, isn't it?!"

"...Ranta, is that how you felt about it?"

"Am I wrong?! Have I said anything wrong here?!"

"You're not wrong... no, but..."

"You were never any *real* use in battle, anyway! Always getting hurt so easily and getting in the way! Because of you...!"

"Stop!" an angry voice roared out and the tavern fell silent for a moment.

Did someone just shout? Haruhiro thought. *Looks like it was Moguzo, apparently.*

Haruhiro was taken aback. He couldn't believe it. Moguzo's eyebrows were raised in exasperation. "Don't fight at a time like this!" he said. We don't have time to be fighting amongst ourselves! Cool your heads!"

Haruhiro sat back down in his chair. "...Sorry."

"No, hold on..." Ranta shook his head. "Aren't you the one who needs to cool his head...? You're way too mad..."

Moguzo glared at Ranta, who shrunk back.

"...S-sorry. It won't happen again. Seriously, seriously. This guy's scary when you piss him off, huh...?"

"—But," said Moguzo, taking a sip of his beer and then slumping his shoulders, "...When it comes to what we do from here, honestly...I feel the same way, I guess."

Haruhiro scratched the back of his neck. "...Yeah, same here, when it comes down to it. For the moment, I don't want to think about it—or rather, I *can't* think about it..."

"Let me just say," Ranta said, tapping the bottom of his mug on the table. "I didn't say what I did out of desperation. I'm saying that, after thinking it through, there's no way we can go on without him. If you count up the number of times he helped you, you've got to see the same."

"And?" Haruhiro looked sidelong at Ranta. "You're going to do nothing? That's not possible and you know it. What will you do for money? It costs money just to eat and sleep. Are you going to search for another job?"

Ranta rested his cheeks on his palms, frowning. "...Well, it's an option, I guess."

"Maybe it would be for me, but you're a dread knight, aren't you? Even if you want to change jobs, you can't quit your guild, can you?"

"Ah..."

"Did you forget?"

"I-I did *not* forget. Y-yeah. M-me? I-I'm a dread knight and I'll always have to be a dread knight, yeah? Dammit...why'd I have to go and become a dread knight...?"

Moguzo sighed deeply. "Other work, huh..."

"Oh!" they heard a familiar voice. When they looked over, they saw a man they recognized waving at them and coming over. "Oh! Oh! Oh! It's you guys! I forget your names, but hey, it's been a while! How've you all been? Living the best days of your lives?"

"Kikkawa," Haruhiro said, blinking.

I'd recognize this chatty guy's face anywhere, he thought. *There's no doubt about it. It's Kikkawa the playboy. But he looks totally different now. It's the equipment. He's wearing armor reinforced with metal plates and he's got a sword with a decorative pommel hanging from his hip. Judging by the way he's dressed, did he become a warrior?*

"Yo! Yo!" When Kikkawa broke into a broad grin and went for a high-five, Haruhiro gave him one before really thinking about it. Kikkawa plopped himself down between Moguzo and Haruhiro without hesitation. "Beer! Beer! I'll have a beer over here! That's beer!" he called out his order to one of the waitresses. "So? Tell me, tell me. How is it? How's it going? How're you guys doing? Like, business-wise? You've been hitting up the Old City of Damuro, or something?"

I heard. I heard. Heard it right here, you know, from my man Manato. I heard. So? So? How's that going?"

It's been a while since I last saw him, but he's still annoying. Way *too* *annoying.*

Overwhelmed by Kikkawa and without intending to, Haruhiro answered honestly. "...It's not going at all, I guess. To tell you the truth, about Manato...he had a little something happen to him. No, it wasn't little. How do I say this...?"

"Whaa?!" Kikkawa stood up and shouted. "Whaa?! Wha?! Whaaaaa?! D-d-don't tell me...! He couldn't have gotten himself...m-married...?!"

"Of course that's not it," Haruhiro corrected him, slapping Kikkawa in the back of the head pretty hard. Kikkawa's eyes nearly popped right out of his skull, but Haruhiro didn't regret doing it in the least.

"...That's not it," Ranta said with a bitter look crossing his face. "He went and died. Yesterday, you know. It was still just yesterday..."

"Wow..." Kikkawa rubbed the back of his head, moving his jaw back and forth. "Sorry, dude. Sorry. Like, seriously sorry, 'kay? I didn't mean anything bad by asking. Not really, you know? I mean, who'd have thought he'd be dead? Manato always seemed like a capable dude. In a different way from Renji, though. But, man... really? That happened to Manato? Hmm. You never know when it'll happen, huh? With people. It's the one thing you can't predict...whoa, you're bringing it now?! My beer! Beer, beer! Okay, chee...rs, okay, yeah, you guys aren't in the mood, huh? It's not a good time. Well, just me then. Phew!"

Haruhiro twisted his head from side to side. He was intensely tired.

"...You seem well, Kikkawa. Did you get into a party?"

"Yup. Yup. Right after that. A guy by the name of Tokimune's party. He's a great guy, actually. Little stupid though. He's here, you know? Should I introduce you? Should I?"

"...No, I'll pass for now."

"You will? Yeah, that figures. Manato was your priest, yeah? The core of the party. They say the death rate's pretty high. For priests, that is. It's easy for them to get targeted after all."

Moguzo slowly turned to look at Kikkawa. "...It is?"

"Well, duh," Kikkawa knocked back his beer. "Phew! Er, where was I? Right, right, priests. The enemy know that priests are healers, too. So, of course they'd go 'take that guy out first,' right? For a warrior like me, my job is, like, what? I run around putting my neck on the line just trying to defend the priest, or something? That's how it goes. Basically."

Moguzo clutched his head. "...I couldn't defend him. He was always helping me."

"No, no, nooo," Kikkawa got a bit too touchy-feely with Moguzo, slapping him reassuringly on the shoulder. "Don't let it get you down so bad, man. We all make mistakes, you know? We use our mistakes and errors to discover the right way. It's fine, it's fine. You're good. You're good."

"...But," Moguzo shook his head. "Manato-kun is never coming back."

"Well, yeah," Kikkawa lifted up his hands like he was surrendering. "Guess not, huh? But, still, still, here's what I think, you've just got to think about the future, don't you? I mean, I may only be able to say that because I've never lost a comrade, yeah? But let's turn that around, okay? I can say it because I've never lost a comrade or something. Huh? It's the same? Well, anyway, stay positive, man, positive."

Haruhiro lowered his eyes to the table full of ceramic mugs.

I guess he means I shouldn't be looking down like this, huh? he thought. *I don't have to listen to anything Kikkawa says, but what would Manato do? What would he have said? Probably, even if he didn't say it directly, he'd try to create an environment where we would all become more positive on our own.*

"Even if we do look forward..." Ranta grumbled. "What is there up ahead for us? Our party's lost its priest."

Kikkawa looked like he wanted to say, 'So what?' "Why not just look for one? A new priest. Ah, hold on, let me guess what you want to say. I know, you were about to say 'Would any priest want to join a party of trainees?' By the way, I'm not a trainee anymore, y'know? I'm a proper volunteer soldier. Wanna see the Corps Badge I bought? Do you? Should I show it to you?"

"...I don't really care about seeing your stupid badge," Haruhiro said with a sigh. "But you're right. I'll bet there aren't any priests who'd be willing to join our party."

"I don't think that there's absolutely none, y'know?"

"Huh...?"

"You wouldn't know it from the look of me, but I've got connections. Lots of 'em. I know a lot of volunteer soldiers. And, there is one. I know one. A priest even you guys could get to join you."

Ranta leaned in. "Wh-who is it?"

"Before. We. Get. To. Thaaaat..." Kikkawa looked at each of them in turn. "What were all of your names again? I've been thinking about it and, yeah, I totally can't remember. Sorry? Could you tell me, pretty please?"

13. An Important Piece

The morning still comes, huh? thought Haruhiro. *No matter who dies, the next morning comes, again and again.*

It was 8:00 the following morning in front of Alterna's north gate. Before the lingering echo of the bells ended, Ranta shouted out, sounding desperate, "—And on that note, *everyooooone!* I want to introduce you all to our new frieeeend! It's the priest, Merry! Okay, give her a nice round of applause...!"

Haruhiro and Moguzo did clap at least, but Yume and Shihoru seemed dumbfounded. It wasn't hard to understand how they felt. They had been shaken awake early in the morning by Haruhiro and the others, brought here, and now this. It would be stranger if they weren't surprised.

Even though it was her first time meeting Yume and Shihoru, Merry made no attempt to greet them. She looked strong-willed and was actively trying to come off as prickly, so it wasn't unexpected. But even so, Haruhiro wondered whether she couldn't have handled this a bit better. Apparently not. That was almost certainly the reason why even they had been able to recruit her.

Ranta gestured to Merry one more time. "Th-this is Merry-san..."

"He..." Shihoru bowed timidly. "...Hello."

"Ni..." Yume was hesitant as well. "Nice to meet you."

Even after that, Merry didn't so much as wave. She narrowed her eyes without a word, staring intently at Shihoru and Yume. Haruhiro had been observed the same way the night before. That had been hard to bear.

She's cute, for starters, he thought. *And not just your run-of-the-mill cute. It's not that her eyes are big, or that she has a shapely nose and lips, or that her glossy, straight hair is pretty. It's something in a dimension far above all that. I have a hard time believing she's human like us. What is it that makes me feel that way? It's probably the balance between all these things. Her little head and her figure. With one glance, you can tell she's just different. She has that sort of aura about her. It's so powerful that at first, I had trouble just standing in front of her. But I noticed something right away. Her gaze is cold. Abnormally cold. This woman is trouble. The kind you're better off not getting close to, just watching from a distance. That's the kind of woman she is.*

But sadly, Haruhiro and the others' situation left them with no choice but to recruit her.

According to Kikkawa, volunteer soldiers who couldn't find a party weren't common to begin with and priests were especially uncommon. There were even fights over who would get a talented priest sometimes, so they must have been in short supply. On top of that, Haruhiro and the others were still trainees and it seemed they had fallen behind Team Renji and Kikkawa, the others who arrived at the same time as them. In other words, they were the lowest-ranked

group within Red Moon and they were still crawling around at the bottom. They were in no position to get picky. Whether it was Merry or anyone else, so long as they had a priest to join their party, they were good. If they didn't have someone, they would need to either give up or one of them would need to change jobs to become a priest.

Merry brushed her hair up, then looked at Haruhiro.

"Is this everyone?" she asked.

"Yeah..." Haruhiro hurriedly looked down. He had been staring at Merry despite himself. She was easy on the eyes, at least. Merry wore the blue-lines-on-white outfit of a priest. It wasn't particularly stylish and it didn't accentuate the lines of her body, but she still looked great. It just wasn't fair.

"Uh, yeah. This is everyone. With you included, there's six of us."

"I see," Merry gave a little, laughing snort. "Well, that's fine. As long as I get my share, I don't care. Where are we heading? Damuro?"

"Y-yeah..." Haruhiro looked to the rest of his comrades.

The mood here is not good, he thought. *It's terrible, actually. Is this gonna work out okay?*

"...I guess?"

"You guess? Be clear," Merry snapped.

"D-Damuro. The Old City. Hunting goblins... As for the rest, I don't know."

"Fine, whatever. Well, how about you get going? I'll follow you."

"...Hey, you know?" Ranta looked up to Merry. "C-couldn't you, uh, do something about the way you talk, your attitude...?

Merry's ice-cold eyes shot through Ranta. "Huh?"

"...No, s-sorry...really, sorry. It's nothing..."

You're scary, Merry, Haruhiro thought. *Way too scary. You're bad news, seriously. You live up to your reputation.*

According to Kikkawa, Merry has a number of nicknames. One is Ill-Tempered Merry. Another is Scary Mary. Merry's primarily a free agent. She's invited to parties that have no priests or not enough priests. Merry never refuses. However, she never stays with a party for long. Merry doesn't think of people as people, apparently. The quality of her work as a priest is iffy, too. Not one of the rumors I heard was good. In any case, she was top-class when it came to looks, but her personality made little room for cooperation. Way too little. Incidentally, while she never refuses an invitation to a party, she'll shoot down invitations for a date at the speed of light. Kikkawa got shot down rather spectacularly himself, I hear. I'm amazed he had the balls to ask her out. You're incredible, Kikkawa.

There was absolutely no conversation during the one-hour walk to Damuro.

This is tough. Way too tough. Ranta and Moguzo are terrified of Merry, and Yume and Shihoru view her with suspicion, doubt, and uncertainty. Why is that? Haruhiro didn't understand. *I'm not sure, but Yume and Shihoru seem bewildered and maybe a little angry. Maybe they're upset I'm bringing in a new priest right after Manato died. Is that it? Especially considering what she's like. Is that it...?*

Honestly, Haruhiro couldn't say he didn't feel the same way.

Couldn't we have at least waited a little longer? We never consulted Yume and Shihoru, either. It's not like we had to decide there, on the spot, that day. I should have thought it over more. If Manato were around, he would never have just gone with the flow and let things turn out like this.

Besides, it's too soon for us to come back here.

To the Old City of Damuro.

To the place where Manato died.

"...What if we run into them again?" Haruhiro mumbled. "If we do," Ranta said, forcing the words out darkly, "we've got to kill them. I won't be satisfied until I've cut their ears off and offered them on Lord Skullhell's altar."

"But..." Shihoru said coldly. "We can't win. Not as we are now."

Ranta scoffed. "We'll fight even if we can't win."

"If we get ourselves killed doin' that," Yume's voice quivered. "...If we die like that, it'll all be for nothin.'"

Moguzo nodded vigorously. "Dying is no good. I don't want anyone else to die."

"Is someone..." Merry started to say, then bit her lip. "...going to go out? Or not? I don't care which, but make it quick."

Ranta looked away from her, clicking his tongue in disapproval. "Let's get on with it, Haruhiro."

"Yeah..." said Haruhiro, then a thought crossed his mind. Who was the leader of this party? Before, there was no question it had been Manato. But now? Ranta wasn't cut out to lead. Moguzo wasn't the type who could pull everyone along with him and neither were Yume or Shihoru. Then, was it him? No, he didn't have the ability to lead people either. He was too indecisive. Manato had told him as much.

At the end, Manato had looked to Haruhiro and said he was counting on him.

Did that mean he wanted me to take care of the others for him? But Manato, that's impossible. I can't do it. I can't be like you.

Haruhiro tried saying, "Let's go," to the others, but it came out with a stutter. That made him feel pretty pathetic.

Following the map they were still making, they walked carefully through the areas goblins often appeared in.

Since Manato was gone, taking on a group of three would be tough. But on today of all days, though they came across groups of three or four, they just couldn't seem to find a group of two or less. By the time they took their afternoon break, they were all filled with impatience, frustration, exhaustion, and weariness, and Haruhiro's stomach began to hurt. At this rate, there were so many ways they just weren't going to last. Haruhiro came to a silent decision. If they found a group of three or less, they'd attack. They had a priest; he was sure they could manage somehow.

The chance for that soon came. There were traces of a campfire in an area surrounded by crumbling walls. There, they found three goblins. One was clad in chainmail and carried a short spear, but the other two wore clothing made of cloth: one with an ax in its hands, the other wearing a short sword. The well-built spear gob seemed to be in charge, with the ax gob and short sword gob following its orders.

We can handle these guys somehow, Haruhiro thought.

"First, Moguzo and Shihoru will launch a preemptive strike on the spear gob," he said. "Me, Ranta, Yume and Merry will keep the ax gob and short sword gob busy, so Moguzo and Shihoru take out the spear gob. If it's hard for the two of you, either Ranta or I will step in to help. Once the spear gob is taken out, this will be easy."

"Hold on," Merry's voice was sharp. "Why am I fighting goblins?"

"Huh..." Haruhiro looked daunted. "W-was that not okay? Huh? Why not...?"

"I don't go up front. I'm a priest; the reason should be obvious."

"Hey..." Ranta was about to snap, but composed himself. "...pal."

Merry's pointed glance stabbed into Ranta. "'Pal'?"

"...Y-you? No, it's weird for me to address you like that...M-Merry!"

"Where's my -san?"

"M-Merry...-san," a vein was pulsing on Ranta's temple. "N-now listen! You priests carry that thing with you. That, uh, what's it called? A priest's staff? You've got one, right? That thing's for whacking stuff with, right? Or is it just for show?"

"Yes," Merry said, puffing her chest up and looking down her nose at Ranta. "This is just for show."

"Why you little..."

"Little?"

"M-Merry...-san, you, couldn't you be a little more, you know, more... uh, I don't know. Forget it! Just do whatever you want..."

"I'd do what I want without you telling me to, you realize?"

"Of course you would! Ha ha ha ha! I figured as much! Dammit, what's this bitch's problem...?"

"Could you refrain from using such filthy words? They soil my ears."

"I'm *so* sorry! My bad! If you really don't like it, why not try some earplugs?"

"Why should I have to trouble myself like that?"

"A-anyway..." Haruhiro said, scratching his neck. "I understand what you're saying. Merry will stand by in the rear until she's needed. Um, maybe near Shihoru would be best. Shihoru's a mage, so she doesn't go up front. That should be fine...right?"

Merry gave Haruhiro a look that made it seem as if she was ready to give up on him as useless. "Sounds reasonable, I guess."

"W-well, we'll go with that, then..." Haruhiro felt reassured, but also upset. Why did he have to defer to her like this? She had only just joined the party today. Yes, she had more experience than Haruhiro and the others, but weren't they all comrades here? Though, that said, he didn't have the nerve to say that to Merry. She was scary. Even when they got in a circle and did their usual *fighto ippatsu* ritual, it didn't really feel like they could do this. "...Yume, Shihoru, please." Haruhiro pleaded.

Yume and Shihoru nodded silently.

Are they too upset to even speak? Haruhiro wondered. *They both have looks of extreme displeasure on their faces. I wish they wouldn't do that. I'm no happier about this than they are, but what choice do we have? They could at least try to understand that much.*

If he said anything, he knew it wouldn't stop there. Haruhiro decided to bottle it all away deep in his chest.

Haruhiro took point with Yume and Shihoru following behind him. They would be in magic range soon. When Haruhiro gave the signal with his hands, Shihoru began drawing elemental sigils with her staff and chanting in a low voice. Yume nocked an arrow and pulled back on the bowstring. An elemental launched forth from the tip of Shihoru's staff.

Go. Yes. It hit.

The spear gob took a hit right in the chest from the elemental and the full-body convulsions made it drop its short spear. Yume's arrow missed, flying off into the distance. From behind they heard a "...That was just *awful*," from Merry and Yume's knuckles went white as she gripped her bow.

"Don't worry about it!" Haruhiro called out to Yume as he pulled out his dagger. Moguzo and Ranta were already about to charge the gobs.

I need to hurry out there, too. We'll defeat these enemies. We'll win this. If we lose, we might die. Winning is our only option.

Moguzo grunted; the ax gob and short sword gob were in his way. The spear gob was trying to use that time to get back on its feet. Ranta slashed at the ax gob with a battle cry and managed to get it away from Moguzo, but the short sword gob was more stubborn. Moguzo just couldn't throw the short sword gob out of his way. *That's my job then,* thought Haruhiro.

"Backstab...!" Haruhiro got behind the short sword gob, immediately stabbing at it with his dagger. The short sword gob shrieked, trying to turn around. The dagger grazed the sword gob's side. The short sword gob drew its short sword.

"Shigyahh! Shigyahh! Shigyahh!" it cried.

"Urkh, whoa...!" Haruhiro leapt backwards, hopped to the right, then backed off quickly. It was a quick little gob. Little wonder Moguzo had been having trouble with it. But with that, the last obstacle in front of Moguzo had been removed. The spear gob thrust at Moguzo. Moguzo struck down the spear gob's short spear with his bastard sword. There were three one-on-one battles now. No, it looked like Yume would come help Haruhiro. She swung her machete, slashing at the short sword gob.

"—Diagonal Cross...!"

"...!" The short sword gob lowered its hips, jumping backwards almost two meters to run away.

Wow, it's agile, Haruhiro thought. *You see gobs like it sometimes. Small, with no offensive power to speak of, but with a ridiculous ability to dodge. They're always a pain to take down. It's a lightweight-class gob. They're trouble.*

"Ohm, rel, ect, vel, darsh...!" Shihoru cast Shadow Beat. A shadow elemental flew towards the spear gob. It dodged. Moguzo followed up immediately with a swing of his bastard sword, but it was a little too far. He caught only air. The spear gob stabbed at Moguzo once, then again. With it stabbing at him so much, Moguzo had no choice but to put some distance between them. It was a short spear, yes, but it was still longer than the spear gob was tall. Moguzo couldn't get in striking distance of the spear gob. On closer consideration, this might have been the first time they'd had a proper fight with an enemy that used a spear. It seemed likely that Moguzo's difficulties were stemming from that. It was a lack of experience.

"—Ow...!" Ranta let out a little cry and jumped backwards. He'd taken a cut to his left thigh and it was bleeding. The ax gob was swinging its ax wildly from its low stature, aiming for the lower half of the body. It looked like it was going to be another troublesome type to deal with.

"Yume, I'll take care of this one, you take the ax gob! Merry, heal Ranta!"

Merry responded "No," without missing a beat.

"No?! Huh? Why not?!"

"It's not a wound that requires immediate treatment. Suck it up."

"...Why you...!" Ranta wailed on the ax gob. "Dammit! Dammit! Dammit! Dammit! Don't get all conceited just because you're a little—okay, *very*—attractive! This is bullshit! Bullshiiiit...!"

Haruhiro and Yume were chasing around the lightweight-class short sword gob, but they just couldn't catch it.

"Aren't you supposed to be in pain, Ranta?"

"I am in pain! Hatred...!" Ranta slashed downwards diagonally at the ax gob, but it nimbly evaded him. "I'm gushing blood here, you know?! Of course it hurts! It hurts, goddammit...!"

With a cry of surprise, Yume landed on her rump. The short sword gob had tripped her.

Oh, crap. That's bad, Haruhiro thought. *Yume's in trouble.*

"Why you...!" he threw himself between the short sword gob and Yume with reckless abandon and—*Hey, wait, you're just running away?!* The short sword gob hopped away, putting distance between them. It was over in no time. Haruhiro's dagger wouldn't reach it anymore.

"You're all worn out," Merry muttered.

And whose fault is that? Haruhiro thought. *If it were Manato instead of you, these enemies would have been easy. Manato could tank like Moguzo, was a healer, a strategist, and our leader. If Manato were there, it might have been an exaggeration to say he was a good as 100 others, but it sure felt that way. Manato wasn't like you, a priest who only heals, and doesn't even do a good job of that. The gap is so wide, it's not even worth comparing the two of you.*

But Manato isn't here anymore. He isn't anywhere. We've lost Manato.

What should we do now, Manato?

14. Silver and the Gold Coin

"...I can't work like this!" Ranta slammed his ceramic mug down on the table.

"U-um," Moguzo mumbled. "Y-you'll break the mug."

"Shut up! I'm holding back! And what about you, Moguzo?! Doesn't she piss you off?! Well, huh?!"

"W-well, yeah..."

"Damn straight! You've gotta be pissed off at that woman! What's with her attitude?! No matter how long we work with her, she doesn't try to get along with us better! Haruhiro!"

"Huh?"

"What do you think about this?! Well, what do you think, huh?! I'm asking you what you think, all right?! How many times have I asked you what do you think now, you idiot?!"

"Why ask so many times in a row...?" Haruhiro sipped his beer. "... Honestly, I'm having a hard time dealing with it, you could say. I wish we could do something to fix that."

"Quit beating around the bush and say what you mean! What?!

Are you acting like that just because that woman looks good?!"

"That has nothing to do with it..."

"No, you're too soft! You're too soft on women! You're a big softie!"

"I'm not trying to be soft on her; you're just weak when it comes to Merry. You'll bash her like this when she's not around, but you'll never say anything to her face."

"Like I could!" Ranta laid his face down on the table. "That woman scares me! The looks she gives, that voice, she's too damn scary! I'm ready to cry here, dammit! You mind if I cry?!"

Moguzo patted Ranta's shoulder. "D-don't cry."

"Stop that!" Ranta brushed Moguzo's hand away. "Don't try to console me! I don't want a man consoling me! It's just too pathetic! I, I... I, wahhhh...!"

"Leave him be, Moguzo." Haruhiro sighed. "He's always like this. If you worry about it every time, there'll be no end to it."

Since Merry had joined the party, Haruhiro, Ranta, and Moguzo had made a habit of visiting Sherry's Tavern together when they came back from the Old City of Damuro. It wasn't because they wanted to drink, but because they couldn't get to sleep if they didn't blow off some steam like this first. They couldn't motivate themselves for the next day without it.

The cost for one beer was discounted to three copper for badge holders, but Haruhiro and the others were trainees, so it cost them four. Even though they only went for one— sometimes two—beers, they were well aware it was wasteful spending. They had dropped to earning half—no, a third—of what they were making when Manato was around, so it wasn't unusual for there to be days when they earned less than one silver each.

I should be more frugal. I know. I realize that much, Haruhiro thought.

His total assets, including what he had stored at the Yorozu Deposit Company, amounted to a little over seventeen silver. A Corps Badge cost twenty silver, so he was almost there. Though even once he did get to twenty silver, he couldn't go out and buy his badge right that second. If he didn't have around thirty silver, he couldn't pay twenty silver all at once. It'd have been nice if they'd let him pay for it in installments.

"A volunteer soldier, huh…" Haruhiro murmured, looking around the tavern. All of the customers had better equipment than Haruhiro and his group. Many volunteer soldiers wore their precious armor to the tavern because they were afraid it would be stolen, but some wore only fancy clothes with expensive-looking swords at their hips. He couldn't help but feel painfully conscious of the overwhelming difference in their positions.

"I know," Ranta lifted his face, sitting in a weird position with his chin resting on the table. "Even if you don't say it, I know, Haruhiro. Let me guess. Buying our Corps Badges and becoming fully fledged volunteer soldiers is our goal for the moment, yeah, but somehow you just don't care. It doesn't get you fired up. That's what you're thinking, isn't it?"

"…I've got real complicated feelings about *you* being able to guess what I'm thinking."

"You're so rude. I could knock your block off! You want that?"

"Sorry."

"Don't apologize so quick. The conversation goes nowhere. It's boring. Banter with me some more. Do it, idiot."

"You're such a pain to deal with..."

"B-but," Moguzo groaned lowly. "...It does feel like we've lost sight of our goal. Kinda. It wasn't like this before..."

"Who'd have thought..." Ranta turned his face on its side, his cheek against the table. "...that it'd change this much. Just losing Manato made everything change this badly."

Haruhiro nearly snapped, tried to hold himself back, but then couldn't. "...What do you mean we 'just' lost Manato? Don't talk like that."

"Yeah," Ranta nodded. "Sorry."

"...Don't apologize so quick, it throws me off balance."

"You're such a pain to deal with."

Haruhiro considered slugging him, but he didn't want to waste energy swinging his fists on someone like Ranta.

"A goal, huh..." Haruhiro looked around the tavern again. As he did, his eyes stopped on a familiar face and it felt like his heart had stopped.

"...Renji."

Haruhiro and the others were seated around a table in a dark corner of the first floor. Renji and his group on the other hand were at a good table in a bright spot near the bar. No, it may not have been a better or worse spot, but Haruhiro could never bring himself to sit in a spot that stood out like that.

It wouldn't suit our position, our status, our rank and many other things, he thought. *That's the sense I get.*

"Whoa," Ranta had spotted Renji, too. "That's one showy getup Renji's got on there..."

Moguzo ducked his head as if he had just been reprimanded.

"I-it's incredible..."

They sure said it, Haruhiro thought. *That's a really showy outfit. Even though his silver hair is already enough to turn heads, Renji's wearing a battle surcoat with black fur trim on top of his armor. That sword leaning against his table looks awesome, too. How did Renji get his hands on that thing? Did he buy it? It looks pretty expensive. Or did he find it somewhere? And if he did, where was that somewhere?*

It's not just Renji. The guy with the buzz-cut next to him, Ron, has some fine-looking armor on and Adachi with his black-rimmed glasses is wearing a lustrous black robe that looks expensive, too. As for Sassa, since she's showing enough skin to remind me of Barbara-sensei, did she become a thief, maybe? She was beautiful to begin with so honestly, she's looking pretty sexy. Chibi-chan, who's kneeling on the floor next to Renji for some reason, must be their priest. But Chibi-chan's priest clothes are clearly different from Manato and Merry's. The fabric is high quality and there are decorative touches on the edges.

"They're rookies, right...?" Ranta stared, dumbfounded. "They've been volunteer soldiers for the same amount of time as us... So how is there such a huge gap...?"

Trainees and badge holders alike, those who hadn't been volunteer soldiers for very long were called rookies. However, nobody who looked at Team Renji would think they were rookies. If someone tried to treat them like they were, that person would be in for a rough time.

We're never going to close that gap, thought Haruhiro. Forget closing it, the gap was only going to get wider. Haruhiro and his party would be stuck at the bottom. They'd always be the smallest of small-fries while Renji's group would just keep rising up. Someday, everyone would look at Renji and his party with deference. Even if he ran into them somewhere, he wouldn't be able to talk to them. Haruhiro and his group would be forgotten while Renji's group would bask in the spotlight.

How would things have been for us if Manato didn't die? Haruhiro thought.

Manato said we had become a good party. Did he really mean it?

Manato frequented Sherry's, so he maybe he knew how Renji was doing. Didn't it frustrate him? Renji keeps steadily rising, but look at me. If I had better comrades, I could do the same. Manato was human too, so it wouldn't be strange for those thoughts to cross his mind. Besides, why didn't Renji invite Manato to join him? He was more than capable enough. If Manato had joined Team Renji, their party might have been even more powerful. If he had, I'm sure Manato wouldn't have died. He definitely *wouldn't have died.*

At some point, Haruhiro had hung his head. Ranta grabbed his arm saying, "H-hey," and Haruhiro looked up to see the silver haired man looking down at him.

"—Huh…?"

"I hear Manato kicked the bucket." It was that low, husky voice of Renji's that he would never forget.

"Bu…" Haruhiro started to say something, but then realized he didn't know what it was. But. But? But what?

"…S-so what?"

With no expression on his face, Renji tossed what was in his hand to Haruhiro. When Haruhiro caught it, he saw it was a coin. Moguzo said, "Whuhh?!" pulling back in surprise. Ranta's eyes went wide and he said, "Wha…!" before falling speechless. When Haruhiro saw the coin in his palm, his right hand began to tremble. It was the first time he'd actually seen one, but it was probably real. "...A-a gold coin?"

"Consolation money. Take it," Renji said, then turned on his heel and walked away.

"...D-don...! Don't you...! Don't...!" Haruhiro rose to his feet. The blood was rising to his head. He wanted to chase after Renji and slug him good. He didn't, though. That seemed dangerous. In the end, he just chased after him and stopped him. "R-Renji, wait! Hey, *wait*, I said...!"

Renji finally stopped, looking annoyed.

"What?"

"...N-no," Haruhiro gulped.

S-scary. He's seriously scary, Haruhiro thought. *What's with this intimidating aura? It's just not normal.*

"...L-listen," he said haltingly, "I can't—well, how should I say this? I can't accept this. It feels, I don't know, wrong somehow..."

"I see," Renji extended his right hand.

Huh? I expected more trouble, but he's not really objecting? Well, I'm glad he's not.

While feeling enough relief to last a lifetime, he placed the gold coin in Renji's right hand. After he did, he regretted it just a little.

A gold coin. One gold. A hundred silver, huh...

Renji then left without another word. When Haruhiro got back to the table, Ranta attacked him.

"—Y-you idiot! You damned idiot! Why did you give it back?! You could've just kept it! If we'd split it three ways, that'd have been thirty-four silver for me and thirty-three silver each for you and Moguzo! You moron!"

"...Why are you getting the extra silver?" Haruhiro asked.

"Because I'm *me,* duh! Dammit, what a waste! If we'd taken the money, we could have easily bought our Corps Badges!"

"I don't think," Moguzo furrowed his brow and frowned. "...I don't think that would be right. I-if we bought our badges that way, M-Manato probably wouldn't be happy...I feel."

"Like I care!" Ranta spat venomously. "He's gone now, anyway. Thinking about how he'd feel isn't going to do us a lick of good. Dammit. That was a gold coin, you know? I'm amazed he can just give it away. Just how much money does that bastard Renji have? Meanwhile, here I am with just three silver..."

"Huh? Three silver?" Haruhiro stared hard at Ranta's curly hair. "You're kidding, right? Why do you only have that much? What did you spend it all on?"

"Oh, shove off. I spent it on lots of stuff. Lots of stuff. How I spend my money is none of your business."

"...Keep it up, and you'll never buy your badge."

"Don't you dare say that after pissing away the best chance I had at getting one!"

"This isn't going to work," said Haruhiro, resting his elbows on the table and hanging his head. "...At this rate, things aren't going to work. I'm not talking about Manato; it's not about that. This is a problem with us. Because on that one point, you're right Ranta. Manato is gone now."

Ranta snorted. "I'm telling you, I've been thinking that all along."

"Y-you just think it," Moguzo said in a strong tone. "That's no good. Just thinking it isn't, isn't enough, you, you have to do something about it."

"...We're all falling apart," said Haruhiro, biting his lip.

"It's not just Merry. Lately, I haven't had a proper conversation with Yume or Shihoru either. It wasn't like this before."

Ranta rested his cheeks on his palms, looking to the side. "Let's all get along, is it? But can we do that after all this time?"

Can we do it or can't we? Haruhiro thought. *That I don't know. But* we *have* to do it.

Grimgar of Fantasy and Ash

15. Sorry

The first thing Haruhiro did was try talking to Yume and Shihoru as often as he could.

"By the way, this morning, how'd it go for you? Did you wake up all right? Huh? The same as usual? I see."

"By the way, last night, what did you have for dinner? The same as usual? Oh, I see."

"By the way, last night, I met Renji. It was amazing. Oh, you aren't interested?"

"By the way, for lunch, what did you bring? Huh? Bread? I see."

"By the way, are you tired?"

"By the way..."

It was starting to look like "By the way" was his catchphrase. They never outright ignored him, but they did the absolute least they could to answer, so it was pretty depressing.

Merry was as unapproachable as ever, so he could barely even talk to her.

Does she even enjoy life? he wondered. *Then again, I'm not enjoying life much at the moment, either.*

In the evening, after heading back to Alterna and selling off their loot from the Old City of Damuro, they had earned one silver, fifteen copper each. Not good, not bad, by their standards.

Haruhiro headed back to the lodging house without stopping by the tavern. After taking a bath, he was squatting in the hallway when Yume walked by, fresh from a bath of her own.

"Oh, Yume."

Yume stopped, but she didn't look his way. She was drying her hair with a towel. She always had her hair up in braids, so she looked like a different person with it down.

The awkward silence continued a few seconds.

"Uh, so...where's Shihoru?"

"Our room."

"I see. Um..." Haruhiro stood up, scratching his neck. "...Are you mad?"

"Yume's not mad."

"Really? But, you seem like it."

"Yume's tellin' you she's not mad, okay? Or did you do somethin' Yume should be mad about, Haru-kun?"

"I might have."

"What'd you do?"

"I invited Merry to join the party without consulting you or Shihoru. I don't think we could have continued as we were, but we rushed things, I think. Really. I didn't make that decision entirely by myself, but..."

"Then whose fault is it?"

"Kikkawa introduced Merry to us and me, Ranta, and Moguzo

made the decision, so…well, I guess the blame goes to all three of us."

"That's not it."

"Huh?"

"It's not, don't you get it?"

"…Yume?"

"It's not, all right?" Yume wiped her face with the towel. "That's not how it is, see? Haru-kun, you dummy."

"Huh? Wait, why—" Haruhiro started to reach out towards Yume, then pulled his hand back. "Huh? Yume, hey, wh-what do you… mean?"

"You don't understand a thing, Haru-kun. It's because you're like that. That's why Yume and Shihoru ended up like this."

"No, but…" Haruhiro looked down. "…I don't get it, not like that. I mean, you two won't talk to me. How am I supposed to know if you won't tell me?"

"Yume's not so good at relatin' her feelings to others. Yume can't do it so well and Shihoru's got it even worse than Yume."

"W-well, neither am I!" Haruhiro came close to shouting, but he restrained himself. "…Neither am I, at talking and stuff. It's not something I'm particularly good at. Besides, I was in shock, too."

"Yeah, so it was the same for all of us, wasn't it?"

"That's right. It's the same…for all of us."

"It's all of our fault, then," Yume said with a sob. "It's not any one person's fault it turned out like this. We're all to blame. It's not just Haru-kun, Ranta, or Moguzo's fault, is it? It's Yume and Shihoru's fault, too, right? Is Yume wrong? I mean, we're comrades, aren't we? With Manato, we were six comrades, weren't we? Was Yume the only one who felt that way? Is Yume wrong?"

"...You're not wrong."

That's right, thought Haruhiro. *Yume's not wrong.* I'm *the one who was wrong.*

Manato had said they'd become a good party. Manato, Haruhiro, Ranta, Moguzo, Yume, and Shihoru. The six of them together had been one party.

It was true, Manato had stood head and shoulders above the rest of the group. Still, Manato couldn't have done anything and everything by himself. At the very least, they had done things as a group that Manato wouldn't have been able to do alone. Manato must have been well aware of that.

That was why, even if Ranta was selfish, Haruhiro was bumbling and overdependent, Moguzo was slow and stupid, Yume was clumsy and awkward, and Shihoru was cautious to the point of cowardice, Manato had never complained.

Because they were all inexperienced or worse, they'd known that if even one of them went missing, the group wouldn't function. That was why Manato had brought them all together. Each one of them supplemented the others' weaknesses. With the six of them together, Haruhiro and the others were one party.

Whether good or bad, everything that happened affected them all. When times were hard, they were hard for everyone. Because individually, they weren't strong, the least they could do was all share their pain and suffering.

But Haruhiro hadn't tried to do that. He had just used the easygoing relationship between guys to commiserate over beer with Ranta and Moguzo.

How had Yume and Shihoru felt about that? They must have felt ostracized and lonely.

"Sorry, Yume, I—" In the moment he started to say that, Haruhiro suddenly understood why Manato had apologized to him as he lay dying.

That day, Manato had praised each of them, but he had said nothing about Haruhiro and because of that, Haruhiro had been worried. Manato must have been concerned about that.

"That guy..."

In an instant, he couldn't see anything. Could the tears really overflow this quickly? What little composure he had was easily washed away. Haruhiro crouched down.

That guy was so silly, he thought. *Manato. What were you apologizing for? It was fine, really. It didn't matter. You should have done something else. You had bigger worries. You were dying, right? You knew it was bad, didn't you? Before you apologized to me, there must have been other things you wanted to say. You didn't have to apologize to me. Though it was so like you to do it.*

You said it yourself, Manato. That you felt like you were not the sort of person that anyone should be treating as a comrade. It wasn't true. Absolutely not. How could it have been? Why? Why did you have to die? Don't die. Don't go dying on us like that.

"Haru-kun..." Yume crouched down and gave him a hug.

Yume was crying, too.

As they both sobbed, Yume patted Haruhiro on the back, the shoulders, and the head. When their cheeks touched, both were soaked with tears.

He heard Yume crying in his ear. Haruhiro held Yume tight and wept. He lost track of how long they stayed like that for.

He felt like he had cried until he could cry no more. Yume had stopped crying a while ago, too.

And yet, they didn't separate. He couldn't find a good opening to break it off. It felt weird; now they were just sort of hugging.

She's so soft, so warm... No, no. Stop. Don't think about it. If I think about it, this'll turn out bad. There's no guarantee I won't get into a weird mood. Of course, I'm pretty sure that's not what Yume wants. Neither do I. How do I say it? To me, she's a comrade, or something like that. Just a comrade.

"Haru-kun," Yume suddenly said and Haruhiro gave such a flustered and awkward "Uh, yeah?" that it made him hate himself a little.

"You know, Yume..." she went on.

"Y-yeah?" he stammered.

"Yume's gonna try her best," she said, hugging him tighter.

Er, no, that feels good and all, but could you please stop...? And what do you mean, "try your best"?

"A-at what...?"

"With Merry. Dunno if we can get along, but Yume will try."

"O-Oh. Th-that. Sure. That's... well, it would help a lot, I guess."

"Do you think Yume can do it? To be honest, Yume's not so sure. Yume thinks Merry-chan hates her, you know?"

"Huh? You think that? I don't think so."

"It's just once in a while, but when Yume looks into her eyes, they're so cold. Like, the looks she gives, and her expression."

"Nah, that's not just for you, Yume. Merry's equally cold to everyone."

"She is? If that's the case, maybe it's okay. Doesn't make her feel any more friendly, though."

"Well...fair enough, you may have a point there."

"Do you think Yume can do it? Yume'll do her best, but Yume has a request for Haru-kun."

"A request? For me? What?"

"Yume just found out that when someone hugs her tight like this, it really calms her down. So hug Yume more. Yume wants you to cheer her up, you know?"

"I-I don't mind, I guess?" he stammered.

He wondered, *Is this okay?* but then decided, *It's probably fine.* He was just encouraging her. He didn't have any ulterior motives. It was purely something he was doing to encourage her.

"...Here goes," he said.

When Haruhiro hugged her tightly—as tightly as he could—Yume let out a little moan.

Don't do that! I'm just doing this to cheer you up! he thought. It felt like something was ready to explode inside his head, but he couldn't very well ask her not to do that.

He couldn't let himself lose here. He wasn't sure what would be a loss and what would be a victory, but he knew that if he gave in here, it would be very, very bad.

Haruhiro closed his eyes. "Do your best, Yume."

Yume nodded without a word.

When he opened his eyes, Shihoru was standing at the other end of the corridor. Haruhiro froze.

"...Oh."

"Huh?" Yume looked in that direction, too. "...Oh."

"Uh, uh, uh, um..." Shihoru started to stagger backwards. She was starting to freak out, but so were they. And... hold on, how long had Shihoru been there? Why hadn't he or Yume noticed Shihoru approaching? Had they been too occupied to notice?

Regardless, this was bad. It would be all too easy for her to misunderstand the situation. Or rather, it would be harder to *not* misunderstand the situation.

Haruhiro and Yume jumped apart at the same time.

"I-it's not what you think!"

"It's not what you think!"

After speaking in unison, they turned to look at one another despite themselves.

"I-I'm sorry, I...!" Shihoru backed away. "I-I didn't realize at all, not before now, I-I'm fat, and d-dense, so I'm really sorry!"

"No, listen, it's not what you think!" Haruhiro protested.

"Th-that's right! Yume was just asking Haru-kun to give her a hug!"

"...Yume, that's really not an appropriate explanation right now."

"Oh? Why not?"

"I-I-I'm sorry for interrupting...!" Shihoru rushed off.

Yume groaned, rubbing her cheek with her hand. "Well, it'll be fine so long as Yume explains it later. Yume and Shihoru share a room anyway, so that's what Yume'll do."

"I'm counting on you to do that..." Haruhiro scratched his neck and sighed. He stole a glance at Yume.

This is no good. I'm feeling kind of embarrassed.

He should never have hugged a girl he didn't really have special feelings for like that. What would he do if those feelings started to grow inside him because he did?

No, they're not going to...but still.

Grimgar
of
Fantasy and Ash

16. When You Aim for the Top

When he left the lodging house the next morning, Shihoru suddenly apologized to him.

"U-Um! I...I'm sorry!" she stammered. "I was convinced you two were in that sort of relationship... I'm sorry I jumped to conclusions! Yume explained what happened to me, so..."

The apology was fine, but he did think he'd have been happier without her bringing it up in front of Ranta and Moguzo.

"Relationshiiiip?" Ranta's nostrils flared as he drew in close to Haruhiro's face. "What? What's this about a relationship? What kind and between what people? Hmmmm?"

Haruhiro leaned back a little. "...It's nothing."

"It's not nothing, now, is it? Tell me. Talk! Spill it!" Ranta shouted.

"Listen, Shihoru said herself that she'd jumped to conclusions, didn't she?" Haruhiro defended.

"Yeah, and I'm asking what happened that would make her jump to conclusions."

"Now listen," Yume interjected.

She'd better not be about to say something she shouldn't again! He would have liked for his fears to be for naught, but things went about the same as always.

"So, yesterday, Yume, she was having Haru-kun hug her, you see, and Shihoru saw that. That's all it was."

Moguzo's eyes bulged out. "Whaaa...?!"

"Whoa, whoa, whoa, whoaaaaaa!" Ranta's eyeballs nearly flew out of his skull. "What, seriously, how did that happen? Are you serious?! When did you and Haruhiro get to second base?!"

"What's second base...?" Haruhiro blustered. "No, whatever second base is, Yume and I didn't go there. That's not it, we were—"

"How is that not it?! You were trying to do her, weren't you?! You two were getting hot and busy when Shihoru walked in on you and you panicked and stopped, right?! You stopped halfway!"

"Haru-kun was crying, see," Yume explained.

"...Yume, you don't need to tell him that," Haruhiro said.

"Huh?! Crying—" Ranta looked from Haruhiro to Yume, then scratched his curly hair. "...Oh, that's all. That's how it is. So, what, let me guess. It was a tearful parting, huh? Stupid Haruhiro got himself rejected and Yume was doing it to console him out of pity. So, that's how it was. I see now."

"You're totally off-base," Haruhiro said testily, "but I don't want to waste any more time explaining it to you..."

"Well, anyway," Yume continued with her usual laid-back attitude. Haruhiro envied her for that. "Yume, she's decided she's gonna try and be friends with Merry-chan. So, Shihoru will too. She said she'd try to cooperate."

Shihoru looked down at the ground, clasping her staff tightly. "...I have zero confidence that I can do it. But I'll try to do what I can, I guess."

"Be friends?" Ranta frowned as hard as he could. "With Merry? That's not possible. I mean, come on, you know she has no intention of being friendly, right?"

Moguzo hung his head. "...B-but it's a bit tough the way things are. I wish we could just get her to at least heal us properly, you know...?"

Merry wasn't just lacking in cooperation; there were issues with her performance as a healer, too. As Moguzo had said, she wouldn't heal them normally. More specifically, she would leave minor wounds untreated.

Even if they asked her to heal them, it was no good. They would either get ignored, or flatly rejected. Obviously, if a wound impacted their ability to move around, or was life-threatening, she'd heal it for them, but they had issues with her willingness to leave a comrade in pain.

Manato hadn't been like that. Whenever someone had gotten a scratch, he'd healed it right away. It let them feel that, even if they got hurt a bit, things would be fine.

They couldn't feel secure that way with Merry. They worried that, when they really needed it, Merry might refuse to heal them. That she might abandon them. The thought gave all of them cold sweats.

"So anyway," Haruhiro looked around to each of his comrades except Ranta. He left Ranta out. "We need a relationship of trust, I guess you could say, with Merry. If we don't start by building that, we can't move forward. Merry may have her own reasoning behind how she does things. Because we don't understand what it is, that may be why things aren't going smoothly."

Ranta scoffed. "It's just her having an awful personality. She's sick man, sick. What she's got is chronic congenital maliciousness syndrome. There's no treating that."

"But we need a priest, don't we?"

"Here's a thought, Haruhiro. *You* be the priest. Okay! Goodbye, Merry! Problem solved! Yeah! Man, am I smart. Awesome. Nice idea!"

Honestly, Haruhiro did consider it an option, but only as a last resort. He felt the thief's job suited him, skulking around on his own to scout ahead and always looking to attack the enemy from behind. He wanted to continue to grow as a thief. Besides, after talking with Yume yesterday, he had realized something.

"Ranta."

"Yeah?"

"It was me, you, and Moguzo who decided to add Merry to the party, right?"

"And that decision was a huge mistake, which is why I'm saying we should just kick her out already."

"We added her to the party, so Merry's one of us now."

Ranta seemed to be looking for a comeback to that, but he shut his mouth and stared at the ground awkwardly.

"Listen, I get it." Haruhiro grasped his right wrist with his left hand. "It's not easy to suddenly treat someone like an equal member of the group. And Merry's not doing herself any favors with the way she acts. Still, if we're ganging up on her five-on-one all the time, she won't be able to fit in even if she wants to. Merry is not just a machine that walks around and dispenses healing magic for us."

"...That's right, huh," said Yume, bringing a finger to her chin. "Merry is cold to Yume and everyone, but maybe Yume and everyone have been being cold to Merry, too."

"Yeah…" Moguzo nodded slowly. "That could be it."

"M-maybe," Shihoru said, mumbling without confidence, "she could actually be a good person…I-like she's a tsundere or something?"

"Hell no!" Ranta looked the other way. "Not a chance. I wouldn't even give you ten thousand to one odds on that. She's a nasty woman and rotten to the core. No matter what you say, my opinion won't change. We should cut ties with her. Stupid Haruhiro can be our priest."

"If I were our priest, no matter what happened, I wouldn't heal you, Ranta," Haruhiro fired back. "I mean, you're a dread knight. The dark god Skullhell and the god of light Lumiaris are enemies, right? I'm not enough of a softie that I'd go healing my enemies."

"Tch. You're disqualified as a priest! Disqualified! Moguzo can… No, we'd be in trouble without a warrior. Fine, Yume! You do it!"

"Yume wants her wolf dog, so she's not givin' up being a hunter."

"Ugh… You self-centered girl! Then Shihoru! How about you?!"

"…I don't think I'd make a very good healer. I'm sure if someone got hurt, I'd start to panic before I could heal them."

"You're useless! All of you! Completely useless! This is hopeless! This is a group of people who are naturals at being useless! If that's how it's gonna be—" Ranta cleared his throat. "…If that's how it's gonna be, there's only one option. Even that woman is better than nothing. Let's just pray that she actually *is* a tsundere… Though, if she were a tsundere, obviously, the one she'd go dere for is me, you know? That's kind of…not so bad, I guess?"

"O-obviously, she wouldn't go dere for Ranta, I think…"

"Oh, shut up, Moguzo! *Moguzo?!* Did Moguzo just hit me with a witty retort?! Hey, seriously?! I can't believe this!"

That was that: a policy had now been set. They would treat Merry like one of them and she would become their comrade.

They could discuss more later. If they didn't clear this hurdle first, Haruhiro and his party wouldn't be able to move forward.

Still, it didn't seem like they would have an easy road ahead of them.

Merry stood waiting for them at the north gate, as per usual.

Figuring everything started with a proper greeting, Haruhiro tried an energetic, "Good morning!"

All Haruhiro had done was greet her. That was all he'd done, so why did she have to glare icy daggers at him?

Right then, Haruhiro felt like she was mocking him, sneering at him. He was sure she was thinking *Go die in a fire* or *Get lost, scumbag* at him.

After tormenting Haruhiro with her absolute-zero stare, she returned a curt "Good morning" and added, "Hurry up and go. I'll follow you."

Things continued along that note.

Even so, on the road to the Old City of Damuro, Yume and Shihoru made a valiant effort, trying to talk to Merry several times. About where she lived, what she'd had for breakfast and dinner, how long it had been since she'd become a volunteer soldier.

No matter how you looked at it, they were harmless questions, but Merry never gave a straight answer. Answers like "Who knows?" and "Food" were on the not-so-bad end, but once she snapped, "What does it matter?" Yume and Shihoru couldn't bring themselves to keep talking.

She's a difficult opponent, Haruhiro thought. *Well, no, she's not an opponent. She's our ally. She's one of us.*

Even if they couldn't get a conversation going, they at least wanted to improve their teamwork. In the morning, they got lucky and encountered a group of three goblins, so they prepared for a difficult battle. If they could come together to pull through a somewhat difficult fight, they might be able to see some way forward.

"—Moguzo, Ranta, each of you take one! Yume and I will take the other! Shihoru and Merry, back up Ranta and Moguzo!"

He tried subtly asking Merry for backup, but even as Shihoru's Shadow Beat and Magic Missile struck the enemy, Merry just stood there. When Ranta took a light cut to his left arm, she ignored him even as he cried out in exaggerated pain. And when Moguzo got scared after a shallow cut sliced his temple open, she shouted, "Don't back down after something that trivial! You're a warrior, aren't you?!" and that was it.

"Dammit, don't act so high and mighty! You aren't doing anything!" Ranta forcibly kicked the goblin away from himself, then stepped into the space that opened up, closing the distance and thrusting his longsword out straight. "—Anger...!"

The goblin squealed as the sword burst through its neck. It thrashed around for a little while then eventually fell silent. The sword skills used by dread knights—the Dark Arts of Battle—avoided close combat, preferring to strike from outside the enemy's range with hit-and-away tactics.

What he did there didn't feel quite like that, but all's well that ends well. Now we're down to only two enemies. No—

With a roar, Moguzo moved from locking blades with the enemy to making it stagger backwards with Wind, then quickly followed up by slamming his blade into it. "Hungh...!"

Its skull split, the goblin crumpled, leaving only one left.

"Marc em parc...!" Shihoru drew elemental sigils with her staff, chanting a spell, and a fist-sized bead of light slammed into the last goblin's chest.

"Gyah...!" it cried.

The bead of light from a Magic Missile spell packed around the same force as being punched by an adult. The goblin was thrown off balance for only a moment, but that created an opening. Yume closed in on the goblin, trying to cut it down with her machete.

"—Brush Clearer...!" she cried.

The goblin was taken by surprise, but nimbly managed to jump back and to the side to avoid it. Its back was now facing Haruhiro.

Now, Haruhiro thought, and his body moved into action on its own.

Without taking a breath, he executed a Backstab. The dagger pierced the goblin's back, as if settling into a place it had always belonged, then burst through its belly.

That's definitely how it feels when I do it right!

The goblin trembled violently as the strength drained from its body. As Haruhiro lowered the tip of his dagger and pushed it into the goblin with his shoulder, the blade slid free. The goblin fell face-first to the ground, unmoving.

"Gwa ha ha ha ha!" Ranta cackled loudly as he cut a claw from the goblin's corpse. "Our teamwork was utter crap, but with my strike leading the way, we won big! That's just how awesome I am! It's become so predictable, it's boring! But come on, my hand hurts!

Merry! Heal it!"

Merry completely ignored Ranta, walking briskly over to Moguzo. "Sit."

"...Okay." Ordered to sit like he was a dog, Moguzo lowered his hips to the ground.

Merry touched his forehead, the back of his head, and then finally his temple. When Moguzo grimaced, she said something in a quiet voice, but Haruhiro couldn't pick up what it was. Merry made the sign of the hexagram and chanted a prayer. "O Light, may Lumiaris' divine protection be upon you... Cure."

"...If we wait until the battle's over, she's relatively willing to heal us, huh?" Haruhiro muttered to himself as he collected the goblin pouches. Inside were two silver coins and two pretty stones as well as a smattering of fangs, gears, and other small things. Depending on the price of the stones, they were looking at about four silver.

"Hey, Merry! You're done with Moguzo! Heal me next!"

"Yours is just a scratch."

"No, it's not! Look, it's bleeding! Even if it's stopping now, it is!"

"Try putting some spit on it. Also, don't address me without an honorific. You're going to make my anger boil over."

"Eek!"

—was about how it went, with her being unwilling to heal Ranta very often. However, Ranta tended to make a big deal out of every little thing, so he would make a big fuss even over minor injuries.

Manato might have looked like he was being generous, but he had actually been pretty nervous. He hadn't been able to feel at ease unless all of them were in perfect condition, so he'd treated every injury right away. Maybe that had been unnecessary. When Haruhiro reflected on it, he realized Manato may have taken it too far. When it came to Ranta, he felt Manato had been too soft on him.

After clearing away the goblin corpses, Haruhiro came right out and asked, "Is it an issue with how you do things, maybe? Like, Merry, do you have some sort of method you've settled on for how you work as a healer, or something?"

"Huh?" she snapped.

That was a pretty scary "Huh?" there. I wish you would stop doing that. Haruhiro somehow managed to stop himself from faltering and roused himself to keep going. "...Well, I was thinking, maybe there are different types as far as priests go... or something. Because, well, I don't know about all that. I don't have much experience."

Merry was about to say something, but then, maybe deciding it was too much effort, she sighed. Then she crossed her arms and looked away to the side.

"Who knows?"

There it was. Her "Who knows?" Haruhiro got upset.

"C-could you explain it to me? I'm a thief, so I don't know about priests, but if I just keep thinking, 'I don't get it, I don't get it,' I'm never going to get it, and I don't think that's okay, so—"

"That's just your opinion. I think it's fine as is."

"It's not fine at...!" Haruhiro hurriedly took a deep breath.

Not good. I nearly snapped there. That was close. I need to calm down. She makes me so mad, though. What is with her? Why does she have to be so hard-headed?

"...I'll respect your privacy and won't try to delve too deep. But our roles in combat, the flow; there are those things to consider. I want to talk more about those things as a group."

"If you don't like my work, why not just come out and say it? I'll leave right now."

"That's not it. I just want to—"

"Then we have no problem here."

"...Right."

Someone please tell me: is there some way to communicate properly with Merry? Maybe there isn't. It sure doesn't feel like there is.

After that, Yume and Shihoru determinedly continued trying to talk with Merry and got crushed every time. Haruhiro tried to start a discussion with her a number of times, but she wouldn't even respond.

By evening, they had taken seven goblins down. Their earnings were two silver, five copper a person, which was kind of okay, if they chose to think of it that way. However, Haruhiro couldn't help but compare himself with Renji, who had thrown a gold coin their way as if he wouldn't miss it, and he ground his teeth as he felt a tinge of pain.

Merry left as soon as she received her share, so the five of them ate and then went to Sherry's Tavern.

"There are a whole lotta folks here, huh? Yume doesn't want to drink alcohol, so Yume will have juice instead."

"...Me too, I don't want alcohol. It's very lively in here..."

This was Yume and Shihoru's first time in a tavern, so they were very busy staring at and being nervous about things.

Ranta acted like a regular, saying, "Hey, girls. Calm down. Okay? It's just a tavern, nothing out of the ordinary. Come on now, seriously," but the two of them probably weren't listening to a word he said.

Soon the waitress came over and they each ordered drinks and paid her. Haruhiro chose to get lemonade instead of beer tonight. It was a drink made by adding lemon and honey to naturally carbonated water from the Tenryu Mountains and he was quite fond of it.

"—The problem is with Merry, really," Haruhiro started.

Yume replied, "Yeah," with a nod. "Yume and Shihoru tried talkin' to her a lot, you know, but she wouldn't give us the time of year."

Shihoru quickly corrected her: "Yume, you mean 'time of day,' not year." But Yume just blinked in confusion.

"It is? Yume, she was suretain that it was year. So that's it. It was 'time of date,' huh?"

"...Not suretain, certain. Also, it's not 'time of date,' it's 'time of day.'"

"Huh? Yume got it wrong again? Yume keeps makin' mistakes like that, huh?"

"*This* is our only choice," Ranta said, drawing a finger across his neck. "*This*. We ought to hurry up and do this to that woman. *This*, got it? *This*."

It seemed Ranta really liked making that decapitating gesture. Maybe he thought it looked cool. If he did, he was even more mistaken than Yume.

"Ah..." Moguzo said, gazing in the direction of the door.

Speak of the devil, as they say, Haruhiro thought.

It was Merry. Merry had come to the tavern.

It was brief, but Merry glanced in their direction. They were almost certain that she had seen them. She pretended not to have, though. Merry went deep inside to an open seat at the counter and sat there.

"Wha—" Ranta slammed the table. "The hell! What's with her attitude?! We're in the same party, for god's sake! Normally, you'd at least give a little nod in our direction!"

"The thing about Merry-chan is," Yume arched her eyebrows and pouted angrily, "normal isn't really somethin' that applies with her, you know. What she did just now stung Yume's heart a little bit, though."

Shihoru kept rubbing her lips together. "...B-but we didn't wave to her or anything, either. I think both sides are to blame... maybe."

"Ahh," Haruhiro scratched his neck. "Yeah, sorta. Like, we expected her to ignore us and we braced ourselves for it. So, lo and behold? Something like that. Maybe it's not good for us to do that, either."

"Don't give me that bullshit! Why do we need to go out of our way to worry about her feelings?"

"See, Ranta, you actin' like this is why us girls all hate you," Yume said.

"Oh, shut up! I don't want to hear a girl with tiny tits acting like she can speak for all women!"

"Don't call them tiny!"

"Tiny! Tiny! Tiny! Tiny! Tiny! Tiny! Tiiiiiiny!"

"Murrrgh," Yume moaned.

"...Ranta, no matter where you go, you never stop being terrible," Haruhiro said.

"It's none of your business, Haruhiro! Like I care about the expression on a girl's face! The only parts I look at are their boobs, their butts, their legs and their upper arms!"

Shihoru looked at Ranta as if she were looking at garbage. "...You sicken me. As a person."

"H-Harsh!" Even Ranta must have realized this was bad. "I don't *only* look at the boobs, butt, legs, and upper arms. I don't care about their expression, but their face is important, too! Because even if you've got a hot body, if your face is all gross, yeah, I'm not touching that! Huh? That's strange, I feel like I'm getting glared at even harder now. Why?"

"Someone just..." Moguzo pointed at Merry. "...started talking to Merry."

"Oh." Haruhiro blinked. "...You're right."

It wasn't anything to be surprised about, but it was unexpected. What's more, the man who was chatting to Merry with a smile was someone Haruhiro knew.

That said, they had only spoken once. That gentle face. The armor and cape. That sword. His generally whitish attire.

"—Huh, that's Shinohara from Orion."

"Orion?" Ranta cocked his head to the side. "Whoa, you're serious. If we're talking Orion, they're a pretty famous clan. And, wait, Shinohara... If I remember, he's the master of Orion. Well, not like it matters. Who cares what that woman does? Oh! Drinks're here. Let's have a toast. A toast. Cheers!"

"Ch-cheers," Moguzo responded. He was the only one who did.

Haruhiro clacked his wooden mug together with just Moguzo, Yume, and Shihoru's, and then took a sip of lemonade. It was sweet, sour, and delicious.

"Hey, hey, Haru-kun." Yume tugged at his sleeve. "What's a clan?"

"Ah, clans are—" Haruhiro didn't know much about clans himself, but they were groups or teams that volunteer soldiers would put together in pursuit of some goal.

Most parties were five or six people and he had heard that was because a priest's all-important Protection, which was a buffing spell, targeted a maximum of six people. However, there were powerful enemies that six people alone couldn't hope to defeat, as well as dangerous enemy territories they couldn't enter with only six people. There were scenarios which required multiple parties to coordinate with each other and the clan framework had apparently been created in order to facilitate that.

"—there are a number of famous clans, too. Like the Berserkers and Iron Knuckle. Or there's the all-female Wild Angels clan, for instance. Oh, right. Orion's famous, too."

"Look," Ranta gestured towards Shinohara with his thumb. "There're seven crests in an X-shape on his cape, right? That's the symbol of Orion. There're probably a few of them around."

True enough, there were customers with the same cape as Shinohara's dotted around. Shinohara had said that they came to Sherry's Tavern fairly often. Haruhiro had always meant to go over and say hi if he ran into them here. Maybe now was the time—

Yeah, no. I don't want to interrupt him while he's talking to Merry. It can wait.

But still, what was Shinohara's connection with Merry? Shinohara seemed to be doing all the talking, with Merry just making occasional short comments and nodding along, but she didn't seem to be bothered by it at all. Actually, if anything, she seemed apologetic.

Eventually, Shinohara walked away and left Merry. She watched his back for a while as he left then looked down and took a sip of her drink.

Ranta chuckled evilly. "Those two are doing it."

"I didn't get that vibe..." Haruhiro said uncertainly.

"Haaaaruhiroooo. You, pal, are seriously blind. No matter how you look at it, that was totally the vibe they had going. They're totally doing it. 100 percent, I guarantee it."

"I'm gonna go have a word with Shinohara."

"Hey, you bastard! Don't ignore me! You're making me sad!"

While thinking Ranta could go ahead and be sad all he wanted, Haruhiro started to get up from his seat and then the tavern suddenly became noisy. The reason why was immediately apparent.

"—Soma."

"Hey, if it isn't Soma."

"It's Soma!"

"Soma!"

"Soma...!"

The volunteer soldiers were all calling out one name.

Who's Soma? Must be that guy. A group of six people had just come into Sherry's Tavern. *He's the one at the front.*

He looked like he was still a young man, but he was different from the rest. Way too different. For a start, his equipment was unique.

What is that black armor that covers his whole body, yet fits him tightly, looks incredibly light, and has no angular spots whatsoever? thought Haruhiro.

It had been probably made from countless little metal plates fitted together, but there was an orange light that leaked out from inside it here and there. It flashed on and off, as if it were breathing.

He wore a long, asymmetrical skirt, which looked like it was part of the armor, and covered his lower body. *But that just makes it look cooler.*

The long sword he was wearing over his back had a curved blade. *If there's anyone who's not completely enthralled by that sinister yet beautiful workmanship, they clearly don't know what they're talking about.*

The small sword hanging at his hip was incredible, too. *Honestly, just that one would be enough for me. I want it.*

The man who carried all those weapons and armor which were clearly on another level had a face that was extraordinary, too.

He's got clear-cut features. They're not especially manly, or beautiful in a more neutral way, it's not like that, but if he gazed at someone with those almond eyes that are so full of cool-headed composure, intensity and sorrow, I don't think anyone could stay calm.

The men and women following Sōma were clearly no ordinary people themselves.

One was a swarthy man with his hair in dreadlocks who had sanpaku eyes and wore silver armor so radiant it was blinding.

He's huge, Haruhiro thought. *He's got to be taller than Moguzo.*

He seemed well-built, but because of his small head, he came across as lanky.

The man walking right behind him, in contrast, was rather small. He had a childish face, but eyes that were thick with too much mucus. *I feel like I'll get cursed if I meet his gaze.*

Was the man with long arms, much too long, who stood beside the little man even human? He wore a terrifying mask, so it was hard to be certain, but Haruhiro felt like he was some other kind of creature. The armor he wore, which looked as if he had wrapped metal and leather around his entire body, was abnormal, and the giant, saw-bladed sword strapped to his back looked dangerous.

Still, when Haruhiro looked at the two women following them, it was a nice refreshment for his eyes and his brain felt like it might just melt away. Soma's party included four men and two women—and both of those women were beautiful.

One was a sexy, older girl of the cool beauty variety. She wore something like a dress that had a bold design which gave a peek at her breasts and legs. She was decked out with necklaces, rings, bracelets, a staff of the finest quality, a short sword, and more, but none of it felt excessive. That was because she herself was gorgeous enough that none of these things outshone her.

The other one looked, in some ways, a little like Merry. It wasn't that their faces were similar, but she had that same, inhuman beauty. Was she a beautiful, young girl or a beautiful woman?

She looked like she could be around the same age as Haruhiro but at the same time looked older. She wore a breastplate with delicate designs carved into it, but was otherwise lightly equipped. But she did have a sword.

Was she a warrior? Female warriors were uncommon. But, setting that aside—

What stunning silver hair.

It was nothing like Renji's hair. Her hair looked as if it had been made by melting real silver and spinning it into thread. Her eyes looked like they had been inlaid with sapphires and her skin was abnormally white.

It was like snow. That was not just an expression: it truly did look like snow. Obviously, there had to be blood flowing through it, so there was the slightest red tinge, but her skin was radiant.

Merry's nothing next to her. This woman's not human. I mean, she's got pointy ears.

"...Isn't that an elf there?" Ranta whispered.

"An elf..." While Haruhiro stared so hard he forgot to blink, he parroted the words back.

An elf. What's that? I don't know, but I do know. An elf. Right. She's probably an elf.

With a "Yo! Yo!" someone raced over to him. Someone this noisy could only be Kikkawa.

"Hey, if it isn't Harucchi, Rantan, Moguchin, Yumepi, and Shihorun! You good? You good? I'm great! Hey, did you see, did you see, are you seeing right now? Soma's amazing, isn't he?! Man, I didn't think I'd get the chance to see him. Talk about lucky! We're aaaall luck-luck-lucky! Yessiree!"

He seemed even more wound up than last time. Was it because of Soma?

"...Kikkawa, who's Soma?"

"*Whaaaaat?* Harucchi, you don't know Soma?! Seriously?! You're kidding me. That's like, no way. Soma's, you know, the number one volunteer soldier. The volunteer soldier of volunteer soldiers. Well, in terms of ability there are some people who'd argue otherwise, but in name-brand value, he's the top, hands down. It's my first time seeing him, too, though. He's different! So different! So cool! If I were a woman, I'd want him to take me now! Soma, I love youuuu! Yup. That's a lie. I don't feel *that* strongly about him. Still, he's awesome. I aspire to that, you know. If I've got to be like someone, I want it to be him."

"And how!" Ranta's eyes were sparkling. "If you're a man! If you're a volunteer soldier! That's what you've got to aim for! Damn! Where do I get me some of that armor? I wanna wear iiiit!"

"...F-for me," Moguzo looked down and mumbled, "I-I'd like

a h-helmet. P-plated armor too, if possible. Then I could do a little more…"

Shihoru looked pained, biting her lower lip. "…I want to learn more magic. Magic that can help everyone. What I have now isn't enough…"

"For Yume, Yume wants armor, too. Maybe Yume should do something about that, shouldn't she? Yume, she's not so good an archer so she has to move up to the front a lot, you know."

"For me—"

What should I say? Haruhiro still couldn't tear his eyes away from Soma's party. But, if he was honest, he didn't want to become like Soma the way Ranta and Kikkawa did. He wasn't even convinced he could close the gap between their group and Renji's.

It's pointless, aspiring to be like someone. When there's no way you'll ever catch up, it's just stupid.

Still, that didn't mean he thought things were fine as they were. He didn't. Haruhiro wanted to move forward.

Even if he couldn't be like Renji, racing up the stairs, skipping one or two steps with each stride, he was sure he could ascend those stairs slowly and carefully, one step at a time. Surely, that was what Manato had been trying to do. They could move at their own pace, making today better than yesterday, and tomorrow better than today. Obviously, just wishing for it to happen wasn't enough. He had to do something.

What should I be doing—and how?

Should he save up money and learn skills? Buy good equipment?

Those things were important, but there was more to it than that.

Manato said he was counting on me. Did that mean what I think?

That he wanted me to do what he had been doing? Basically, to become the leader of the group?

Can I do that? Someone probably has to, I know. But does it have to be me? I don't want to do it. I don't want to carry that burden. It's too much hassle. What about Manato? Did he choose to do it because he wanted do it and was happy doing it? Maybe not necessarily. Maybe it was hard and he wanted to give up, but he gritted his teeth and pulled us all along. How can I say for sure that that wasn't the case?

"Oh, but, but, but!" Kikkawa had thrown his arm around Ranta's shoulder and started laughing at some point.

Being able to do that with Ranta is impressive.

"I didn't think I'd get to meet Soma! I heard Old Ishmal is his main stomping grounds, and he rarely ever comes back to Alterna! That's me for you, though! I'm so lucky I scare myself! No, I'm not actually scared of myself, though!"

"Hey, Kikkawa! Let's go become buds with Soma and his gang! The way we are now, we can do it!"

"You wanna go?! You going?! Ranta, are we going?!"

Kikkawa and Ranta stood at the same time.

They couldn't seriously intend to talk to Soma, could they? Haruhiro lifted himself up in his chair, glancing around the tavern.

Soma and his group were sitting at a table next to the counter and a crowd was starting to gather there. Merry was alone, drinking something, alcoholic or otherwise. He couldn't see Shinohara anywhere. Had he headed off somewhere else?

Sitting back in his seat, Haruhiro drank his lemonade. When he raised his face, his eyes met Yume's.

Yume tilted her head to the side as if to say, *Is something up?*

Haruhiro shook his head as if to say *Nothing*, and took another sip of his lemonade.

Well, no, it's not nothing. A leader, *huh. Is that something I can be?*

17. Precious

Whether he could or couldn't, for as long as he was breathing, time would continue to flow. When he went to sleep, the sun would rise. When the morning came, he would have to go to the Old City of Damuro.

They ambushed two goblins, wounding one with the preemptive attack. Ranta and Yume took on the wounded goblin while Moguzo and Haruhiro faced the unharmed one.

The unharmed goblin wore a dented helmet and rudimentary chainmail and was armed with a damaged sword. It was a pretty tough opponent, but, that said, Moguzo was far larger than it and had the upper hand in terms of strength, as well. It seemed like he should have been able to ram his way through its defense, but Moguzo didn't do that.

Why not? Because Moguzo was afraid?

True, Moguzo wasn't as reckless as Ranta. However, he had good reason to be cautious.

The goblin happened to be wearing a helmet, so Haruhiro noticed something while watching the two of them. With a helmet, you wouldn't die from a slight blow to the head. However, without one, even a grazing blow could cause serious injury, so you couldn't help but be cautious.

The night before, Moguzo had said he wanted a helmet and plated armor. Not a sharp, new bastard sword; it was defensive gear he wanted. With equipment that defended him better, he could throw himself into the fight more fully. That was probably what he'd meant.

Haruhiro spent most of his time thinking about how to get behind the enemy. He didn't wear armor, so every enemy attack was scary to him. It was only a little bit of an exaggeration to say that one slash could be the end of him, so he avoided them with everything he had.

However, Moguzo had to face the enemy in a straight-up exchange of blows. If Moguzo were running around like Haruhiro, everything would turn into a total mess.

Because their roles were different, Haruhiro hadn't understood that. He hadn't seen anything. No, he hadn't tried to see anything.

"Moguzo...!" Haruhiro called out to Moguzo, slashing at the goblin as he did.

The goblin turned in his direction. Haruhiro backed away.

The goblin hesitated for a moment.

Just a moment.

The goblin spun back around to face Moguzo, but he was already thrusting his bastard sword at it.

"Hunghh...!"

The bastard sword buried itself deep inside the goblin's flank. But living creatures don't die that easily.

The goblin shrieked, "Gyagyahh!" and tried to swing its sword.

I won't let you do that! Haruhiro attacked the goblin from behind. *The goblin's sword hand. Aim for its hand. The wrist.*

"—Slap...!"

He wasn't able to lop it off, but his dagger reached the bone and the goblin lost its grip on its sword. Moguzo grunted and gave his bastard sword a twist. The goblin screamed, trying to grab a hold of Moguzo. Haruhiro grabbed hold of the goblin's helmet with his left hand, tearing it off with all his might, then slammed his dagger in under its chin.

"—There!"

Even after all that, it took some time for the goblin to stop struggling.

There were lives at stake here. Both sides were serious. It didn't get any more deadly serious than this. There was no way it was going to be easy. Hadn't Manato said that?

Just like they didn't want to die, the goblins didn't want to die, either. They killed them, taking their stuff, eating, and living on.

For the other goblin—Ranta and Yume's—Shihoru weakened it with magic and Ranta struck the final blow.

Once the battle ended, while Haruhiro was collecting the goblin pouches, Merry brought the five fingers of her right hand to her forehead, pressing on her brow with the middle finger.

That was really quick! I nearly missed it. However, he did manage to see it properly.

That's the sign of the hexagram. Manato often did that after we beat the enemy. I'm a little surprised, she doesn't seem like the type to do that. Then again, I don't really know her. I don't know anything about Merry.

I've never tried to learn.

During their afternoon break, he said to Moguzo, "Hey, I'll pitch in a bit. Moguzo, it doesn't matter if it's a cheap one, but buy yourself a helmet. Maybe look for some used armor in your size, too. Even if you can't find any, see what it would cost to have it fixed up. That will give us an idea of the price."

"...Huh? Really? But...I couldn't. I don't think you should have to pay for it, Haruhiro."

"It's fine, really. For now, this here is all I need," Haruhiro said, tapping his dagger. "If you don't have all your equipment together, it's a problem for everyone. So, it's in my own interest to pay, see? Iron armor is expensive, right? If we were making a lot of money, I'd let you handle it, but since we aren't, it's a bit much to expect you to be able to pay for it all yourself."

"Ahh, when you say it like that, Yume agrees," Yume gave a relaxed smile. "Moguzo, if you buy defensive gear, Yume'll donate to the cause. Let's all go lookin' for a cute helmet together, okay?"

Shihoru hesitantly raised her hand. "...In that case, I will, too. I can't spare much, but I can put in a little."

"No matter what happens, you aren't getting a single copper out of me, okay?! Just saying!" Ranta declared.

"That's fine. No one expected anything from you, Ranta," Haruhiro said.

Then he glanced over to see Merry's reaction.

Merry was staring off into the distance as if to say it wasn't her concern. Still, was it just Haruhiro's imagination when he thought she looked a little sad and lonely?

It occurred to him that, if he could afford to next time, he should watch Merry during combat. *She's just holding onto her staff, she never moves up, she barely ever heals us, she has no motivation, she's basically just standing there,* was his current impression of Merry. But was it really true?

The first goblins they encountered in the afternoon were a group of three, so things were too hectic for him to observe what Merry did in combat.

After that, they couldn't find any groups or individual goblins that looked like good targets, but on the way out of the Old City of Damuro, they stumbled into a pair of two goblins.

They had been walking right past each other, so it turned into a sudden melee. Shihoru and Merry, the rear team, didn't even have time to fall back.

One of the goblins lunged at Merry.

She gasped.

"Don't just stare off into space—" Ranta body checked the goblin, knocking it to the ground. "—you stupid bitch!"

"I wasn't staring off into space!" she snapped.

True, it hadn't looked like Merry was staring off into space.

The other goblin tried to jump on Shihoru. Merry shouted out, clobbering it with a hearty swing of her priest's staff. That was the priest's self-defense skill, Smash. It was one Manato had learned too, so Haruhiro was sure of it.

There were two enemies, so they were in a good position from the very beginning. While Haruhiro was eyeing the goblins' backs, he occasionally glanced over at Merry.

I thought so. The staff isn't just for show. She's learned the proper self-defense skills. She doesn't want to move up front, but she still protected

Shihoru.

What's more, when a goblin latched on to Moguzo, headbutting him in the chin, Merry watched everything that happened closely. Right after that, she turned away. As if she were thinking, *He's fine. No need to heal him.*

Merry's just standing there? She has no motivation? That's not it at all. Merry was watching the situation from the rear, making judgment calls every time a comrade was injured. She would even use her staff if she had to.

With the battle over, Shihoru went and talked to Merry. "Um, thank you for earlier."

Merry looked away from her. "What are you talking about?"

She doesn't have to say it like that, Haruhiro thought. *If she would just say, "You're welcome" or smile, then everyone, guys and girls, would like Merry. It shouldn't be difficult. I'm sure doing it would make life easier for Merry, too. So why doesn't she do it?*

After they went back to Alterna and sold their loot, he called out to her. He noticed she was about to leave without telling them. "Ah, Merry, hold on a second!"

Merry scratched at her hair, turning around like it was a bother. "Did you still have some business with me?"

Like I said, you get scary over every little thing, Haruhiro thought. *I'm starting to think you want to be hated. Still, we're members of the same party, aren't we? It's got to be better to be liked than to be hated. I wish I had the guts to say that to her, but I can't. If I try to get too involved with her, Merry will probably run off. I get the feeling she'd say, "That's enough! Goodbye!" and drop out of the party.*

"I wouldn't call it business, but would you like to come grab a meal with us? We can hit the tavern or something after that."

"No, thank you."

"...Why so polite?"

Merry looked down and away, furrowing her brow ever so slightly. Was she angry? She seemed embarrassed somehow. "...There's no real meaning behind it."

"Oh, I see. Sorry to poke at you over a little thing like that."

"I don't really..." Merry began to purse her lips but stopped, looking down and shaking her head left to right. Then she said, "See you—"

Probably, the next word she had been about to utter was *tomorrow*. For Merry, who always left without a word, this was unusual. Or it would have been unusual but, ultimately, it never happened. Stopping with only those two words, Merry turned her back on Haruhiro and the others.

Merry's a fast walker, but the way she's walking is strange. Like she's getting flustered.

Ranta scoffed. "Yeesh, what an unlikable woman. Seriously."

"Really...?" Moguzo stroked his chin. It was slight, but he had a beard growing.

Your beard sure grows in thick, Moguzo, Haruhiro thought.

"I feel like, today, she was a little different."

Yume nodded along. "Yeah, yeah, she was different today, huh? Today's Merry-chan was just a teensy bit cute. That's just a vaaaague feeling Yume had though, y'know."

Ranta gave Yume the side-eye. "Don't just call anything and everything cute, cute, cute. Your 'cute' applies to such a broad range, I don't even know what it means anymore."

"I don't need someone like you to understand, Ranta. I don't want you to understand me."

"That is so not cute."

Once they managed to calm Yume and Ranta down, they went looking for a helmet for Moguzo. There was a shop out in the marketplace selling used iron helmets and one type called a barbut was cheap.

Barbuts were forged from a single sheet of iron, so they were as low-priced as they were simple. They were shaped like the big toe of a person's foot and when you wore it, your eyes, nose, and mouth were exposed through the T-shaped opening.

At first glance, it looks like it'd fall off easily, but there's leather wrapped around on the inside, so I guess not, Haruhiro thought.

Ranta stubbornly haggled the price down and they got a barbut that was a perfect fit for Moguzo—even if it was scratched and dented all over—for eighteen silver when the original price had been forty-two. Of that, Haruhiro paid three silver, Yume and Shihoru three silver each and Moguzo paid eight silver.

While they were eating at a stall, Ranta said, "Well, I effectively put in twenty-four silver, got it?! You'd better be grateful, guys!" and puffed out his chest proudly which made Yume and Shihoru furrow their brows.

Haruhiro was appalled, too, but when he thought about it, Ranta may have been right. Probably no one but the shameless Ranta could have haggled that hard. Twenty-four silver might have been an exaggeration, but they had probably saved around ten silver thanks to him.

"Yeah. Thanks, Ranta," Haruhiro said seriously.

Ranta blinked in surprise and said, "S-Sure," then looked down.

"...A-As long as you get it. It's my, what, merit? My value? My true worth? Something like that, anyway. Since you guys tend to look down on me. Take this to heart for future reference. Seriously. I'm begging you to, honestly. Well, no, I won't beg..."

They had planned to look around at armor after they ate, but it was already late, so they went to the tavern. Merry didn't seem to be there. Haruhiro had invited her to come, so that might actually have made her decide not to show herself here tonight instead.

"That woman is seriously uncute. She's even worse than Yume," Ranta muttered. He seemed to be bitter that Merry hadn't said a single word of thanks after he'd helped her. "I mean, she can't even give a proper hello or thank you or sorry. She's hopeless. Looks are all she's got going for her. Just her looks. Her looks are top-notch, though. Well, she's got nothing on that elf from Soma's party, though."

"B-But..." Moguzo stammered. He was still wearing his barbut. It seemed he was quite fond of it.

It's not going to be easy to drink in that thing, Haruhiro thought.

"Before, when she healed me, she said sorry. Merry-san did."

"Huhhh? Don't you lie, Moguzo. Like she'd ever do that," snorted Ranta.

"I-It's true. It was when I hurt my head. Merry-san's hand touched the wound and I groaned in pain, so she said sorry."

"Yeah, that did happen." Haruhiro remembered it, too. He hadn't been able to hear her, but Merry had definitely said something to Moguzo that time. "I see. That was an apology."

"She protected me, too," Shihoru nodded. "She's hard to approach, but I don't think she's nasty or heartless. She's not that sort of person."

"Merry-chan's a real cutie-pie, too, y'know," added Yume.

"So, I was watching Merry more closely today," Haruhiro said, "and—"

He described to the others what he had noticed in combat. Merry was working hard to fulfill her role in her own way. It was just that she didn't tell them what she was thinking, she didn't speak nicely to them, and she had attitude problems. That was why they misunderstood.

"—Now, this is just probably, but, if we understand Merry's method, I think we can use her well. Still, I'm not sure if that's good enough."

"What's wrong with it?" Ranta guzzled down some beer then snorted derisively. "If that woman's doing her job, like you say, it's no problem. Though I'm not convinced she really is."

"If you feel that way, Ranta, it's already a problem."

"Does how I feel even matter to you guys? You're always ignoring me, aren't you?"

"Don't get sulky."

"I'm not sulking at all. Just stating the truth. That bitch is an outsider in the party, but I'm not much different on that front, am I?"

Had Ranta been feeling that way? He'd never noticed. It hadn't just been Merry; Haruhiro hadn't been looking at Ranta, either. Was that what this meant?

Now that I think about it, Ranta's human, too. If they treated him badly, he wouldn't just be fine with that.

Though in that case, maybe he should have tried to do something about the way he spoke and acted. It did feel like he was getting exactly what he deserved. Still, even if you told someone to fix their personality, it wasn't something that could be fixed that easily.

Even as he is now, Ranta has some good points. Well, not absolutely none, at least.

"My bad," Haruhiro lowered his head. "I'm sorry, Ranta. I'll be more careful in future."

"Y-Yeah! Y-you'd better be more careful, moron!"

"...The 'moron' was uncalled for."

"What's wrong with calling a moron a moron, you moron?"

"Man..." Haruhiro scratched his neck. He couldn't even get mad at this point.

What is Ranta, a child? Yeah, he definitely was. Maybe it was better not to pay attention to every little provocation and just let it go instead. *Manato handled him that way, come to think of it.*

While he sighed and looked around the tavern, an Orion cape caught Haruhiro's eye. It was Shinohara. He was climbing the stairs up to the second level.

"Ah. I'm going to go say hi to Shinohara-san," Haruhiro said.

"Whaaaat? Let me guess, Haruhiro, you're trying to get into Orion without the rest of us, aren't you?!" Ranta demanded. "I won't let you do it! I'm going, too!"

"...Well, no, I have zero intention of doing that, but sure, you can come along."

"Th-then, me too."

"If you're all goin', maybe Yume'll go too."

"Huh... W-well then, me too... It'd be a little awkward to be the only one left behind..."

Haruhiro had his doubts that they should be doing it this way, but the five of them went up the stairs together. Shinohara noticed them before Haruhiro could call out to him and he rose from his seat.

"Hey, Haruhiro-kun. It's been a while. Are these your comrades with you?"

Whoa. I only met this guy once and he remembers me. That's kind of incredible. And, hold on, almost everyone sitting around Shinohara is part of Orion. There's got to be more than twenty... no, thirty of them. Most are guys, but maybe a third or so are women and they're all wearing Orion's cape.

"Y-Yeah... N-nice to see you, uh..."

"Come along, right this way. Hayashi, could you get some seats for them?"

"Okay, Shinohara-san." The short-haired, slim-eyed man he'd called Hayashi brought some tables and chairs from nearby.

"Join me here," Shinohara said. He sat down at one of the chairs surrounding the table Hayashi brought over and Haruhiro and the others did the same.

The members of Orion didn't gawk; they just continued quietly talking amongst themselves.

They're too well-mannered, too pleasant, Haruhiro thought.

Even though they hadn't ordered yet, drinks came for them. Forget Moguzo, Yume, and Shihoru—even Ranta was being as quiet and meek as a lamb.

Orion's amazing, Haruhiro thought.

"Well, how is it, Haruhiro-kun? You don't seem to have bought your badge yet, but are you starting to get used to the lifestyle?"

"Huh? How do you know I haven't bought my badge yet?"

"I'm always interested in what the rookies are up to. You're frequenting the Old City of Damuro, right? It seems some people have started calling you guys the Goblin Slayers behind your backs."

"Ahh... We've been targeting nothing but goblins all this time, so that's fair enough."

Shinohara paused for a moment then adjusted his posture. "What happened to your comrade was regrettable."

"...Yeah." Haruhiro lowered his eyes to the table, clenching his hands together. He even knows about that, huh. Then again, maybe that's just how it is.

Alterna had felt huge to him at first, but in reality, it was a fixed space with everything packed tightly into it. The world volunteer soldiers occupied was an even smaller portion of that. If they didn't go to great lengths to hide it, news of pretty much anything would get around in no time. *I should probably keep that in mind.*

"...I mean, I was really disappointed about it, too," Haruhiro said. "He was a great guy."

"It may be conceited of me to say this, but I know what it's like losing a comrade," Shinohara told him. "I've experienced it, too."

"I...see. That's..."

"Please, never forget that pain," Shinohara said, looking at Haruhiro and the others. His eyes were peaceful but filled with a deep sorrow. "Even as you carry that pain, you can still move forward. I want you to carve that deep into your hearts. Also, I want you to treasure the comrades you have now. Treasure the time you spend with them. Because once it's passed, it will never come back. You'll no doubt have regrets, but please, work hard to leave as few regrets as you can."

As he was listening to Shinohara speak, Haruhiro unconsciously brought a hand to his chest. *Treasure the comrades I have now.*

If only he had done more to treasure Manato while he was alive. If only he had done more to understand Manato. However, that was no longer possible. That was all the more reason that he needed to value the time he had with the comrades he had now. So as not to leave himself with regrets.

There's no telling when I might die myself, he thought.

It was the same for Moguzo, for Ranta, for Yume, for Shihoru, and even for Merry. He didn't want to be left thinking about how he should have done this or that differently if someone died again. *I don't want any of us thinking that.*

"Shinohara-san, I have something to ask your advice on."

"What might that be? I hope I'll be able to help you."

"It's about Merry. Yesterday, you went up and talked to her, yeah? You know Merry's in our party now, too, right?"

"Yes. What about her?"

"We want you to tell us. About Merry. Anything you happen to know. I may be coming to the wrong person, but I don't think she'd tell us herself even if we tried to force her to."

Shinohara tapped the table just once with his index finger. "— Rather than me, Hayashi's the guy to talk to about that. He was in a party with her at one point."

"Huh...?" Haruhiro glanced over to the next table where Hayashi was currently knocking back a goblet. Hayashi noticed Haruhiro's glance and gave a silent bow.

18. Her Circumstances

Hayashi spoke and this was the story he told:

Merry and I were comrades from the time we were trainees.

Michiki and I were warriors. Mutsumi was the mage, Ogu was the thief, and Merry was the priest. I think our party was doing fairly well for itself.

We targeted goblins in the Old City of Damuro, just like you guys, and ten days later we bought our badges.

We got our equipment together, learned skills, and even after we started hunting kobolds in the Cyrene Mine about eight kilometers northwest of Alterna, we hardly ever ran into a dangerous situation. At the time, I thought that was just how things were. I didn't notice it at all.

The one giving us a sense of stability in battle was Merry. Even though she had such perfect looks, she wasn't full of herself because of it. She was always cheerful and energetic and she smiled all the time, to the point where there was never room for a dark moment in our party.

What was more, she learned self-defense skills in addition to light magic and she fought shoulder-to-shoulder with Michiki and I.

Of course, she never neglected her job as a healer, either. If we got even the slightest scratch, she healed it right away.

In our party the front-liners were me, Michiki, and Merry. That meant Merry could heal us right away when we got hurt. If Mutsumi or Ogu got in trouble, Merry would hurry back to help them right away. Basically, Merry was doing the work of three people.

Despite that, we fought assuming that we had five. So of course it was easy. We were effectively a group of seven.

It happened to be that there were a lot of volunteer soldiers who arrived in the same period as us and some of them were even more extraordinary, so we didn't draw much attention. Still, the more we fought, the more our confidence grew. We weren't afraid of anything back then. We hadn't run into much that could scare us, so of course we weren't.

However, I know now that it was different for Merry.

Every time we got hurt, she must have been on-edge. That was why she was so quick to heal us. Once one little thing goes awry, the rest can come tumbling down in an instant, so she may have been desperate to prevent that.

She probably knew. She probably knew that, honestly, the difference between victory and defeat was paper-thin for us.

The rest of us didn't realize that. We had gotten arrogant.

There were other parties aiming to clear the Cyrene Mines and we didn't want to lose to them. We thought we wouldn't lose. So we went deeper. Ever deeper. And finally, on that fifth layer of the mine, which I'll never forget, it happened.

You may already know, but kobolds are a furry race with doglike faces. They're built just a little smaller than humans. However, in the lower mines, there are lots of big kobolds around 170 centimeters tall and those ones are relatively tough.

While they're not as smart as humans, they've built a society with a rigid class structure. They have skilled smiths and their magic is developing as well. They're good at working in groups and at least some of them are fearless warriors.

We had gotten used to cutting down those kobolds, heading down to the fifth level over the course of a full day. To be honest, we thought we were stronger than the kobolds, that we were superior.

Still, we never let our guards down.

But even without us letting our guards down, it was stronger than us.

Its hair had black and white spots and, because of the fact that several volunteer soldiers had fallen at its hands, those were known as the spots of death. The kobold itself was called Death Spots.

We had heard it went around the mines, bringing a small number of followers with it.

If you ever run into Death Spots, don't hesitate, run immediately! Sometimes, it even comes up as far as the entrance. Even if you aren't that deep in, you'll still need to watch out.

We knew all that, but we weren't careful. Because we'd never seen hide nor hair of Death Spots.

Now, that said, when a large—much too large—kobold that looked like Death Spots came at us, we weren't so thoughtlessly optimistic that we expected to win.

It's just... we were on the fifth level. It was a long way to the surface and we couldn't get away easily. We thought we had no choice but to fight.

Michiki and I would take on Death Spots in turns while Merry, Ogu, and Mutsumi took care of its followers. That was the plan we followed. It went well, at first.

Death Spots was as strong as the rumors had said, but between Michiki and myself, we were able to keep it in check and Merry and the others were gradually whittling down the number of followers. If someone got hurt, Merry healed them immediately.

The moment all its followers were gone, I thought we could do it. After all, Death Spots was already wounded, but we were uninjured. To be accurate, even after taking countless wounds, we were uninjured.

I misread the situation due to my inexperience. If we had run away then, we might have been able to shake off Death Spots and hidden ourselves somewhere. But we didn't do that.

We attacked Death Spots, staining its spotted fur with blood. However, no matter how many times Michiki and I slashed it, Merry bludgeoned it or Mutsumi struck it with magic, it refused to fall. We weren't even slowing it down.

It had boundless reserves of stamina and the pain from its wounds wasn't weakening it; if anything, the pain was just making it madder.

It was an outlier, while we were ordinary.

First, it slashed open Ogu's face with its claws. While Merry was healing Ogu, Michiki took a hard blow that broke his left arm. While Michiki was being healed, it punched me hard and I lost consciousness.

I was out for thirty seconds at most. But in that time, Ogu had gotten killed.

Merry was desperately trying to keep a near-dead Mutsumi alive a little longer. Michiki was covered in wounds and trying to hold Death Spots off.

When I opened my eyes, I desperately drew Death Spots's attention to me, letting Michiki fall back.

With the last spell Mutsumi let off before she breathed her last, Death Spots looked like it was faltering.

No, maybe that was just what I wanted to think. With every second, Death Spots was pushing me closer to the edge.

"Hurry, Merry! Hurry, heal Michiki!"

That's what I shouted. Again, and again, I shouted.

Until Merry screamed back at me, I didn't realize.

"I'm sorry, Hayashi! I'm sorry! I can't use any more magic!"

You can't just use magic as much as you want for as long as you want. For mages and priests to use the power of the elementals and gods, they expend a spiritual power called magic power. Even I understood that much.

No...I hadn't truly understood it.

Even though I'd known Mutsumi and Merry occasionally meditated to regain their magic power, right then, things like how much magic power they had left, whether they could spare any, whether they were almost out...those were things I didn't have a firm grasp on. Mutsumi and Merry hadn't let us trouble ourselves with those things.

Anytime we needed it, magic came flying. Our wounds were healed. That's what it felt like. We never even thought about how much the two of them were struggling to do that.

Even by the time we finished off its followers, Merry must have used a lot of magic power. And after a long, drawn-out battle, it had finally run out.

Michiki was the one who saved Merry and me. He worked up the last of his strength to stand facing Death Spots. Throwing one skill after another at it, he told me and Merry to run.

Merry refused and she went to charge at Death Spots.

I stopped her.

I ran away, dragging her with me.

I won't make excuses for what I did.

I abandoned a comrade.

Michiki wasn't going to make it with those wounds. I wanted to at least grant the last wish of the friend who was risking his life so that we could get away.

I'm still amazed that we made it back from the fifth level to the surface alive. We almost died many times on the way and it took a day and a half.

But...we had lost them. Our precious comrades, our friends... three of them at once.

Merry was in a terrible state. She was the priest, a healer in charge of saving her comrades, and she had let three of them die, then had her own life saved by a comrade.

Since then, I've never once seen her smile. Maybe she thinks she doesn't have the right to anymore.

After that, we were picked up by Shinohara and joined Orion, but Merry dropped out right away. I think, probably, the comfortable atmosphere of Orion actually made it more painful for her.

Since then, Merry has joined any party that asks her to. However, she never sticks with any of them for long.

Everything I'd heard about her was completely different for the

Merry I had known, so I got worried and went to talk to her. She only kept telling me she was fine and I couldn't help but feel a wall between us.

Seeing me was painful for her; that was what her eyes told me.

For her, I must be a symbol of the past she lost.

What she needs now is a future. That can't be me.

Michiki, Mutsumi, and Ogu are dead and I might as well be a ghost to her. We're just her past.

She needs to find a future for herself. Otherwise, someday, she'll sink into the swamp of depression, stop being able to move and, eventually, she'll stop breathing.

19. For Now, Tomorrow

What do we do? What do we say to her? What are we supposed to do? Those questions were all Haruhiro had been able think about since before going to sleep last night. All he had been able think about until they had met Merry at the north gate at 8:00.

He didn't come to a conclusion.

Once they reached the Old City of Damuro, he needed to focus on work, so he wouldn't be at leisure to worry about anything else. The time he needed to hold precious flew by quickly and after returning to Alterna, Haruhiro was finally able to look her straight in the eye for the first time.

"Merry. I've been wanting to talk to you," Haruhiro began as they were leaving the merchant's.

Merry said, "I see." She wrapped her arms around herself as if bracing for something. "Make it quick."

Haruhiro knew he had been acting strangely today. He didn't know how to act towards Merry. Everyone must have felt that way. Of course, it was because they heard her story from Hayashi yesterday, but she didn't know about that. Merry had likely noticed something had changed and she had a premonition that something was coming.

Like a parting. An end.

Sorry, but could you leave the party? Haruhiro would say.

Merry would immediately say *I understand,* leaving at once, without further drama.

That was what Merry was getting ready to do now. That was how it looked.

Was it always like this for her? Every time, in every party? That was just too sad.

"Merry."

You're wrong, that's not what it is. As if to tell her that, Haruhiro called his comrade's name, never looking away from her eyes.

Merry furrowed her brow just a little.

It wasn't just Haruhiro. Moguzo, Yume, Shihoru, Ranta, they were all looking at Merry as well.

Merry noticed that, stiffening uneasily.

Seriously, that's not it. That's not what's happening here, Haruhiro thought.

"Merry. We had a priest in our party before. His name was Manato. Manato died. It might be more accurate to say that we let him die. We relied on Manato too much. Manato was a bit of a perfectionist, see. If we got injured, he would heal even the slightest scratch. He was a reliable healer and a tank as well. He was always on the front line with Moguzo. On top of that, he was our leader, so we were making Manato take on three roles by himself. I thought he was amazing. But we took that for granted. It wasn't easy on Manato. But he never let that show. So we never imagined how Manato was feeling. Now, all we can do is imagine it. Because Manato died. He's gone now."

It was probably occurring to Merry that she and Manato were similar. Quite possibly, she was assuming that Haruhiro had heard about her past and was telling her this because he knew that.

Haruhiro had been at a loss for what to do. He had heard the story from Hayashi. He knew roughly what happened long ago and had a rough idea why she had turned out like she had. Should he tell Merry that? But somehow, that felt wrong.

He knew what had happened and why things were like this. But Haruhiro didn't think people were that simple and he couldn't see into Merry's heart. He couldn't say that he understood her so easily. *The only one I can open up about is myself.*

"When we lost Manato, honestly, I thought we were finished. That it was impossible to go on without him. But even after Manato died, we were still alive. If you're alive, you can't just do nothing. For now, we have no choice but to keep ourselves fed as volunteer soldiers. Even if we are just trainees. So we invited you to join us. Because without a priest, we can't do anything at all, you know. That was the only reason. There wasn't anything else to it.

"But, me, Ranta, Yume, and Shihoru, we were the leftovers to begin with. Moguzo managed to get into a party with some guy named Kuzuoka, but he got thrown out and they even took all his money. With Manato bringing us together, it wasn't perfect, but we managed to become a party. We became comrades. That was all it was. But we became comrades. Sometimes things don't go so well and sometimes we get angry and fight with each other. But in the end, we're all still precious comrades. Rather than dwelling on why we became comrades, right now, the important thing is that we are comrades. As for me, Merry, I think of you as a comrade."

Merry said nothing. Aside from blinking occasionally, she just stared back into Haruhiro's eyes.

"...I feel the same." Shihoru raised her hand. "I think of you as a comrade."

"That's right," Yume grinned. "Merry-chan's a real cutie-pie, after all."

"I-I do." Moguzo was still wearing his barbut. "Of course I think of you as a comrade. It's reassuring, having you there."

Ranta snorted. "Yeah, me too, well, you know... The way I make a fuss over little injuries. It's not like I haven't reflected on it at all. Doing that kind of stuff... Anyway, you're a comrade, I guess?"

"I guess it'll snow tomorrow," Haruhiro said, looking up at the darkening sky. "Since Ranta says he's reflected on something. Hopefully, snow is the worst that happens."

"Even I reflect on things sometimes! My ability to learn is crazy high! After being with me all this time, you still haven't figured that much out?!"

"Well, setting that aside..."

"Hey, Haruhiro! Don't try to just move on! You're making me sad!"

"I think it's about time we settled on a goal. Our current objective, I mean—"

Haruhiro looked at Merry. Merry was the same as before. She just kept staring at Haruhiro.

It's probably not out of rejection. She's not rejecting us. I want to think that. That's enough for a start.

"—since it's been kind of vague up until now. We don't seem to be working hard to save enough to buy our badges; we seem to just be living day by day. I want to stop doing that and choose a direction to focus on."

"Our goal is to become billionaires! Also, world domination!" Ranta burst in.

Haruhiro ignored Ranta and continued on with what he was thinking. Aside from the noisy Ranta and silent Merry, they all agreed at once.

"I'm only interested in money and power," Ranta broke in. "I wanna be popular with girls, too, though. But, once I've got the money and the power, then the rest'll work itself out... Well, as a goal, that's a step before being a step before being many steps before that goal, but I guess it's fine, really."

Yume sighed. "Blah, blah, blah, blah, he just keeps goin' on."

You said it, Haruhiro thought as he looked Merry in the eye. "Merry, do you have an opinion?"

Merry cast her eyes downward.

She tucked her chin in a little. *Was that a nod?* He decided to take it as one.

"Will you join us for dinner?" he asked.

"No," Merry said, adding in a quieter voice, "...not yet."

"I see."

He couldn't expect it to happen right away. Even if he spent some of his precious time, something he could never know how much he had left, to take the next step, by the time he did, the end could still be right around the corner.

So of course, I want to be in a hurry. Considering that. Still, this was a step forward.

For Haruhiro and the others, who were still all inexperienced or worse, they had to move forward with little steps like this.

Just as Merry turned to go, she said clearly, "See you tomorrow."

For now, tomorrow would come.

20. The Little Pride of the Goblin Slayers

They woke before the bell rang at 6:00 and began to prepare. They ate whatever seemed good for breakfast, heading to the north gate for 8:00. They met up with Merry and headed to the Old City of Damuro. They still weren't done making their map of the Old City yet. They mapped out more of it while searching for goblins.

If it was just three goblins, they had gotten to the point where they could handle them without too much issue now. However, when the lightweight-class goblins that specialized in evasion were thrown into the mix, they had to be careful.

Sometime the goblins had ranged weapons as well. Mostly, it was crude shortbows. Their arrows were slow and didn't have much force, so they weren't that scary, but crossbows were dangerous. If they took a hit from them in the wrong place, crossbows could be instantly lethal. And heavily equipped goblins were sometimes strangely strong, so if they underestimated them, they would be in for trouble.

For groups of four or more, unless the conditions were exceptionally good, they let them go. Four goblins was about their limit.

If they saw a group of five, they pretended they hadn't. If there were five, six, or more goblins, it was safe to assume they were a family or a clan or some other group with their own territory. There were often similar groups nearby, so attacking one was like stepping on a tiger's tail.

Most of the goblins acting alone looked poor, but sometimes they had valuable items hidden in their goblin pouches. That made them a target.

Once a day, they would go to *that place*.

The goblins of the Old City fell into two broad categories: those that stayed in one place and didn't move around much and those that traveled from place to place. Those guys were the latter of the two. They were only in that place occasionally.

When the party saw them from a distance, they had a hard time just sitting still.

But, no. Don't rush it. It's not time yet, Haruhiro would think.

Currently, Haruhiro's was the only party using the Old City of Damuro as their hunting grounds. They didn't need to worry about anyone stealing them from them. Now was the time to build their strength.

When they returned to Alterna, though not every day, they would go to Sherry's Tavern.

Not to do anything in particular. They just drank and talked. Merry didn't do much talking, but that was a million times better than Ranta, who talked far too much.

The other volunteer soldiers sometimes poked fun at them, saying, "Hey, Goblin Slayers," or "How's it hanging, Goblin Slayers?" or, "Is

Damuro fun, widdle Goblin Slayers?" Actually, any time they went to the tavern, they could count on being called that once or twice.

Ranta would say, "Oh, shut up!" but if they got mad each and every time, there would be no end to it.

Haruhiro didn't mind the name that much actually. He thought it didn't have such a bad ring to it.

Goblin Slayers. It's nice. I quite like it. If they're calling us that, we'll become the best goblin slayers in the Volunteer Soldier Corps.

Day after day, it was goblins, goblins, goblins. Goblins goblins goblins.

At first, all goblin faces looked the same to him, but now Haruhiro could tell them apart pretty well. The vast majority were male and females were exceptionally rare, he noticed. According to Merry, most of the females were kept in the New City by upper-class goblins as wives.

"*There's* one harem I'm not at all jealous of..." Ranta said.

"Even goblin girls wouldn't take you, Ranta."

"You moron, Haruhiro, don't you know? I'm hot stuff even with the gobs! Don't take the Wandering King of Hotness Ranta so lightly!"

"You say that, King of Hotness, but Yume sees you talkin' to girls in the tavern and gettin' ignored, y'know."

"Th-that's just...well...you know...even an invincible guy like me has that happen occasionally..."

"The King of Hotness gets shot down too, huh? Even though he's supposed to be the hot, hot King of Hotness."

"Quit saying 'King of Hotness' over and over! Besides, if those idiots can't understand my charm, they aren't worth snot! The people who get it really get it! Merry, if you were forced to choose one of the three of us, who would it be? Totally me, right?"

"If I *had* to, Moguzo-kun."

"Wha...?!"

"Huh? M-Me...?" Moguzo opened his eyes wide; he seemed more astonished than shy.

"Hmm..." Haruhiro looked back and forth from Merry to Moguzo.

Yume said, "Hoh!" She seemed impressed.

Shihoru looked at Merry, blinking.

"Wha, Wh-wh-wh-wh-wh-whargh!" Ranta bit his tongue stuttering over his words. "—Wh-why?! Not me, but *Moguzo* of all people?! That choice is unbelievable, you know?!"

Merry was calm and self-possessed. "He's big and lovable."

"...You chose him by size... W-well, I can't compete there... There's nothing I can do to beat him there... Still, to think I would lose... And to stupid Moguzooooooo... Dammiiiiiiiit!"

"Too bad, huh, King of Hotness? Huh?"

"I told you, stop calling me King of Hotness, Tiny Tits! You're just rubbing salt in the wound..."

Haruhiro was a little shocked about losing to Moguzo, too. It seemed Merry cared about more than just a pretty face. Perhaps because she saw her own gorgeous face in the mirror every day, she wasn't that concerned about other people's faces. But, no, neither Haruhiro or Ranta had especially attractive faces, so that wasn't the issue, either.

Haruhiro was the epitome of mediocrity when it came to his looks and abilities, but after this many days in a row of facing goblins, he had confidence in his goblin-fighting abilities, at least.

But still, don't get cocky, Haruhiro reminded himself. *I'm not special like Renji, Manato, or Merry. When Manato was alive, he carried me like a baby. Now, I'm taking my first steps as a goblin slayer. If a mediocre guy like me gets careless, I'll definitely fail. Even if I don't get careless, it's still dangerous. So at the very least, I can't let my guard down.*

On good days, he could make over ten silver in a day and even on bad days, he could make around two silver. Merry was living in a pretty good lodging house apparently, but Haruhiro and the others were still living in the terrible but cheap volunteer soldier lodging house. They kept their spending on food to within twelve copper a day, investing the money they had managed to save towards the party as a whole.

One of the places those investments went was towards equipment. The other was towards skills.

In Haruhiro's case, for defense he bought a second-hand chest protector and a belly band, as well as hand and leg armor. They were all made with tanned leather, so they were light and wouldn't encumber him. The boost to defense was little more than a placebo, but it was important that it made him feel safer.

For weapons, he could go to a sharpener to improve the edge on them and he was already used to using the ones he had. So for the moment, he had no intent of buying new ones. If he had money, it was better spent on equipment for Moguzo.

Moguzo was trying to assemble the full set of plated armor he wanted. Normally, plated armor was made to order, but if they ordered it from an armor blacksmith, even at its cheapest, they would be looking at paying not just a few gold coins, but over ten. Of course, that was out of reach, so they'd find something cheap used and have an armor blacksmith resize it. Even then, they were still in the realm of spending tens of silver on each of the parts.

Moguzo currently had the cuirass, backplate, spaulders, and vambraces, as well as half greaves, which covered just the front of the shins, and he wore all of this over a mail hauberk. For the helmet, he was still using his barbut. His sword was also still the bastard sword he received from his guild. It was getting damaged and he needed to replace it soon or something bad would happen.

Ranta bought a chainmail shirt, wearing leather armor over top of it for some reason. His leather armor had the crest of Skullhell on it, and he seemed awfully proud of it. He'd fallen in love with a weird helmet that looked like an upside-down bucket called a heaume, so he wore that, too. For weapons, he had found a nice-looking longsword in the market once and bought it on impulse so Ranta was flat broke for a time.

What an idiot, Haruhiro thought.

Yume had gotten a tanned leather coat and pants and they looked pretty good on her. With a hooded cloak over top, she was starting to look like a serious hunter.

For Shihoru, the mage's robe and hat she had been given by her guild were starting to come apart and get holes in them, so she'd bought new ones. She still had the same staff. Apparently, unlike the other schools, the shadow magic Shihoru was mainly focused on, Darsh Magic, wasn't affected by the qualities of the staff she used. In fact, she said she could use it even without a staff.

Shihoru had also learned a new spell, Sleepy Shade.

Haruhiro had learned the Sneaking and Swat skills from Barbara-sensei, while Moguzo had learned War Cry. Ranta had learned Avoid and Exhaust. Yume had learned Quick-eye, bringing up her accuracy with the bow and, with the Pit Rat skill, she had learned to swiftly dodge enemy blows.

Merry was already a priest whose power and experience was several levels above Haruhiro and the others, so the party's abilities were definitely improving. The problem was, by how much?

In the Old City of Damuro, there was a place they called the smithy. It was half-collapsed, but with what looked to be a furnace and anvil, that roofless building still had a number of traces suggesting it had once been a smithy.

In that building, there was now a group of five goblins.

They had come to the smithy a number of times before now, even taking a break and eating lunch there. Up until this point, they had never spotted a single goblin.

It seemed there was a great disparity between the goblins of the New City and the ones that made the Old City their home. Goblins from the New City that lost power struggles or were otherwise ostracized would be forced to come to the Old City, apparently.

These goblins must have been newcomers that drifted here from the New City that way.

Newcomers would first choose a place and, if they were a large group, they would try to establish their territory. The five new goblins had likely chosen the smithy as their base of operations.

After scouting, Haruhiro returned to the spot a little ways away from the smithy where the others were waiting.

"Let's try it," he proposed. "There are five of them. The one in chainmail's got a crossbow. The rest are all in leather armor, one with a spear, one with a short sword and buckler, one with a hand ax and one with a sword. The crossbow gob is probably the boss and the four other gobs follow its orders. They're strong enemies, but it will be a good test."

"Sounds interesting." Ranta licked his lips and grabbed the bucket helmet—the heaume—that sat beside him. "Let's do this thing. I'm just about to cross forty-one vices. Once I get there, I can summon my demon Zodiac-kun at noon. Heh heh heh..."

Yume showered Ranta with a cold look. "What will Zodiac-kun be able to do for us this time? Right now, all he does is whisper in the enemy's ears *occasionally*, gettin' in their way."

"Don't let this shock you, okay? Now, the even more powered-up Zodiac-kun will, incredibly, pull the enemy's arms or legs once in a while, disrupting them for us! When it feels like it."

Shihoru looked exasperated. "...In the end, it's all on its whim."

"Oh, and one more thing. It only does the leg-and-arm-pulling thing starting in the evening. Until evening, well, you know. It'll do the whisper attack, tell me if there are enemies and tell demon jokes. —When it feels like it."

Merry gave a nasal laugh. "That's way too capricious."

"Oh, shove it." Ranta put on the heaume and was now dressed bucket-style. "What do any of you know about Zodiac-kun? You don't have to understand. I must be the only one who understands Zodiac-kun. Heh. Dread knights are lonely. Or aloof, rather?"

"I-I'll..." Moguzo gave a big nod. "...pull as many of them to me as I can. Two, definitely. If it comes down to it, I'll intimidate them with War Cry."

Shihoru hugged her staff, tucking in her chin. "I'll start by putting one of them to sleep with magic."

"Yeah," Haruhiro nodded. "Okay, then—Shihoru will put the

crossbow gob to sleep. It will make a big difference whether you hit it the first time or not."

"...I know. Leave it to me."

"When Yume's done takin' her preemptive shot, she'll do her best to take one of them in melee combat."

"I'll keep getting behind them and if a chance comes along, I'll finish one. Merry, you—" Haruhiro glanced over and Merry gave a silent nod.

It felt like she spoke even less now than before, but if he asked her something, she'd answer and she did what she was supposed to and did it well. While her style wasn't like what Hayashi had described, Merry must have learned from her big... much too big... mistake and changed the way she did things. She never went too easy on them, but Merry was a priest they could trust.

Now if she would just smile once every few days, it would be perfect, he thought.

"This is a dry run." Haruhiro looked to each of his comrades, stretching out his right hand. Ranta, Moguzo, Yume, and Shihoru placed their right hands on top of Haruhiro's. Then Merry did the same. They weren't that far from the smithy, so Haruhiro spoke quietly.

"Fighto," he said in a whisper and they all responded as one.

"Ippatsu."

Haruhiro led the way, bringing Yume and Shihoru with him. Ranta, Merry, and Moguzo followed after.

Lowering his hips and loosening his knees, Haruhiro used Sneaking to move without making footsteps. Not being thieves, Yume and Shihoru couldn't hope to imitate him, but they could follow him, stepping where he stepped. Even that made a great change.

They moved from the shadow of a broken building into the shadow of the remains of a building. Following a wall that seemed ready to crumble any second, they stuck close to a mountain of rubble. Sleepy Shadow had a range of roughly twelve meters. It would reach from here.

The smithy only had two walls, which were full of holes, left standing. The others had almost fully collapsed. From where they now stood, they had visual confirmation of four of the five goblins, so they could choose their targets as they pleased.

When Haruhiro gave the signal with his hands, Yume and Shihoru poked their faces out from the rubble.

Yume readied her bow and nocked an arrow, closing her eyes and breathing deeply. Her eyes opened. She had activated Quick-eye. Apparently, using special eye exercises and self-hypnosis improved her ability to see at a distance, even improving her kinetic vision on top of that. That was the true nature of the Quick-eye skill.

Shihoru drew elemental sigils with her staff and began chanting in a low voice.

"...Ohm, rel, ect, krom, darsh."

A black, mist-like elemental flew forth from the tip of her staff. It wasn't as fast as Shadow Beat, so if the enemy detected it, it would be pretty easy to avoid.

It's going. It should be good. It's going. It's gone, thought Haruhiro.

The shadow elemental attacked the crossbow gob's face, forcing its way into the gob's nose, ears, and mouth. It started to stagger. The spear gob, who had been sitting against the wall, noticed and went to jump up. That was when Yume let her arrow fly.

The arrow buried itself in the spear gob's shoulder. The spear gob, previously standing, fell back on its rump. Haruhiro shouted out.

"—Moguzo! Ranta!"

Moguzo and Ranta bellowed loudly and charged at the smithy. The crossbow gob collapsed on the ground.

It was sleeping. It was deeper than normal sleep, but if someone pinched or kicked it hard, it would still wake up. They needed to clear out the other gobs to keep them from shaking the crossbow gob awake.

Haruhiro and Yume chased after them, as did Moguzo and Ranta.

Moguzo bellowed, "Thanks!" to intimidate the hand ax gob with his Rage Blow that they called the Thanks Slash and Ranta stabbed at the sword gob with Anger. He missed, though.

Moguzo paid no heed to the off-balance hand ax gob, attacking the buckler gob instead. When the buckler gob backed away, blocking the bastard sword with its buckler, Moguzo swiftly turned back to hand ax gob, slashing at it.

Moguzo intended to take on both the hand ax gob and buckler gob by himself. Ranta was trading blows with the sword gob. Yume charged towards the spear gob that she had already wounded with an arrow.

Haruhiro glanced back to Shihoru and Merry quickly. Merry was surveying the battle situation with a frighteningly serious look in her eyes, her priest's staff at the ready. If any enemy were to approach Shihoru, she'd be there to intercept them. As a mage, Shihoru was practically defenseless, so it was reassuring to have Merry protecting her. *Not that I intend to make Merry go to the trouble.*

"I'll take it down!" Haruhiro shouted. He once again checked the positions of his comrades and the gobs. *Which one? Choose a target. That one. The hand ax gob.*

Neither walking or running, Haruhiro kept his posture low, moving across the ground as if he were sliding. It was the same idea as Sneaking. Soon, he had gotten behind the hand ax gob. That was the moment it happened.

His vision zoomed in on the ax gob's scrawny back and he saw something like a light. It was only something that was *like* light. It probably wasn't an actual light. Regardless, it drew a colorless line, indicating a point in the ax gob's back.

What that was, Haruhiro had no idea. It didn't happen every time or even frequently, but recently, once on a rare occasion, without any reasoning behind it, he would think, *Right there.*

Haruhiro moved his dagger along the line that had suddenly appeared and just as suddenly disappeared. The blade went in incredibly easily and it brushed against *something*.

Right here, thought Haruhiro. By the time he thought that, he had already pierced through it.

When he pulled out the dagger, the hand ax gob gave a short groan and collapsed. It was already dead.

Having lost what could be called its partner, the buckler gob stood on the balls of its feet, taking one... no, a half step back. Immediately, Moguzo cried out and struck the buckler with all his might, knocking it away and then continuing to charge at the plain gob, who was no longer the buckler gob. The gob flailed around with its short sword, but there was no need to bother dodging.

Moguzo's armor deflected the sword. He pushed the gob down, hefted his bastard sword high and with a "Hungh!" he brought it down on the gob's skull.

It split open.

Three left to go.

"Tch! Exhaust!" Ranta clicked his tongue, leaping backwards at an incredible speed.

Exhaust was a skill that used special movements to instantaneously open a wide gap between the user and their opponent. The sword gob chased after Ranta, as if being sucked in. That had been Ranta's trap. Breaking into a smirk as he backed away, he thrust his sharp longsword forward.

"—Avoid!"

The sword gob couldn't stop its momentum to avoid the blow.

Its throat.

Ranta's longsword impaled the sword gob's throat. Ranta gave his longsword a twist, kicking the goblin to the ground. "Bwa ha ha ha ha ha!" he laughed loudly. Shihoru's chanting was half drowned out by that loud... no, that stupid laugh.

"—Ohm, rel, ect, vel, darsh!" It was Shadow Beat. The elemental was launched from the tip of Shihoru's staff, slamming into the spear gob.

As the hyper-vibrations caused the spear gob's entire body to shudder, Yume closed in. First her machete knocked away its spear and without missing a beat, she said, "Hah!" and slashed at the base of its neck. Unable to dodge fully, the spear gob shrieked as it took a deep cut to the shoulder. At that point, the battle had already been decided.

"Thanks...!" Moguzo stepped in powerfully, slamming the Thanks Slash into the spear gob.

"...We can do it. Like this," Haruhiro nodded. "Time to carry out the plan."

"Finally, huh," Ranta walked over to the sleeping crossbow gob, swinging down his longsword. Would there ever come a day when that theatrically cruel smile suited him? "Well, whatever. This is the end. Not just for these gobs. —for *those* guys, too."

21. Paper-thin Innocence

But things were never that easy.

Haruhiro, who had gone to scout out *that place* full of spirit, couldn't help but gulp. Then "...You're kidding me, right?" he whispered. He hadn't anticipated this at all. "—There are more of them now...?"

On the second floor, which was more like an open balcony of that broken-down, two-floor building made out of stone, sat a goblin in plate armor trying to look important. On the first floor, wearing a helmet and chainmail, was a member of a larger subspecies of goblin, a hobgoblin.

This much he had expected. The problem wasn't inside the building, it was the two goblins outside, both in chainmail and helmets. They each carried a shield and spear with another sword at their waist. They looked like guards.

The plate armor gob wasn't sitting on the floor. It was kneeling on top of a chair. That chair hadn't been there before. It must have gone to procure it from somewhere.

He dreaded to think it, but could the plate armor gob be increasing the number of minions it had, scheming to expand its power? He wouldn't know unless he asked. Well no, even if he asked, he wouldn't be able to find out, but if that was what was happening, it meant trouble.

Haruhiro went back to his comrades to report in. "—So, we aren't looking at two enemies. It's four now. Also, this is only my prediction, but there may be more of them soon."

"Four of them..." Merry furrowed her brow, casting her eyes down.

Yume puffed out her cheeks with a "Murrgh," while Shihoru hung her head and sighed. Moguzo lightly tapped the top of his barbut.

"What, what?" Ranta scoffed. "Are you all getting scared now, guys? You're hopeless. As servants to the great Ranta, you should be ashamed."

"Since when were we your..." Haruhiro started to say, but stopped himself. "Whatever, doesn't matter."

"Yes, it does. Don't stop things halfway. You're supposed to push back there. Come up with a witty retort. You're no fun. You're just Haruhiro, so don't take away the one thing I live for."

Haruhiro ignored Ranta, looking to Moguzo, Yume, Shihoru, and Merry in turn. "Now, if we assume that I'm right and there will be more of them coming, we need to make a decision. Not right here and now, maybe, but in the near future. Do we give up or do we strike quickly? As for me, I don't want to give up. Besides, as we are now, I'm sure we can handle four of them."

Merry fixed her eyes on Haruhiro. It was a gaze that would not permit him to look away. "What's your basis for that?"

"Moguzo's defense has improved considerably. Because it's

hardened, he doesn't need to focus on defending. That's led to an increase in his attacking power, as well. Shihoru can incapacitate one of them with her magic. We can rely on Yume to actually hit things with her arrows now, too, and for short periods I can handle an enemy in combat using Swat. Also, we have you, Merry."

"Hey, what about me? Isn't my name going to come up? Isn't that strange? Well?" interjected Ranta, to no response.

"As for me..." Merry cast her gaze down and to the side. "...if you're going to rely on me so much, that troubles me. I'm...a priest who let her comrades die, after all."

"We let our priest die. That's why we never want to let another person die. Ever. No matter what happens. It's probably the same for you, Merry. I believe in you." Haruhiro said.

Merry didn't respond. She bit her lip, holding something back. Yume and Shihoru laid their hands on Merry's shoulders.

"Just gonna say this," Ranta pointed to himself with his thumb, "but I'm immortal, so I won't die even if they kill me. Don't waste your time worrying over silly things."

Merry looked up, loosening her lips a little and narrowing her eyes slightly.

Had that just been a smile?

It was so reserved, Haruhiro couldn't be sure. But he thought it probably had been. Haruhiro regretted that it had vanished so quickly. *I should have burned the vision of it into my memory,* he thought.

"Got it," Merry nodded. "I'll never let a comrade die again. I'll protect your lives, so you can feel safe."

"Good," Haruhiro stuck out his right hand and everyone placed their own right hands on top of his.

"Fighto, ippatsu!"

After their usual rallying cry, Merry cocked her head to the side. "...I've always found it odd, but why is it *fighto, ippatsu?*"

The other five laughed a little. Then they focused themselves, going over the plan.

Going over the plan. Yes. They were going over it.

Haruhiro and the others had been preparing for this day. There was no need to formulate a plan from scratch. They would need to make adjustments to account for the additional enemies, but the main thing they needed to do was keep the plate armor gob and hobgob, which were incomparably stronger than the other goblins, in check. This was their highest priority.

They would finish the two guard gobs as quickly as possible then take down their main targets. They had discussed strategies for how to overcome the plate armor gob and hobgob over the course of many planning sessions. They could do this. They would definitely win.

Like always, Haruhiro led Yume and Shihoru in first. Ranta, Moguzo, and Merry followed behind at a distance.

The first trial was getting within twelve meters, the approximate range of Sleepy Shadow. There was a wall that provided perfect cover until they were fifteen meters away, but past that point would be difficult. Still, through studying the layout, they had learned that if they circled around to the other side, there were the ruins of a building within ten meters of the two-floor building that they could just barely hide themselves in.

This was the place. Here was where the attack would start from.

When Haruhiro gave the signal with his hands, Yume readied her bow and activated Quick-eye while Shihoru grasped her staff and steadied her breathing.

It's finally time. We'll take them down. The plate armor gob and hobgob. They killed Manato. I've done my best not to think of this as revenge, as avenging him. That's because I felt like hatred would muddy my thinking and make my hands go astray. This isn't about a grudge: they're enemies. Strong enemies. A wall we need to transcend.

Haruhiro poked his head out from the ruins. "—!" He didn't so much suck his breath in as stop breathing. He hurriedly pulled his head back in. It had been looking. The plated armor gob was looking his way.

"...Were we noticed?" But why? Had they detected them before? Had he just been found? Or was it a coincidence? Had it just happened to be looking this way and then its eyes met with Haruhiro's? He didn't know and that wasn't what was important.

Haruhiro stuck his head out once more, immediately lowering it again. He breathed heavily. The plate armor gob had a crossbow and it was aiming this way.

"...Wh-what do we do?" Yume loosened up on her bowstring. Shihoru's face had gone stiff and very pale.

Did Ranta and the others, who were at a spot not far away, understand the situation? They were hiding in the shadows, and Haruhiro couldn't see them from here, so he didn't know.

What should I do? Haruhiro thought. *What am I going to do? Retreat? No, not an option. The plate armor gob shouted something. That was an order. I'm sure the hobgob and guard gobs'll be coming to attack us. We can't retreat. We have to do this. The problem is that crossbow. If we get hit, one of us could die.*

"Leave this to Yume."

"—Huh?"

Before he could stop her, Yume left her bow on the ground and jumped out from the ruins.

The plate armor gob fired its crossbow. Yume curled herself into a ball, rolling forward at an incredible speed.

Pit Rat. It was a skill where she moved like those rats they had encountered in the forest, avoiding attacks as she advanced.

Did Yume manage to avoid the arrow? It looked like she had.

Haruhiro tapped Shihoru on the shoulder. "Magic!"

"R-Right!" Shihoru leaned out from the ruins, drawing elemental sigils with her staff and chanting a spell. "Ohm, rel, ect, krom, darsh...!"

A black, mist-like elemental flew towards the plate armor gob. The hobgob had only picked up its club, not left the building, but the guard gobs were closing in on them. Still, if she could just put the plate armor gob to sleep—

"Ah!" Haruhiro raised his voice. The plate armor gob had jumped down from the second floor. The shadow elemental passed through the spot where it had been before, dissipating and vanishing.

We've botched this. Botched it badly. This is no good. No good at all. No. That's not true. We can make up for it. Don't panic.

Haruhiro drew his dagger. "I'll face them! Shihoru, you get over to Merry's side!"

Shihoru responded, "Right!" again.

Ranta and Moguzo came out of the shadows. Yume used Pit Rat again, avoiding a guard gob's spear. The other guard gob came at Haruhiro.

Where are the plate armor gob and hobgob? Damn. I don't have time to check. The spear. The guard gob's spear.

Haruhiro struck aside the incoming spear with his dagger. If he hit it hard enough, the attack would go aside and with some luck, he might damage the weapon, make the gob drop it or knock it off balance. That was what the thief fighting skill Swat did, but the guard gob was pretty strong. No matter how much he hit its spear with his dagger, it kept thrusting at him. This was no average gob.

"I'll take both!" Moguzo shouted out.

No way... was he planning to take on the plate armor gob and hobgob at the same time? That was crazy.

However, when it came to both the plate armor gob and hobgob, only Moguzo could fight them properly. That's why they had planned to neutralize the plate armor gob first.

That had been the party's plan. You could even call it the root of the plan. It had fallen apart so easily.

Maybe they should have run away without a second thought. It was too late now. Regretting not doing it wouldn't change anything.

Haruhiro pulled back while using Swat. Back and back. It looked like Ranta and Yume were handling the other guard gob. Shihoru launched another Sleepy Shadow, but this one hit the hobgob, not the plate armor gob.

The hobgob staggered on its feet like it was going to fall asleep. Before it could, the plate armor gob used the flat of its sword to slap it in the butt and wake it up.

That one knows about magic. It knows what we're capable of.

"Yume!" Ranta shouted angrily. "If you just keep running around, we'll never kill this thing! Hit back, you dolt!"

"Oh, shush! You're the last one Yume wants to be hearin' say that—" Yume must have tried to escape with Pit Rat again, but she was a little too slow. Besides which, the guard gob may have been getting used to Yume's movements. "—Urkh!"

The guard gob's spear grazed Yume's right shoulder. No, it gouged into it.

"Why, you...! How dare you do that to Yume?!" Ranta threw himself at the gob. He jumped in, swinging his longword down diagonally. "Hatred...!"

"—Gahh!" The guard gob guarded with its shield. Then, holding its spear so it was shorter, it thrust. It was blocked. It thrust again.

"Oh, wha, whoa?!" Ranta managed to barely parry its repeated attacks with his longsword, backing away with those unique movements he used. "—Exhaust! Bring it! ...Huh? Why aren't you coming after me?!"

"Because you're too obvious!" Haruhiro spat the words as he Swatted, Swatted, and Swatted again.

Merry chanted a prayer. "O Light, may Lumiaris' divine protection be upon you... Heal."

Unlike Cure, Heal didn't require the priest to hold their palm over the wound. It could heal people at a distance and it affected the whole body. It was a spell Manato hadn't learned.

Yume was right-handed and the wound was in her right shoulder. Merry must have determined the wound was serious enough to heal right away.

Now Yume was able to return to the front line, but Moguzo was in danger. He was managing to avoid the hobgob's club somehow, but the plate armor gob's sword kept hitting him hard.

There was no time to waste. Haruhiro needed to take out one of the guard gobs and go help Moguzo or things were going to turn sour.

Isn't there anything I can use? A plan of some kind?

He had to do more than just think: he needed to keep Swatting the guard gob's spear. He was running out of breath and his hands were going numb, but if he missed once, it would all be over. He felt like he might start to panic. *Bear with it. I have to bear with it. Bear with it, and then what? What will I do?*

"Haru!"

Someone was calling his name. *She's never called me Haru before, but that's Merry. It was Merry's voice.*

I can't afford to look over there. But she called me. It probably means she wants me to go over to her.

That was what Haruhiro did. While continuing to Swat, he headed over towards Merry and Shihoru. He lured the guard gob in. *This is what you wanted, right? It's fine, right?*

When Merry shouted, "Switch!" Haruhiro jumped to the side. Merry moved up, blocking the guard gob's spear with her priest's staff. No, she did more than just block it. "—Hit Back!" she cried.

For a moment, it looked like the spear had been knocked away by her staff, but that wasn't it. She had used the recoil from its attack to jab the guard gob in the chest. The guard gob groaned and backed away.

Now. This is our only chance.

Sensing Haruhiro's intent, Merry continued her onslaught against the guard gob. Since the guard gob had shifted its stance to focus entirely on defense, she couldn't break through, but it was still enough.

Haruhiro got behind the guard gob.

Let me see it, he prayed. *Let me see the light. No good, huh. I can't see it. But I don't have time to be disappointed.*

Haruhiro rammed his dagger into the guard gob's back with the force of a tackle. He managed to pierce the chainmail, but it was a shallow hit.

The guard gob cried, "Gugyahhhh!" and thrashed around wildly. In the spur of the moment, Haruhiro threw his left arm around the guard gob's neck and pulled his dagger halfway out. Then he stabbed it back in again. He pumped the dagger in and out—in and out—repeatedly. Until the guard gob went limp, he stabbed it again and again with reckless abandon.

"...You're a lifesaver, Merry!" Haruhiro shoved the now-motionless guard gob away and looked around, his shoulders heaving with labored breaths. Ranta and Yume were still unable to kill the other guard gob.

"—Hungh!" Moguzo blocked the hobgob's club using his bastard sword. He staggered.

"Moguzo!" Haruhiro dashed towards him, but there was no way he could make it in time. The plate armor gob leapt at Moguzo with a cackle, not so much trying to cut him with its sword as to slug him with it. It went for the head.

Sparks flew between Moguzo's barbut and the plate armor gob's sword. Even with a helmet on, he couldn't shrug that off. Moguzo reeled from the blow, but managed to hold firm and, with a cry and a swing of his bastard sword, he made the plate armor gob and hobgob back away.

Moguzo's breathing was ragged. He wasn't bleeding, but when he took off his armor, there were going to be bruises everywhere. Obviously, this was hard on him. And yet, Moguzo swung his bastard sword around with a hearty laugh.

"This? This is nothing! Me? I'm fine! Wah ha ha!"

He was acting like an entirely different person. Things really were bad, after all. There was no way Moguzo could hold out on his own.

Should I support him? But Haruhiro's dagger probably couldn't pierce plate armor nor could it deal a fatal blow to the large hobgob. It may have been practically impossible.

"—Ranta, help Moguzo! I'll handle that one!"

"Hmph! Time for the real star to do his thing, huh?" Ranta immediately ran over with a hop, skip, and a jump, thrusting his sword at the plate armor gob. "—Anger...!"

"Keh...!" The plate armor gob easily knocked his longsword aside, but it looked like its focus had thankfully shifted from Moguzo to Ranta.

"—Oh! Oh! Oh?!" Ranta was on the receiving end of a one-sided onslaught. In no time, he was stuck purely on the defensive.

Hang in there, Ranta. Don't die.

Haruhiro looked around and thought, *Things are a little easier for Moguzo now, but this guard gob needs to go down already or we'll slowly get ground down. The way it's holding its shield firmly, it looks like it's focusing on defense. Yume can't tank for me, so if I want to get behind it—*

While Haruhiro was thinking, the guard gob turned towards him and threw its spear—

Wait, huh? This way? Me? No way?!

"Oh, whoa!" He tried to twist out of the way, but the spear took a piece out of Haruhiro's flank and buried itself in the ground. Almost doubling over, he tried touching his side and it was all wet. The pain was great enough that he groaned despite himself, but it wasn't anything he couldn't get past.

Merry called out, "Haru?!"

She sounded a little worried so even though it seemed stupid, he was a little happy.

"—I'm fine! We've got to take that guy down...!" he cried.

"I'll do it!" Shihoru said, charging at the goblin.

Hold on, what are you doing? What are you doing?! Haruhiro thought.

"Wha—" Merry was speechless as she chased after Shihoru. The guard gob, which had drawn the sword that was at its hip, noticed Shihoru.

While Shihoru was running, she started to draw elemental sigils. "Ohm, rel, ect, vel, darsh...!"

With a *vwong* sound, the black mass of seaweed launched out of the end of her staff.

In that moment... *Oh, right,* Haruhiro realized.

Shadow Beat wasn't as slow as Sleepy Shadow, but it still wasn't fast enough that the enemy couldn't dodge it. In that case, why not fire it from up close? Even if the speed was the same, the closer she was, the harder it would be to dodge. Basically, Shihoru had done what she did to increase the odds Shadow Beat would hit and it looked like it had been worth it.

"Fogh...!" The guard gob was hit right in the face by the shadow elemental. Its entire body began to convulse.

Yume dashed in and swung her machete. "—Diagonal Cross...!"

Yume's hard slash knocked the guard gob's shield away, cutting deeply into its right arm. Thanks to that, even once it recovered from the shock caused by the hyper-vibrations, the guard gob wouldn't be able to use its sword properly.

"Hah, hah, hah…!" As if seeing her opportunity, Yume attacked and attacked. She attacked incessantly without stopping to breathe.

Haruhiro easily slipped behind the gob and though he couldn't see that light, he handled it the same as he had the last one. Ramming his dagger into the guard gob's back, he pulled it out a little then stabbed it in again. Wrapping his arm around its neck, he repeatedly stabbed it. He hadn't felt anything when he'd done the first one, but this time he felt bad.

This is a cruel way to kill them. Even though it made him sick to his stomach, Haruhiro didn't stop. *You guys might have killed me the same way. Sorry, but we're both in the same position here.*

When he finished off the second gob, he felt exhausted. His side ached, but he didn't have time to whine about it. *Finally. Finally, the time is here.*

Stressing his abdominal muscles, Haruhiro raised his voice. "We're almost there! Let's show that everything we've done hasn't been in vain!"

I know it's weird to say about my own words, but who are we going to show? he thought. *Manato's gone. What we've done hasn't been in vain? Really? Maybe I just want to think that. I wish I could have come up with a cooler line. I want to get to the point where I can. I don't want this to be the end. It's not that I especially* want *to be a volunteer soldier, but I want to have a tomorrow. I want to live. I don't want to die. At the very least, I don't want to die yet. Manato, you must have felt the same. You can't have been satisfied. You should have been able to do so many more things. Since I'm lucky enough to still be alive, I'm gonna live. I'll move forward. I'll find a tomorrow with everyone else. But in order to do that, we have to win. We need to take these guys down.*

"I'll take the hobgob first!" Haruhiro ran in, eyeing the hobgob's back. Yume looked like she was planning to attack from the side.

With a "Hunngh! Hunngh!" Moguzo gave the hobgob a powerful two-hit combo. The first strike was deflected by its club but the second slammed into the hobgob's left shoulder. While it didn't split through the chainmail, the hobgob groaned "Obohh!" taking its left hand off the club it had been holding with both hands.

It's feeling it.

"Pile in on it!" Haruhiro cried.

Then it happened.

It's the plate armor gob.

"Gyahhhgah...!" The plate armor gob left Ranta behind, swinging at Moguzo. Getting in close, it swung down diagonally at Moguzo.

No way, was that Rage Blow? You're just a damn goblin.

Moguzo blocked with his bastard sword and they locked blades. However, attacking from that position was one of Moguzo's specialties. With a "Hungh...!" Moguzo tried to catch the plate armor gob's sword and use Wind. When he did, the plate armor gob sprung backwards, turning to slash at Ranta immediately.

"—Oh...!" Caught completely by surprise, there was a loud echo from Ranta's bucket helmet being struck. In rapid succession, the plate armor gob followed up with a thrust, an upwards slash and then another downwards slash. Ranta could only shout, "Ah! Hey! Whoa!" and run away. He was so pressed that he couldn't even use Exhaust to retreat.

This is bad. He's going to get killed at this rate.

"Ohm, rel, ect, vel, darsh...!"

Shihoru was the one who saved Ranta. It was Shadow Beat. The black ball of seaweed struck the plate armor gob's shoulder. The plate armor gob cried out and shuddered for only a moment, but in that time Ranta was able to put some distance between them and catch his breath.

"...Tch! I didn't need your help!"

"We need a decisive blow...!" Haruhiro held his side. *The pain's too much to ignore. Maybe because I'm rushing too much and can't focus. Look at Shihoru. She looks like she's having a hard time. She's pretty tired. She used an exhausting spell like Sleepy Shade twice near the beginning and just now she used Shadow Beat for the second time. How many more times can she use magic? Besides, if I recall, Sleepy Shadow doesn't work well on targets that are excited. Shadow Beat doesn't seem like it can strike the decisive blow, either. In which case, there's only one thing left. We'll decide this. Right here. Before this drags on and we fall apart, we'll kill the hobgob.*

"Moguzo, do it...!"

"Mhm!" Moguzo immediately braced himself with both feet and roared. "Ruohhhhhhhhhhhhngh...!"

He was loud enough to make their skin crawl. It was the warrior's War Cry. If someone heard it at close range without being ready for it, it was guaranteed to shock them. It wouldn't just shake them up, but also make them shudder in fear. That was what happened to the hobgob. It went rigid, as if suddenly paralyzed. It would recover quickly, but every second was precious, precious time.

Yume slammed her machete into the hobgob's waist area. "Brush Clearer!"

Moguzo took a step back, then, stepping into it, he let loose a slashing attack with his full weight behind it. "Thaaaaaaanks...!"

With a terrifying sound, Moguzo's bastard sword dug into the hobgob's shoulder. It probably reached the collarbone.

"—Fugohh...!" The hobgob dropped to one knee but it tried to stand up.

For as long as it's still breathing, we can't let our guards down. We won't.

With a "Take that!" Haruhiro landed a flying kick on the back of the hobgob's head.

With the hobgob reeling again from that blow, Moguzo unleashed a flurry of blows on it. "Ungh! Ngh! Hungh! Gah, gah, gah! Ahhhhh! Uwahhhhhhhhhhhhhhhhhhhhhhhh...!"

It's not easy. People can die so quickly, but taking a life isn't easy.

It was gruesome to watch, but Haruhiro was part of this. He couldn't look away just because it was horrible.

When the hobgob stopped twitching, Moguzo fell to all fours. His back was heaving, his breaths labored. It was more than just fatigue. He must have hurt all over.

"H-H-Hurr...!" Ranta screamed. "Hurry and s-s-save me! Hu... rry!"

When they looked, Ranta was bent over backwards parrying the plate armor gob's sword. He was unsteady on his feet.

He's at his limit. Actually, he's probably well past it.

"Nice going! Good job, Ranta!"

"Yeah! Yume'll praise you just this once!"

Haruhiro and Yume tried to catch the plate armor gob in a pincer attack. However, the plate armor gob struck a blow against Ranta and then ran.

It's running. Running fast. Does it plan to escape? No. That's not it. Shihoru is over that way.

"Ah...?!" Shihoru's eyes went wide and she thrust her staff out in front of her.

She's scared stiff. She can't fight like that. But there's no need to worry.

"Out of the way!" Merry got in front of Shihoru, putting her priest's staff and body at an angle.

It was Prepare. A defensive stance skill.

The plate armor gob lifted its sword to swing. Would Merry knock it away or turn it aside? She couldn't do either. The plate armor gob's sword arced low, close to the ground. It dug hard into the ground, kicking up dry dirt. Merry was surprised and shut her eyes.

In that moment, the plate armor gob jumped away, throwing something with its left hand. A knife. A throwing knife?

Merry backed away, bringing her hand to her belly. It was lodged in there. The throwing knife was. Deeply.

"Merry...!" *Stop. What are you doing? Manato. Merry's going to end up like Manato. Don't do this to me.*

Haruhiro charged in.

I'm not thinking. What should I do? I don't know. I have no idea what to do.

The next thing he knew, he was closing in on the plate armor gob.

The sword.

The plate armor gob's sword came at him.

Above and to the left. It's coming down at me diagonally. I can't avoid it. Well, what can I do? Plunge in. Keep going. Before the sword reaches me.

He thought he might die. But Haruhiro wasn't dead. He wasn't dead yet.

He ended up hugging the plate armor gob from the front. His face bashed into the plate armor gob's helmet, but he didn't care.

"—Gwahh...!" He pushed it down. The plate armor gob said something. It wasn't human language, so he didn't understand.

The sword. Stop the sword.

He desperately held down the plate armor gob's right arm, which held the sword. The plate armor gob punched Haruhiro in the jaw. It punched him over and over. His head shook and he felt his consciousness was about to fly away.

Don't fly away. Don't fly. You're not a bird.

Talking to himself like that, Haruhiro switched his dagger with a backhanded grip.

The plate armor gob screamed. He felt like it was telling him stop.

Like I'm gonna stop. There's no way I'd stop.

The plate armor gob's helmet covered its entire head, but there were holes for the eyes.

There.

He tried to stab the dagger in there, but the plate armor gob stopped him. It stopped him by grabbing the dagger's blade with its left hand. Both of their hands shook. Just a little farther. A little farther and it would go into the eye hole. That "a little farther" felt so far.

"Dammit! Damn, damn, damn...! Why do you have to be so strong...?!"

"Haruhiro-kun...!" It was Moguzo's voice.

Footsteps. Moguzo was running over. Before Haruhiro looked to Moguzo, the plated armor gob had jumped away from him.

"Hunnnnnnnnnnngh...!"

Moguzo arched backward, bringing down the sword he held aloft so hard that it looked like he might fall forward. There was a loud sound that resonated in his gut and Haruhiro thought, *Moguzo, that was awesome.* Moguzo's bastard sword had severed the plate armor gob's head. Of course, the plate armor gob was no longer breathing. It was dead.

"Did you...kill it?" Ranta whispered nervously.

Yume slouched to the ground, exhausted. "Yeah...Yume thinks so."

"...I can hardly believe it," said Shihoru.

"Whoahhhhhh?!" Moguzo lifted up his sword and gave a cheer, but he still couldn't believe it himself so it was kind of half-hearted.

"...Sorry to say this now." Merry raised a hand. "But do you mind if I heal this? It kind of really hurts."

"What are you apologizing for?" Haruhiro laughed, then clutched his side. He nearly groaned. Would it be better if he didn't touch it? It still throbbed with pain if he left it alone. He didn't think he could stay standing much longer, so he crouched down.

"...Sorry, Merry. I can wait, but heal me, too. Ouch..."

Grimgar of Fantasy and Ash

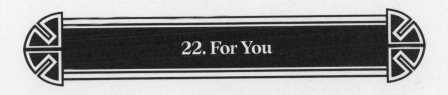

22. For You

I've been thinking all along about what to say when this moment came.

It feels like we've spent so long together, but the truth is, we haven't. Actually, we've only known each other for a short time. Too short a time. That's why I feel like I know you, but I don't know you at all. You were good with people, easy to talk with, smart, able to do anything, and I always felt I could depend on you. I thought you were flawless. But it may just be I never noticed your shortcomings. You may have been hiding your weaknesses. If we had spent longer together, I might have seen another side of you.

I wish I could have known. Known what kind of guy you really were. I wish we'd had more time. With more time, I'm sure so many things would have happened. We might have gotten mad at each other and fought. We might have come to hate each other or to like each other even more. One day, suddenly, Shihoru might have confessed her love for you. What would you have done then?

I don't want to think that, once someone's gone, there's no point in talking to them, that your words can't reach them.

But the more I think about it, the more my heart aches.

Because I know that the friend I still recall when I close my eyes has stopped moving, was burned in the flames—whether that was a mercy or not—and now was reduced to ashes and now is in this grave which casts its shadow in the evening.

"We've become volunteer soldiers now."

In the end, that was what Haruhiro said to the grave which bore his friend's name and the crescent moon, holding up the Corps Badge that looked like a silver coin as he did.

Ranta, Moguzo, Yume, Shihoru: each of them pulled out their own badges, showing them to their departed friend.

Merry stood a little away from the other five, her eyes cast downwards with one hand at her chest.

"It's not that we didn't have the money to buy our badges before." Haruhiro gripped his badge tight. "But we wanted to make a clean break with the past and tie up loose ends first. We all decided we would wait until then."

Ranta snorted. "Honestly, I didn't really care. But you guys wouldn't shut up about it."

"Stupid Ranta." Yume slapped Ranta on the shoulder. "You don't have to say such heartful things at a time like this, do you? People already hate you enough."

"That's fine by me. After all, I'm a dread knight. We live to be hated."

"...Actually, Yume," Haruhiro tugged lightly on Yume's cloak, "you meant

'hurtful,' not 'heartful.' No one would hate him if they were heartful..."

"Oh? Really? Yume always thought it was heartful up until now."

"U-Um." Moguzo turned to Shihoru. "Isn't it time for that?"

"Ah... Yeah."

Shihoru walked forward, crouching in front of the grave. Pulling one more badge out of her pocket, she hesitated for a moment and then...hold on, was she trying to force it into the crescent moon carved in the grave?

"No, Shihoru, that's a bit much..." Haruhiro went to stop her only for Shihoru to turn around saying, "Huh?" her face turning a bright shade of crimson. "...I-I'm sorry, I was wondering where I ought to leave it and I..."

"Well... It's fine, really. But I don't think it's going to fit there. The shape isn't the same."

"...O-Oh, yeah. I... I guess not. I'm sorry. Even though I'm fat, I'm a bit airheaded, too... Um, w-well, here, then." Shihoru gently placed the badge next to the gravestone.

"This one's for you, Manato-kun. We used the money you left behind and everyone chipped in to cover the rest. Merry-san helped, too. Please accept it."

If you could hear this, would you laugh and say we didn't have to do it? Haruhiro thought. *That it's a waste of money and we should have spent it on improving our equipment instead? "I'm on this side now, so you guys who are on that side should use the money." You might have said it calmly like that. But no matter what you said, we wouldn't have listened.*

After all, Manato, we can't hear your voice. If you want to make us do what you want, say something. Let us hear you.

I know. You can't.

When I die, I wonder what will happen to me. Is there someplace like heaven and will I be able to meet you there someday? I don't know. There's no way to know. No one knows what comes after death. But, at the very least, we won't be able to talk until then.

There's a wide, deep, and fast-running river between the living and the dead. Once you cross that river, no matter what happens, you're never coming back. It's a one-way trip.

The tears wouldn't flow.

But all of them wanted to stay a little longer, so Haruhiro sat on the grass, hugging one knee.

Shihoru placed her hand on the grave, her back trembling.

Yume crouched next to Shihoru, putting an arm around her shoulder and patting her on the head.

Ranta put his hands on his hips, looking up into the sky.

Moguzo took a deep breath, exhaling slowly.

Merry held her hair back, looking off into the distance somewhere.

"We've become a good party."

With those words to the friend who would never return, Haruhiro looked towards Alterna. A bell was ringing. Probably telling them it was 6:00 in the evening.

A red half-moon floated near the horizon. Now that he thought of it, why was the moon here red?

—Here?

Haruhiro glanced at the tower that looked down on them from the hilltop.

A tower. That tower. Strange. I feel like I'm forgetting something. Haruhiro and the others had come *here* and after that, they had become volunteer soldiers.

What about before that? Where was I? What was I doing? I don't know. I don't remember.

It wasn't just Haruhiro. It was the same for all of them.

Regardless, when Haruhiro and the others had woken up, *here* was where they were.

Here.

Which is where *again? If I recall, it was dark—dark? I don't know. Where exactly was that place? A tower. The tower. That tower is involved somehow. But how is it involved? I don't know. The more I think, the less I understand. If I reach out and touch it, it disappears.*

Hey, Manato.

Why are we here doing all this stuff...? Even that doubt is starting to feel hazy, as if it might melt away at any moment.

23. Prologue

A bell was ringing. The bell telling them it was 6:00 in the evening. When the last echoes of the seventh chiming of the bells reluctantly sank into the town and disappeared, night fell on Alterna.

The bells only rang until 6:00 and they would not be rung again until 6:00 in the morning the next day. It was the time when craftspeople who woke up early in the morning for work would be chowing down on dinner and having an evening drink. Many businesses took the 6:00 bell as a sign to close for the day.

It was a time of day when food stalls did more business and the taverns began to fill up.

At Sherry's Tavern, where a great many volunteer soldiers gathered to refresh their spirits for the coming day, from now until late at night were truly their busiest hours.

Even considering that, tonight was especially lively.

It wasn't just volunteer soldiers. Old craftsmen, young trainees, portly merchants, glamorous ladies of the night and even soldiers of the Frontier Army were there.

People, people, people as far as the eye could see. To the point that the sizable, two-floor establishment began to feel cramped.

Of course, all the seats were taken. Those without seats stood. Not just the first and second floor, but the stairs were filled with people, as well.

Everyone had crowded into Sherry's Tavern after hearing a certain rumor.

Famous volunteer soldiers were usually referred to as So-and-So of Clan Such-and-Such.

Setting aside the area around Alterna, as you went further from the human race's sphere of power, the monsters and hostile races became stronger or relied on their greater numbers to kill humans. Clans were an organization born of necessity and those seeking to achieve more than a certain degree of success knew they should participate in one. They had to. You could even call it necessary.

And yet, one group that had yet to join any clan: a group of four volunteer soldiers, one elf, and the golem Zenmai, who had been created by one of the volunteer soldiers, the necromancer Pingo. Six people in total had survived their battles.

As a result, they were praised as the greatest of all volunteer soldiers and their fame had spread throughout Alterna. To this day, they were the only volunteer soldiers ever invited to dine with the Margrave of Alterna, Garlan Vedoy. What's more, they had turned him down.

"Soma, don't you think it's about time?"

When the alluring woman spoke to Soma, he rose from his seat. Just because of that, the noise died down and a silence fell over the tavern.

This was a given, of course. Each and every one of them was here to hear Soma's announcement. If they didn't quietly listen when Soma opened his mouth, what would be the point? After all, today was a day to be commemorated.

That Soma would finally be forming a clan. As a result, he would be recruiting comrades, they said.

But was that true? After all, they were just rumors. False ones, possibly. Of course, there were doubters, but Soma himself had appeared in Sherry's Tavern. And now, finally, he was about to speak before the masses.

"Shima."

When Soma called her name, the alluring woman smiled and nodded slightly.

"Yes."

Then Soma turned to the man with dreadlocks.

"Kemuri."

"Yeah," the man with dreadlocks said, twisting his neck left and right lethargically.

Soma turned to look at a childlike man.

"Pingo."

"...Yeah," Pingo looked downward and sighed. "I don't like that sort of thing."

"I see," Soma's lips loosened slightly and he cast a look at the golem wearing a frightening mask.

"Zenmai."

Zenmai slowly nodded his head.

Lastly, Soma fixed his gaze on the elf.

"Lilia."

Lilia's vivid, sapphire eyes stared back at Soma.

"Yes, Soma."

Soma closed his eyes for a moment, taking a deep breath. Then, moving only his lips, he called another name.

Nino.

She was gone now.

After Soma and the others had lost Nino, who had once been their party's priest, Kemuri had changed classes from warrior to paladin. Shima had given up on being a thief, learning to become a shaman in the Shadow Forest where the elves lived. Lilia had joined the party.

Nino was dead. Soma had begun searching for a way to bring her back, but he hadn't found one yet. He thought there might be some lead in the hinterlands of the territory of the former Kingdom of Ishmal, where the remains of No-Life King were said to sleep.

Though that said, nothing was for certain. There might be no means of reviving the dead in this world.

Not in this world.

However, what was *this world,* really? Where had they come to *this world* from? To begin with, this ridiculous world, where the moon shone red and aberrant monsters ran free like it was perfectly normal, was it actually *real?*

It had been a while ago, but Kemuri had said, "You know, it's almost like a game," and Soma had responded, "Yeah, it is." At the time, he had certainly thought so, but the two had quickly found they didn't understand what they meant.

What was a game?

Something was wrong.

Those feelings of wrongness grew weak and he nearly forgot them, but now Soma carved them into his heart.

If this world was not real—if it was fake—where was the real world to be found? And if Soma and the others came from there, what had become of Nino, who had died in this fake world? If they could return to their own world, might Nino still be there?

It was a possibility. Just a possibility. Still, it was a possibility. They couldn't say for sure that it wasn't possible.

Soma opened his eyes.

"—We have decided to form a clan."

A commotion arose and the whole tavern shook.

"Our goal is to invade Undead DC in the former Kingdom of Ishmal." Even without having to raise it, Soma's voice carried well. Just by issuing a low shout, timid monsters would turn tail and flee. Any monster that could hold firm before Soma was a big deal. "We have information that there are omens suggesting the revival of No-Life King. We will investigate this and if No-Life King has revived, we will immediately destroy him once more. Of course, this will not be easy. We will need to find a method to accomplish that. We will need power, as well. The six of us alone are not enough. We need a greater power."

The volunteer soldiers raised their voices in joy while the curious onlookers cheered. The air was ready to burst with all of the voices, clapping, and whistling.

Soma was half-deceiving them. However, for those he recognized as trustworthy, he intended to eventually tell them his true objective.

"Please, lend us your hands! If you feel this is for you, come and offer to participate!"

"The name! What's the clan's name?!" someone shouted.

Soma nodded. "—From this moment onward, we call ourselves

the Day Breakers! You who are brave, you who are wise, you who are noble, you who are decisive and awe-inspiring, come unto me! If you fear not death, will fight death and seek life when faced with death, whoever you are, brave ones, I will welcome you!"

Nino, Soma whispered in his heart, standing the center of the excitement. *I will solve the mystery of this world. Then, someday, I will go to meet you.*

—That his fate would become entwined with theirs, Haruhiro had no way of knowing.

Dragon Quest, *Wizardry*, *Final Fantasy*, *Megami Tensei*, *Metal Max*, *Romancing Saga*, *Breath of Fire*, *Live A Live*, *Chrono Trigger*, *Arc The Lad*, *Tactics Ogre*, *Suikoden*, *Tales of Phantasia*, *Wild Arms*, *Final Fantasy Tactics*, *Star Ocean*, *Atelier Marie*, *Saga Frontier*, *Xenogears*, and many more console RPGs, or games that included RPG elements, saved me.

Even I, who couldn't get into shooters, sports games, fighting games, and other action games because I was bad at them, could focus on RPGs and immerse myself in their worlds.

That I could enjoy them on my own, at my own pace, was important to me. Throughout my life, I haven't been the kind of person with many friends. It might be fair to say I had very few.

Of course, it's not that I had absolutely no friends, but I'm incapable of enjoying playing as a group or having a good time talking about something. Honestly, I want to do those things, but I can't seem to do them well.

When I was a child, when the new *Dragon Quest* or *Final Fantasy* went on sale, everyone would start playing it. They would talk about how far they had gotten and what level they were now every day at school. I couldn't get involved in those conversations.

All I could do was cut into my sleeping hours to play the game, get farther than everyone, then when I heard someone boasting, "I got this far!" I could quietly think,

"Oh, only to there? That's nothing special. I'm further than you," and smile to myself.

Basically, I was a gloomy kid. But even I could become the protagonist, go on incredible adventures, become stronger and save the world. It was always RPGs that saved me.

Then, something brought about a change for that gloomy, solitary gamer. *Diablo... Ultima Online... EverQuest... Dark Age of Camelot*—these are all American games, but domestically there were games like *Dark Eyes* and *Lifestorm*, too.

It was online RPGs.

Using the internet, you could play an RPG with someone else. If we're talking about playing RPGs with other people, there are tabletop RPGs, as well. However, for someone not so good at dealing with other people like I am, that was too high a hurdle to get over. In online RPGs, I didn't have to be face-to-face with anyone.

If I knew some small amount of English, I could play with people overseas. I went crazy for it. This was an era when the internet wasn't as widely deployed as it is now. I connected to the internet not over fiber or ADSL, but over the phone lines, so the telephone was unavailable while I was playing games.

Using a service called Tele-hodai, which charged a fixed monthly rate for unlimited calls to select numbers late at night and early in the morning, I used every single one of those minutes for playing games. There were times I accidentally went outside that time period or well outside it, causing my phone bill to cost an incredible amount.

At that time, for me, online RPGs were reality and everything else was just time to sleep, eat, lay about, or think about games. Every night, I dove into the thrilling world of online RPGs and when morning came, I returned to the mundane world. I lived in games. Games kept me alive.

Occasionally people ask what led me to start writing. As you would expect, games were a major influence. If I hadn't encountered RPGs, I'm sure I never would have written novels.

In particular, had I not spent that time immersed in online RPGs, my debut novel *Bara no Maria* (Kadokawa Sneaker Bunko) would never have been born, neither would have this book.

Furthermore, had I not read books based on RPGs, such as Ryo Mizuno's *Lodoss-tou Senki* (*Record of Lodoss War*) or Benny Matsuyama's *Tonariawase no Hai to Seishun*, even if I had become a novelist, I don't believe I would have written this sort of book. Even the Japanese title of this book, *Hai to Gensou no Grimgar*, was inspired by *Tonariawase no Hai to Seishun*, and the title for the novel that eventually became *Bara no Maria* was *Bara no Maria Senki*.

Online RPGs, and RPGs in general, stirred up my creativity, or perhaps my delusions, and led me to novels deeply involved with RPGs. That's how I got here. Because I played so many RPGs for such a long period of time, I can no longer play games with the same feeling I did during "that time."

Even so, I fervently hope for games that will bring "that time" back to life for me. While ruminating on my feelings from "that time," I wrote this novel. I believe, beyond doing that, a world I have yet to see surely awaits. If I have further opportunities, I think I will write more "that time" novels.

At this time, I offer my heartfelt appreciation and all of my love to: my editor, K, who gave me this opportunity; to Eiri Shirai, the illustrator who drew such transparent, atmospheric, modern, cute, cool and lovely illustrations; to the designer and others who compiled this novel into such a fine book; to everyone involved in production and sales of this book—and finally, to all of you people now holding this book. Now, as I hope we will meet again, I lay down my pen for today.

Ao Jyumonji